# JIGGLING
## *A Gradual Release*

**Eugene Lowe**

"The water's running.
Be a good boy, honey, and
jiggle the commode."

# One

# A Lasting Impression of Peas in Key West

Luckily, I was wearing black pants when I escorted my Maw-maw down the aisle. The pee ran down my leg so fast, there was nothing I could do. I hoped no one had noticed. I peeked to check if it showed. Maw-maw scowled; looking straight ahead, she yanked me forward, her crooked arm locked in mine. *Straighten up and fly right,* I could feel her say. I bet she hated that her daughter was getting married for the second time, and in a Lutheran church. *Why couldn't they get married Southern Baptist? All that chanting and jumping up and down. My word!* Nevertheless, even though I was nervous as hell and stained with piss at twelve-years-old, on June 17, 1967, Mom and the Dive-bomber got hitched. And we all hoped for the best.

Mom had met the Dive-bomber on a husband-reconnaissance mission in Key West. She had wandered into the Waterfront Playhouse. The Dive-bomber, on R&R, was painting scenery for "A Streetcar Named Desire." Mom was taken with the dark-complected, paint-speckled man perched high above her. "He looks Greek," she would say. With barely a pause after "Hello," she told him she had been in shows herself: *The Music Man* and *Damn Yankees* up at the St. Pete Music Box. She missed the theater so much. Oh, how she yearned to get involved in some small way. She poured on the charm, and he was hypnotized. They chatted like that—above and below—for a little bit until the

3

Dive-bomber let if fall that they just might need someone to play Eunice, the Kowalski's upstairs neighbor. He could talk to the director for her. She was delighted.

Maw-maw and Paw-paw were more than a little bit paranoid. She worked for the State Attorney, he for Wackenhut Security in Miami. Not just our main doors, but all the bedrooms were dead-bolted and chained from the inside. And Paw-paw kept a loaded .38 between the box springs and the mattress. A pee can waited in the corner. The rule for everyone was: No leaving the bedrooms after dark. So what was Mom doing out after curfew in Key West? When she dyed her hair red to become Eunice, she had to confess that the reason I hadn't seen much of her was because of *Streetcar*. She promised I could watch the dress rehearsal in just a few weeks. I could sit in the balcony, right next to the guy who worked the spotlight. And, by the way, after the show, she wanted to introduce me to someone very special.

The Dive-bomber played Pablo Gonzalez, the no-nonsense poker player in charge. I was anxious about learning whatever I could about this guy. I figured he'd become my new dad. He dealt the cards and guarded the beer. That's about it. He didn't have a lot to say. Maybe it was the makeup, but he scared me. Mom told me he didn't even want to play the part. The director pushed him into it, she said, because he looked kind of Cuban. They put a mustache on him and had him let his bristle get rough and dark for the show. He didn't want to be thought of as "Cuban," he said. And he didn't like hearing Eunice call Stanley a "Polack".

Eunice seemed to own the place. She was always looking out for everyone like she was everybody's mom. I don't know why. Some moms must be big like that. Anyway, whenever Eunice and her husband, Steve, argued and fought, which was all the time, it was usually about other women and staying out too late. They were very noisy. From their place upstairs you'd always hear yelling and things breaking. Then he'd hit her, and there was more screaming and swearing. But they always made up. They would kiss and hug, slipping down a spiral staircase. Then Steve would ask if anyone wanted to go bowling and have a drink, like nothing had ever happened. I guessed they loved each other. It was the same with the people downstairs. Stanley and Stella fought and carried on just like Steve and Eunice. You'd think they were going to kill each other, then, all of a sudden, he'd get down on his knees and beg her to come back. Of course, she would. Both women would. Every time. It even seemed like instead of wanting to get away, they fought so they could get worked up and hot inside, just for the thrill of it.

Mom was right there in the beginning of the show, telling this fancy woman, Blanche, "This here's Elysian Fields." And then Eunice was gone.

I kept watching for her to come back, but it turned out the show was mostly about Blanche. She was really kind of pitiful. She talked about how her husband had blown his brains out because of something she had said to him or a problem he had had with another guy. I didn't understand, but it still made me cry a little. I hoped the guy on the spotlight couldn't see me. Then Eunice showed up to take care of Stella or her baby, kind of the way Maw-maw would take care of Mom when she'd fight with Dad. Anyway, I watched Blanche. The painful smile on her face reminded me of the way Mom looked when my sister told her she didn't want to live with her, anymore. Sis said she preferred to go back to St. Pete and live with Dad. When I asked Mom about it, she said my sister was just going for a visit and that she'd be back soon. Mom, like Blanche, liked to tell what ought to be the truth.

Maybe Blanche was pretty lonely and afraid she wouldn't have anybody to help her get by. And maybe that's why Mom got married again so soon after divorcing Dad. She sure didn't want to stay at Maw-maw and Paw-paw's. She had often complained that she wasn't getting any younger. It made me feel weird when she told me *I* had to look after her since, at the time, I was all she had left. And then she'd get all soft and hug me and make me kiss her. It was almost like she wanted to marry *me*.

I guess the thing that pushed Blanche over the edge was when Stanley attacked her. You could see it coming. But what was worse and really awful to watch was when the people from the hospital came to take her away. Meanwhile, Pablo and the other men in the show just kept playing cards like nothing was happening. Eunice went along with it, too, and pretended that Blanche was just going away on a little trip. Eunice had to be strong and keep everybody calm. According to the script I read, Eunice was supposed to say to Stella, "You done the right thing, the only thing you could do. She couldn't stay here; there wasn't no other place for her to go." But my Mom suddenly started bawling her eyes out. I began to cry, too, and I didn't even care anymore if the spotlight guy could see me. I just thought about when I was little: *They took her away. They took my Mommie away. She said she got bit by a scorpion. And my sister saw blood from Mom's wrists flowing into the sink. Mom said she had cut herself on a jar. And so we rode fast at night through the rain to the hospital. Mom hung out the window screaming bloody murder. And Dad yelled for me and my sister to hold on*

6

*to her, for God's sake. And then there was no Mom for a while.* They had to put her in a padded cell, my sister told me when I was older.

So, I cried and Mom cried, and finally, the director came onto the stage and put his arms around Mom. He held her close, patting her bright red head against his chest. And he warned her that she wasn't allowed to cry like that during the real show.

After the wedding and the cake reception, some guy in military uniform drove me home and told me I should call the Dive-bomber, "Dad" from now on. A couple of hours later, the newly-weds got home to change before leaving on their honeymoon. To get his attention I called him "Dad" just to see what he would do. It made him weep. Then they left.

With no one around I could do whatever I wanted. There was a baseball game on the other side of the island where I knew this girl would want to kiss me using her tongue, French style. I rode my bike over to meet her. I liked that she was happy to kiss like that; that she wanted to, and that she was so affectionate was the important thing. It made me feel happy and warm and friendly. But all that weird slobbery jabbing was kind of dumb. It was worth it though, because I could tell she liked me by the way she touched my face and said nice things to me. And I liked touching her, too, and saying nice things to her. The tongue thing just seemed to be what you had to do to get the other.

That night I cut my foot pretty bad. I almost never wore shoes in Key West. And even though my feet had started to grow sideways like some kind of animal, the warm at times and cool at times textures of Florida were too much of a pleasure to resist. It was great until you stepped on something like a horseshoe crab,

7

or a Portuguese Man-o-War washed up on the shore, or on a broken bottle.

I had to ride home on my bike, bleeding and wondering if this new dad-guy was going to get mad about it. But no one was home. I couldn't stop the bleeding, and got scared because I was getting blood all over the apartment. I tried to bandage it with rags and clean up the mess, but I bled where I had just wiped up. I didn't know what to do to make it stop, and I wished Mom and "Dad" would come home. But they didn't that night. So I wrapped my foot up real tight in an old t-shirt and went to bed. So what if I bled to death.

Okay. It stopped. And the next morning my foot didn't bleed as long as I didn't walk on it. I wanted to go see if I could find that girl again, but, instead, I stayed home and watched TV. There was a lot of fighting going on. The announcer said they were in Chicago. I saw smoke and cops beating people for no reason. I waited. I waited all day. I began to wonder if I would ever see them again. I really wanted to be happy and hopeful. Late in the day, as much as it embarrassed me, I even prayed they would come back soon. But then I gave up and went looking for that girl. I couldn't find her, and my foot started bleeding again. So I went home. Nobody was there.

That evening, Mom finally called to ask if I was all right. I didn't say anything. They would be out a little longer, she said. I was not to worry. They were having a good time.

The following afternoon, they finally showed up. They had been invited to a luau at the Polynesian Tiki Hut up on US 1 and were having the time of their lives, Mom said. They talked about going back out. They just needed to change clothes. When, at last, they shut up, Mom noticed the bloody t-shirt on my foot.

"What happened?" Their party mood popped.

"I cut it," I said dismissively. I glared at both of them. "Dad" became pissed off that I was putting a damper on their honeymoon. But he could not meet my eyes. It was just then I realized that this so-called "Dad" was nothing of the sort. He was an intruder. Soon enough, I would find a more appropriate name for him.

We lived on Grinnell St. about 1/4 mile from Tennessee William's house, Mom said. But I never met him.

Chameleons frequently scooted into our apartment, but sometimes I found them flattened into the doorjamb when the door got shut on them. Once in Miami, I saw a guy pry their little jaws open and then let them snap shut on each of his earlobes. He would then pose in front of different color shrubs to make the lizards change colors.

The foliage of Key West, that's what Mom called it, was bright and luxurious and full of surprises. The Key limes puckered me up, and a big banana tree out back had ripe spotted fruit, but the bananas were always too bitter to eat. The sea grape trees had delicious tiny purple treats at the end of their wide and flowing limbs that I loved to climb. Once, I collected enough grapes to make juice. But after a few days, it got kind of bubbly and tasted sour like vinegar.

We lived on the first floor of a two-story stuccoed white apartment house that the Dive-bomber had found through an Air Force referral. Our neighbors were almost all military people. I shared my room with the Dive-bomber's electronics workshop of many drawers and cabinets filled with capacitors, resistors, diodes. He also had a big HAM radio. He started to show me how it worked, but he seemed to quickly lose interest.

When no else was around, I played my first album ever—Jimi Hendrix's "Are You Experienced?" I bought it in Miami just before we had to leave for the wedding. The cover was what made me buy it. It was like staring through a porthole at three guys dressed like a garden. I played that album over and over, screaming along and hopping around. Nothing made me feel better. At night, Mom and the Dive-bomber played their music—Johnny Mathis and pop tunes like "The Girl from Ipanema". They sometimes had loud parties that lasted way past my bed time. I couldn't sleep and it pissed me off. Once I got brave enough to confront them. I walked out to the living room and just stood there, facing a bunch of weird military people. The Dive-bomber called out my name, and then Mom did, too. But I did not respond, so they figured I must have been sleep-walking. They teased me about it for a long time afterwards. I didn't bother to tell them the truth.

One weekend I was riding in the Mustang, going downtown to the movies, when the Dive-bomber snapped at me. "What the hell you doing back there?"

"Cleaning my belly button," I said. My tropical lifestyle was a messy business.

"Stop that right now," he swore. "If I ever see you doing that again, I'm gonna tape your hands shut."

Now that's a strange idea, I thought. "How am I supposed to get it clean then?" I asked, which really fired him up.

"You better watch it, boy, or I'll tape your damn little smart-ass mouth shut, too," he barked at me.

Mom shushed him then turned on me herself. "You still want-ing to go to the movies?" she said. "Then don't get smart with your..." she stumbled, "your step-father."

The Dive-bomber had begun to scare me enough to think he really would tape me up into a useless little ball. I swore to him that I'd never touch my belly button again and quickly got out of the car. I was told by Mom we would need to have a little talk about my attitude when I got home.

I slipped into the musty cinema. As usual, the guys were in the back debating who got to try to cop a feel with which girl. It was kind of like choosing who was going to be on whose baseball or football team. As long it was the guys deciding, I was sure to be picked last. Why did the girls never have a say? But, I won-der, did the guys choose her for me, or did the girl who had braces choose me herself? It was her first time at the Cop-a-Feel, and she was very nervous. But I liked her. She seemed smart and she was real quiet. We both knew what we were there for, so right away we gave kissing a try. It went okay. I didn't have to struggle with her too much, so that was good. She made me swear I wouldn't try to feel her up. "Okay. We'll just kiss." She liked that, and it seemed like we might even become friends. But then a really strange movie came on, and I couldn't concentrate on kissing anymore.

The movie was about a mad doctor who shipwrecked travel-ers onto his jungle island. Then he hunted them down as they ran from him in terror. He released a man and a woman that he had caught who were definitely in love. The madman told them they had better run, because, if they didn't, he would kill them right there. At least they would have a chance if they ran. As the black and white jungle—it looked a lot like the King Kong movie

—threatened them with tigers, snakes, and quicksand, the woman screamed so shrilly it made your teeth curl.

Meanwhile, the girl next to me was waiting a little impatiently. But I couldn't take my eyes off of the screen. She probably thought I was bored with her. I wanted to show her I liked her, even though she had braces and wouldn't let me feel her boobs. I didn't mind. But the movie kept pulling me back. She was getting pretty restless, so, I said something stupid like "this movie is really cool." But she thought it was "gross" and "stupid," she said. She turned my head to face her and puckered up. I kissed her once more without any feeling. So she jumped out of her seat and ran up the aisle to her girlfriends.

Alone and up close to the screen, I lost myself to delicious, flickering fear.

Although her papa never let her go downtown, and so we never went to the Cop-a-Feel Cinema or anywhere together for that matter, my new favorite girlfriend in Key West was named Rosa. I met her at school. She was about the only thing interesting at school, except maybe that mural of silver-coated Spanish explorers trudging through the Florida woods. I even flunked geography because I refused to read about Vietnam. I thought it was boring and not important.

Rosa was a lot taller than me, and she had short dark hair and soft figgy lips. Even though her skin wasn't that dark, I couldn't tell my white friends about her because she was Cuban. Her papa would be very angry, Rosa told me, if he even saw us together. But Rosa and I liked each other a lot. We made each other laugh, and we liked to hold each other close and tell stories.

As time went on, we became more and more brave and started kissing right in her house, while her papa was out doing construction. One Saturday, Rosa surprised me; she opened her blouse and offered me her warm breast to kiss. Sadly, that was a half-work day and her papa came home at that very moment to drop off some lumber. When we heard him pull up, in a panic I ran outside right in the direction of him and his helper. Thankfully, they didn't see me. With nowhere to go I ducked under the house. Unfortunately, that's where they needed to store the wood. I could see Rosa's papa and his helper bend down to guide in the planks, sliding them in next to me with great force. I trembled and had to bite my lip so as not to breathe too heavily. Crouching in the half-light, plank after shadowy plank scraped towards me. Her old man never saw me, but after our close call, Rosa and I were just too scared to see each other again.

As if to practice for the day we would leave Key West for a mysterious land far away—Berwick, Pennsylvania—Mom, the Dive-bomber and me made several trips on the one road out of town. Over the first bridge we would pass the dump on Stock Island, followed by the Naval Air Station at Boca Chica. That's where the Dive-bomber was stationed. The Navy had been leaving steadily since the Cuban missile crisis had died down, but the Air Force had no intention of giving up its radar site. The Dive-bomber was a staff sergeant in the Air Force. He was responsible for tracking hurricanes and guarding the straits. He told us how in 1965, when he first arrived, he was standing outside the big golf ball that he said housed radars, when the eye of hurricane Betsy passed over. What amazed him, he told us, was that when he lit a  cigarette, the smoke went straight up without

13

shaking in the slightest. In 1965, my sister and I had watched Betsy from the motel we had been evacuated to out of St. Pete. The wind howled, and it spooked us. We watched the motel sign dance in the wind and the rain. We made a nickel bet on when the sign was going to swing all the way up and over like we always feared *we* would do on our swings. But it never happened.

Usually, we left Key West to visit Maw-maw and Paw-paw in Miami. US 1 from Key West is a road of bridges. From the back seat of the Mustang, if you scrunched down, it looked like you were gliding over the water with no bridge beneath you at all. You could see the white sandbars poking out from the glassy water, and they joined the swirls on the pale blue coral reefs further out. The continuous heat and salty breezes were soothing, unless you looked down and saw where some driver who had been either drunk or hypnotized by the view, had gone over the edge.

The Dive-bomber, against Mom's mild protests usually wanted to stop for a pint of Seagram's Seven and a bottle of Seven Up. On our Christmas trip to Miami, he switched from his usual Seven and Seven to Seven and eggnog with a little Schilling's nutmeg on top. I got to try some of that, and I liked its sweet, thick punch.

Somewhere around Marathon we stopped to pee. I stood politely, fearfully staring ahead, when he drew my attention to his dong.

"Look at that, boy," he said proudly.

His seemingly enormous tube hung dark out of the black fur crowding his jeans. "Ever see anything like that?"

Of course I hadn't. I had seen that idiot's in junior high gym class who used to jump around the locker room naked, showing it off. It stuck out hard, and it was pale white and it had almost no hair around it.

"No, sir," I said.

"Well, don't you worry. Someday you'll have one just like this," he assured me. "Maybe not as big as this one here," he chuckled. "But that don't matter, does it?"

By the time we arrived at the grandparents, we were all laughing and singing. When we went inside, everybody could smell what the Dive-bomber had spilled on himself. He was swaying from the second pint of Seagram's, picked up in Islamorada. Maw-maw especially was pretty upset with us all.

"You know I won't have that in my house," she said. "You should be ashamed, drinking in front of the child. And at the Lord's time. Shame, shame on you." Maw-maw had had some trouble with a drinking man in her past, but she didn't like to talk about it. Since Christmas had soured before we even got started, we had to go back to Key West as soon as we finished opening presents.

Another time, on the way to Miami, we stopped at Bahia Honda park where the seven-mile bridge begins. I played in the sand, making dripped-sand castles the way my sister had taught me. Meanwhile, the not-so newlyweds went out to a sandbar to frolic. It made me sad to have to play alone; my sister was long gone. As I dug further into the sand, it began to stink more and more. It smelled like vomit or human shit, or something worse. I couldn't stand it anymore, and got up to see if we could go. When I looked out to find Mom and the Dive-bomber, I saw the tide had risen around the sandbar, and sand sharks were circling them. A sand shark won't hurt you, but none of us knew that at the time. I remember one afternoon at Garrison Bight, a charter boat captain hoisted a twelve-foot pregnant hammerhead onto the spikes. Horribly, he slit her open and a half dozen baby hammerheads flopped out, squirming alive onto the dock. Not knowing what else to do with them, he threw them into the Bight, making it impossible to swim there anymore.

As I was saying, Mom quickly became hysterical while the Dive-bomber tried to frighten the sharks away. He looked for things to throw at them, and he shouted at me to search for something to throw, too. It was just like when we stopped in the Everglades once, and a huge snake came up and scared us half to death until we frightened him off with sticks and stones. But this time, we couldn't find much to throw at the sharks. So, the Dive-bomber and I just screamed at them from opposite sides while Mom cringed and withered. On their little island, Mom and the Dive-bomber seemed to float further and further away as they were corralled by circling sharks. I stopped shouting. Maybe I wished I could resign myself to losing my new family, again. It would be the second time in a year if you counted the honeymoon. But then the sharks left them alone and just swam away.

Mom was noticeably annoyed when the Dive-bomber tried to assure her that our year apart from him would be pleasant. To make the transition easier, he said, and to give his parents a dream vacation in paradise, he would have them drive down to Key West to help us move up north.

The day after the Dive-bomber announced the plan. I remember sitting down to eat dinner, surveying the meal and waiting for the blessing. A bowl of peas, some mashed potatoes and meat loaf looked pretty good.

Mom said to him, "Honey, you want to return thanks?"

But the Dive-bomber didn't answer. He just hung his head silently. Was he praying to himself? I sat there, wondering what to do. Should we start without him? I sought Mom's eyes and I noticed she had been crying. Slowly the Dive-bomber looked at her, too. He had that look I would learn to spot—his stare fixed sharply at nothing, silently brewing and stinking of rage. I saw the veins in his forehead bulge.

"Honey, what's the mat—?"

Before she could finish asking, I saw peas fly across the kitchen and crash against the Frigidaire. The pastel yellow serving dish in pieces rocked gently where it had landed amidst what seemed like thousands upon thousands of peas. The Dive-bomber let out an awful roar as he exploded from his chair, swiping the rest of the meal onto the floor.

I pulled back from the table as fast as I could and turned to see Mom terrified and confused. Who knows what he was mad at. The Dive-bomber stood silently for a moment, asking himself what to turn to next, I guess. I was relieved that he flew away into the living room, shouting at no one in particular, saying something stupid like, "You want more? I'll give you more." And then he pulled the bookcase apart, causing the books to avalanche onto the floor. For a moment, he stared at his precious WW II German attack plane he had made as a kid, and then he carefully passed it. Instead, he turned to the TV-stereo-cabinet console and kicked the screen as hard as he could.

"Fuck," he screamed.

The attack was over. Mom approached him cautiously. He had broken his big toe. He pushed her away and hopped toward his bedroom in silence.

Peas were everywhere. The TV unit had been knocked into its cabinet about an inch. Peas. Mom grabbed me out of my stupor and told me to get into the car.

She drove us fast to her friend's house. She lived in a trailer on Stock Island close to the base. Mom cried to her friend about what had happened, and asked if we could stay overnight. The friend said it would be better if we went back home, or the Dive-bomber might get worse. It was better to try and make up now. Men had these flashes of temper. "That's just the way they are," she explained. So we left. When we got home, I was sent to bed early. When I tried to sleep, I could still see those damn peas flying across the room. Soon, whether we liked it or not, we would be going to Pennsylvania.

Strangely, the only thing I remember about the trip north was having to pee somewhere around Key Largo. Repeated requests to the Dive-bomber at the wheel produced no response. Finally he told Mom he wanted to wait until we got to Miami, another 60 miles away. He did not want to disturb his folks who were following behind us. I pleaded with Mom to make him stop the car.

"Now, Honey," she said. "You can wait."

"No, I can't," I said. I warned them that I would have to let it go if they didn't stop. I got the usual response whenever I challenged idiocy.

"Don't you get smart with me, young man," she always said.

At last, she compromised and had me pee into a Dixie cup. "I'll hold it for you," she offered.

After that I just retreated into a corner for the next 1300 miles. I must have been stunned, and now, I'm unable to remember a single instance about my first real trip out of the South.

Later on, in the summer of '68, we rode with the Dive-bomber to Fort Dix, New Jersey to see him off and launch Mom's mustang overseas. We rode over the smoking cracked streets of Centralia, PA, where the coal fires still burn out of control down below. And then through Easton where the industrial sky is always ablaze. The Dive-bomber was in a terrible hurry. He raced the Ford maniacally across the uterus of our collective pain. The whole day he sulked, except once when he lit up briefly to hint where he would be stationed at the border somewhere near the Soviet Union and Iran. He was not allowed to tell us exactly where, and we weren't to talk about it. He'd just be somewhere over there. That was enough for us to know. He'd be waiting and watching us, he said, plugged into microwaves.

# Berwick-upon-Susquehanna

At the Pond Hill 4th of July Picnic I had vinegar on french fries for the very first time. Mom, the Dive-bomber and me watched the old fire trucks parade. We tossed hoops around hungry bottlenecks. And, believe it or not, we had fun. At least until the Dive-bomber drank himself monkey stupid, again.

Just the week before, too, he got sticky drunk at his grandpa's wake. That night, all the adults and some of us kids drank and danced around the corpse. I didn't care. I didn't know the guy. They propped him up in a tall-back chair and stuck him in a corner. All the grownups kept laughing as they stumbled to the outhouse, saying they needed to "dot the 'i' on Valentino." But the Dive-bomber spoiled it all. He kept wanting to hug me and slobbered about having to leave us behind because of the "goddam military."

He was long gone when one day I, myself, got really smashed for sure. That was the day my new friend, Andie said I should come over and meet Sally. Andie and her boyfriend Skip had already started to ball. Andie decided her best friend, Sally needed a boyfriend, too. Was I interested? Hell, yes.

So. One morning Skip snuck the key to his parents' fancy liquor cabinet. He invited me over and fixed us a screwdriver breakfast complete with runny scrambled eggs. "You should never drink on an empty stomach," he said. Then we hopped onto our bikes, swerved down Loblolly Street, crashing into each other about a million times, before falling down laughing into

Andie's tiny yard. Sally and Andie just stood there up on Andie's porch all superior-like. Those two acted disgusted, but we knew they thought we were funny, and real cool, too. I climbed up the quivering steps. At the top I smiled at Sally and admired her long straight mermaid hair. I didn't think she would be so tall. I grinned and introduced myself with a gentlemanly bow, and then I puked a yellow puddle at her feet.

A couple of weeks later she said she had forgiven me. Still, we didn't have a lot to talk about. Instead, we just kissed. She was kind of shy in the beginning, but it got better pretty fast. She even let me feel her up a little, but it was always a big fight. Anyway, I mostly liked to pat her soft hair. But more of that later.

At first, I accepted having to share a bed with my mother. She would arrive late from the cigar factory, and, anyway it was dark when she crawled into bed. I didn't mind much, not until the time of my surprise. You know, it suddenly got bigger and erupted. After that I tried to stay as far over to my side as possible. I hated it when our bodies accidentally touched. I was scared it could happen again—hard and warm. It kept me awake for most of our stay in Berwick.

I was told there would be mountains in Pennsylvania. But where I expected craggy lacerators and the flat tops of western movies, I found soft, gentle rising bluffs and notches. These mountains were old. I thought they looked worn and abused. They no longer reached beyond themselves. A long time ago there had been Indians living thereabouts, it was said. I searched through the fog across the river toward Nescopeck, but I saw only blanketing silent trees. No Indians.

The trains still ran along the river. There, me and some guys built forts made of abandoned railroad ties. Over the low bank, we spotted giant stepping stones stretching across the Susquehanna. They say that an impossibly long and low covered bridge used to lie there; but it was ripped apart by ice floes. I kept an eye on those grassy stepping mounds. They spooked me. I didn't want any Indian ghosts jumping over to our side.

One day, I stumbled down the trail to the forts my friends and I had built, and I found some of the walls caved in. A bunch of old guys were hanging around, sitting on the fallen ties. They were cooking something. Hobos! I couldn't believe it. I had never seen people like that for real. They were scruffy and worn just like on TV, their skin dark and wrinkled. They looked like our old hound dog, Woebegone, with eyes sunken into raccoon shadows. We hardly said anything to each other. They told me that it was now their "jungle." I stared at them as they looked at me with eyes of longing. Maybe they wanted to switch places, I thought. But they weren't going to budge. I could tell they wished I'd just run along. They had their ripened despair to attend to. They weren't going to hurt me. Probably not. But why should I go, I thought? Dammit, who was the trespasser?

Before he left on his secret mission to Turkey, the Divebomber, in true military fashion, had clearly defined the perimeter. I was ordered to live within the territory of a few hilly streets that seemed to shrink day by day. I was strictly warned not to explore, not to cross the cemetery, or even to go uptown unaccompanied for a cherry Coke or lime phosphate—strange new treats he had introduced me to.

At one end of 8th Street West, one block down from the cemetery, and then over one, stood American Car & Foundry. Across the street was the barber shop, and above it, a mysterious hotel. Who lived there, I wondered? I was only allowed to approach it with an adult, and only then to get my hair cut. That boundary neighborhood the Dive-bomber called "the rough part of town." In the distance you could see the foundry yard strewn with rusted railroad cars, tanks and other debris of past wars. The heavy trip hammer kept the pace for all of us, as it restlessly shook the neighborhood houses. Some times, I watched the photos of my recently acquired extended family tremble with the aftershock of each slam.

I first met Andie on 8th Street West as I was picking at the bark of a big maple out front. She just came up and started talking to me. Her aunt and uncle lived at the other end of the street, closer to the cemetery.

"I was watching you," she said. "I hope you don't mind. You're new, aren't you?"

I was dumbfounded. Tongue-tied. Finally, I got my mouth working. I said, "Hi," but didn't tell her right away I liked her.

Her aunt and uncle kept spying on us. They wanted to make sure we didn't get too friendly. Andie laughed a lot and she wasn't afraid. Not a bit. She was short like Mom with red hair. We talked for hours under the sycamore tree and tried to catch helicopter pods, spinning down to the street. When it got dark, we watched bats and flycatchers swoop like dark particles, never colliding.

Across from Andie's people lived one of the two white trash families on 8th Street West. Andie and I liked to listen to them, because they had funny accents. The other neighbors hated them. Who wanted to look at all that squalor and listen to their foul loud mouths, they wanted to know? But one particular day, when Andie and I heard the mama screaming at her toddler, we couldn't take it. It wasn't funny anymore.

"I told you, didn't I?" she shouted at her baby. The poor little creature stared up at her and whimpered. "I ain't cleaning you up again," she scowled. "How many times I got to tell you?"

She wouldn't stop yelling. "You think I enjoy cleaning you up, day after day. I'll be damned if I do, you little brat." And *smack*, upside his little head. He teetered a moment, then started to bawl. "I know what you're up to," she started into it again. "And you ain't getting away with it this time." She huffed up real proud at the good discipline she'd 'learned him.' We watched her turn away and go inside, leaving the baby screaming for mercy, "Mama, mama," and saw him banging at the door.

Andie and I got out of there. We both felt pretty bad. We walked around by the cemetery to calm down. About an hour later, we came back and saw the toddler still wandering around the yard by himself. Pitiful. His shit ran down his legs and caked up in the sun. Flies were buzzing him. Andie said how disgusted she was with the mother, and how she wished someone would take care of that poor child. I liked hearing that. Too bad Andie already had a boyfriend.

A climb uphill and you were at the school, where I desperately wanted classes to begin. But school turned out to be much worse than just hanging out with Andie, secretly wishing she loved me. Besides, next semester, I would meet Sally. The school day alternated between pressure to achieve new levels in dull graded birdie-readers — I made it as far as "Cardinal — or   debates about whether it was more sanitary to store glasses upright or rim down in a clean cabinet. I went out for the wrestling team, but everybody who wrestled was always slippery from sweat, and I was required to wear enormous gym shorts with a useless built-in jockstrap. That, of course, was before *the change.* To add to my humiliation, the shorts were emblazoned with the likeness of the mighty Berwick Bull Dawg that I doubted I would ever be.

Mom and I had been assigned by the Dive-bomber to live with his folks. Because they were strangers to us, it was easier to pass most of the time out of sight. Mrs. Dive-bomber Grandma spent a lot of time on the porch swing. Florida people rarely sat on their porches to yak with their neighbors. The bugs would have eaten us alive. I wanted to join this new social delight, without bugs, on the porch, but Mom said it was the Dive-bomber Grandma's only time, besides church, to visit with her friends. My new grandma was nice to most neighbors, but usually cranky with Mom and me. I guessed we were an imposition. She did make strange, fascinating food though. Mom said, politely, that it was Polish food. I liked the chopped cabbage salad that Mr. Dive-bomber Senior minced in the hand-held Vegematic. There were pickled cucumbers, onion, and rhubarb from the garden. I eventually learned to like that fresh rhubarb made into stringy pies and purple salads.

Mr. Dive-bomber Senior cut the hedge, all the time, despite his missing a toe and his old age. He would climb up his ladder to sculpt a ten-foot wall was meant to protect us from the other white-trash folks who lived just across the alley. He could also climb down to the cellar, another place I was not allowed to explore for fear I would fall and be eaten alive by preserves, I guess. I always wondered what he did down there. Yet, with all that climbing, he could somehow never make it to the second floor to be with his wife. I once asked about this discrepancy, but was severely hushed. He was very tall, had olive skin and a high-Herman Munster brow along with deeply set dark eyes. He rarely spoke, but when he did, his rumbling stern voice could invoke terror. This was not because he roared, but because his voice was barely audible, like swallowed distant thunder.

Zizi, their gray poodle, had many toys and many pleasures, but, by far, her favorite was to curl at the feet of Dive-bomber Senior and lick. Mr. Senior had lost his big toe in an accident over at the foundry. Something heavy had fallen or was intentionally dropped on it. I never got the story straight. And the toe had to be amputated. A yellowish bit of bone that the amputator had missed still stuck out from his foot. That nub, where the toe had been, was Zizi's favorite part to lick. The Dive-bomber Senior would recline on the downstairs couch, that had become his bed. He'd kick off his brown corduroy slippers, and after his wife had kissed him goodnight, master and dog would relax into a delicious tickle-lick fest.

When spring arrived, I was alone upstairs beginning to inspect myself, as I have already revealed. I was standing naked from the waist down before the full-length mirror, checking out how my pale-green mail-order Nehru shirt with the large peace medallion went with my new throbbing mystery. And, Bam! I heard a shot and the sound of breaking glass plow through

Grandma Senior's room. I quickly slipped on my pants and peeked down the hall. Shattered glass formed a puddle of glass at her door. Was she in there? I inched my way toward her room and went in. No. No mutilated bodies. I stepped over the glass and looked out the broken window. What? Did I think that cheap medallion would protect me? I realized the hedge wasn't high enough after all. And the gun went off again. Bam! It didn't get me. I ran downstairs and outside. Across the alley, I saw that while a whole had been blown through the white-trash wall, the Dive-bomber house was only slightly injured.

The cops came and arrested our drunk and half-naked neighbor—he had his pants on—for scaring the shit out of us. He was just cleaning his gun, he said when it went off. Twice.

"Lord only knows what goes on inside that house," I heard someone say, and the rest of the crowd agreed. They hissed and snorted as the cuffs were slapped onto our neighbor. And the officers pushed him down into the car for the ride uptown.

Dive-bomber Grandma was beside herself with all the attention she was getting. "Yep-pert. I could have been killed, I could," she said. "He shot right through my bedroom window."

By the time the press arrived, she was gussied up and ready to embellish her story. "I was upstairs getting fixed up to go out, and I just stepped out of the room for a second, when, Boom!"

I tugged at my mother. "But, Mom, *she* wasn't even up there," I said. "*I* was."

My mother hushed me. "You just be quiet and let her have her time," she said.

I went back upstairs and into grandma's room. I watched the shards vibrate on the floor, syncopated to each release of the trip hammer. So this is what the Dive-bomber had left us to. While he trundled over communications at a remote site, somewhere, I listened to his song of humming glass.

# Sally, I Love You
# and The Mockery of Certain
# Metaphors

Mom and I had to leave Berwick immediately. The Air Force had informed the Dive-bomber that at an "undesignated time in the near future," he and his dependents would be transferred to the Taunus Mountains microwave sector north of Frankfurt, Germany. There was no time to lose. We had to be ready, Mom said. We had to go back to Florida right now.

Andie and I quickly hatched plans for a farewell romp with Sally. Andie said she'd make sure her Mom was out for the night. The next evening, that was August 19, 1969, my Mom nervously let me go say good-bye to my friends. "Don't be gone too long," she said. I think she was afraid I wouldn't ever come back.

I ran across the cemetery to Andie's house. We hugged and said we already missed each other and how horrible it was I had to go.

Sally floated in. She complained about how difficult it had been to escape her suspicious parents' fortress, and then, as always, she clammed up. Andie turned back to me, and asked about Germany. How would it be?

"Hell if I know," I said. And Sally winced a little. She had decided she hated it when people swore.

"I wish I could go," Andie said, frowning at Sally, trying to get her to say something. Anything. Did I see Andie wink at her? But Sally just drooped toward the Formica table.

"Don't you want to go, too," I wooed her. If I could get her to talk a little, it might be nice to marry her someday. She was my girlfriend, and she was very pretty. I wouldn't mind looking at her forever.

"Don't ask me that," she pouted.

"I didn't mean nothing bad, Sally," I said.

"Come on you guys," interrupted Andie. "This is your last night together. Make it nice."

Sally looked up at me and forced a little smile. I reached out to touch her hair, but someone was at the door. I'd wait until Andie left the room. Sally stretched toward me like a swan. I understood, and I moved closer. I kissed her sweetly before I heard Andie.

"Guess who's back?" she squealed.

Skip followed Andie into the kitchen. He'd just returned from a camping trip at some festival in upstate New York. He had invited me to go, but Mom wouldn't let me. In less than a week, he'd really changed. His walk was smoother somehow. No more jerky, clumsy boy. He kind of cocked his head and bobbed it, as he showed off his new way of talking.

"Hey man, I hear you're taking off, like, tomorrow." His voice was lower, and he spoke slowly. "Far out," he said.

"How was the camping?" I asked. "Was it cool?"

Skip let out a slow intolerant hiss. He shook his head and ignored the question. "Man, I saw Hendrix," he said triumphantly. His voice quivered a little bit. His eyes darted, searching the memory.

"No shit? Really?" I could feel Sally recoil. I knew Skip was going to go to a folk festival or something, but nobody had said anything about Hendrix. Damn. Why didn't Mom let me go?

Skip was excited. "Like the sun was coming up and Jimi played the Star...Spangled...Banner, man, on his guitar. Wow! It was like, fantastic. He made bombs bursting and machine-gun sounds." Skip shook his head in disbelief. But I didn't know if that was because of what had happened to him, or because we were staring at him, not knowing what to say.

Skip put on *Axis: Bold as Love*. "You gotta hear it with these," he said. I had heard it before, but not with headphones. It was a "whole new trip," Skip said. I listened: it started off with a weird radio voice. "That's Hendrix's voice at the beginning." And then that exploded into a crazy frantic guitar, sliding back and forth, from ear to ear. While I listened, Skip dug into his new worn-out army surplus bag and produced some incense. He asked Sally to light it in a little brass burner he'd brought along. He told Andie to turn off the damn lights and light some candles. Then he ceremoniously opened a film canister and gently shuffled out a green powder.

"What's that?" Andie asked.

"Kif," Skip said.

He could have said, "floof," and it would have meant as much. He put some of the powder into a little pipe and sucked while he lit it up. It smelled like the Florida woods burning. Each time he inhaled, Skip held in the smoke, threw back his head and shook it rapidly. He told us that was how it was done.

"But what is it?" Andie persisted.

"It's kif," he said impatiently, looking at us as if we were dumber than yesterday.

"It's some kind of drug, isn't it?" quivered Sally, nearly in tears.

Skip shrugged, and Sally jumped up and ran out of the room. Andie scowled at Skip, and followed her girlfriend.

He handed me the pipe. Even though I dutifully puffed and held it in, shook my head around, and then collapsed on a pillow, nothing much happened. I could hear Sally, crying in the kitchen, and blubbering something about going home. I looked at Skip who took the pipe and headphones back. He wobbled his head over and over, trying to coax the kif.

Skip kept hogging the phones. I felt kind of stupid siting there, listening to a muffled Hendrix bleed through. And I missed Sally, so I got up to go back to the kitchen. Skip grabbed my ankle. I heard the screeching guitar shout at me as he pried the headphones off his head.

"Wanna give it another listen," he said.

I shook my head, no. Skip got up off the floor and unplugged the phones. I heard, "If the sun refuse to shine, I don't mind. No, I don't mind." Skip followed me into the kitchen, muttering something about oregano.

Meanwhile, Sally cried. She said that she would never be able to forget this terrible evening. All of us had been exposed to drugs! She feared that God was losing to the Devil. It was written somewhere, she said. She couldn't remember where exactly. I put my hand on her shoulder, but she brushed it away. She wasn't done pouting yet. She stood up and glared at Skip, who rolled his eyes and pulled Andie into his lap. He kissed her and grabbed her boobs. They whispered to each other and Skip and Andie laughed. I grinned at Sally. Her mouth began to twitch. Her eyes flooded up, but this time she quickly dried them. Andie whispered something to Skip. He made a goofy face, and she giggled again. I tugged at Sally's arm. I wanted to do like them, but Sally gently slapped my hand. Andie giggled some more. I pleaded with Sally to kiss me. Andie interrupted with the announcement that she and Skip had decided that Sally and I should do it on my last night in Berwick. It would be Sally's going away present to me. Skip thought it would be good for Sally, and Andie thought it would be good for me. My heart dropped. I was afraid to look Sally in the eye. She would never agree. But when Andie asked her straight out if she wanted to, without hesitation, Sally bowed her head and nodded slightly. Yes, I was stunned for a moment, but quickly recovered. I mean Sally and Andie must have discussed this all along, right? I jumped from my seat. I took Sally's hand, and, as slowly as I could manage, I led her upstairs. We went straight to bed.

First, we tried kissing a bit to start off with something familiar, but Sally seemed tense and grumpy again. I sat up, and she turned her head into the pillow. What should I do next? I had no idea. I felt like a little boy searching for home. Sally didn't know what to do either, but she knew who to ask. She jumped up from the bed and ran downstairs to find Andie. Just as quickly, she came running back to me and plopped herself down, but said nothing. She just kind of moved her breasts from side to side, and I figured she wanted me to take off her blouse. At first she was helpful, and then she resisted. Her resistance made me a little mad, but also made me tingle. She fought me until she thought I was about to give up, and then  allowed another button to be unbuttoned. As soon as I got her blouse nearly open, she tried to button it back. I became determined to see  her breasts, yet I was careful not to hurt her or make her mad or rip

33

the damn thing off her. And then, out of nowhere, it seemed, she just fell back into the bed and surrendered.

"All right," she said, "but you have to promise not to look."

What? I thought that was the whole idea. So, I promised and she finished taking off her blouse herself, and quickly hid under the covers. We kissed some more, and I ventured to poke blindly at her breasts padded by a soft bra. Eventually, I got the courage to kind of knead them like biscuits. I was surprised she didn't try to stop me. She just lay back about as rigid as the headboard.

I figured it was time to go to the next step, so, I tried to take off her bra. Oh, well. What a fight! Finally, we calmed down and negotiated:

"But I really want to."

"No, I can't let you."

"Why not?"

"I just can't, that's all."

"Come on."

"Well. Maybe later."

"But I'm leaving tomorrow."

Suddenly, she jumped up again, turned her back to me and put on her blouse. Then she fled out the door.

My desire was starting to numb. Was it worth this? "Why can't she just love me a little?" I softly moaned. Why do we have to fight about it? I was about to go after her when I heard her footsteps softy treading up the carpeted stairs.

I decided I would get down on my knees, and plead with her. But I didn't need to. Andie had gently eased Sally back into pleasure. She scooted back into bed and confidently kissed me. She did not want to stop kissing. I needed a breath. I wanted to move on. I pushed her back, and I told her how pretty she looked. I kissed her softly, just a little bit, and I stroked her hair. I really did like her, whoever she was. I would certainly miss her kisses, her touch. She took off her blouse, then she turned over on her stomach. That was to allow me to work on getting that bra off. I pulled and tugged and wished I had a pocket knife. I groaned. Sally pushed me off of her, and she unclasped the bra herself. Once again, she made me promise not to look. I pretended to promise, and then, she took it off, and when she hesitated—giving me a brief pose—I looked as much as I could before she completely disappeared under the covers.

I took off my shirt, to be fair, and lay next to her in silence. Slowly she poked her head out, and I looked at her, and we smiled sweetly at each other. For a few minutes we lay there together, so gently terrified. What else was there to do? I kissed her, and I caressed her, but only under the covers. I wanted to see the way this all looked. I loved to watch her eyes shutting slowly and then open to my curious gaze. Her expression changed to a quizzical smile, and turned away, embarrassed by our eyes meeting, and our mutual affection. At last, I was in bed with her, and now I was touching Sally's breasts, and she liked it. She whispered to me, "You looked, didn't you?"

"Yes. A little bit," I cooed.

"I can't believe you," she snapped. "I told you not to."

Out of bed she leapt. I got a real good look as she abandoned caution, facing me, and she made a big show of getting dressed. But she did not put her bra back on. And she rumbled down the stairs.

My god, this was confusing. I stared at the ceiling for a while, and I let my mind wander over the whiteness of the room. It was almost like a hospital room. So sterile. I began to feel lonely.

Why couldn't she just stop running away? It would be so nice to hold her close and *naked* and kiss her over and over again. Maybe I was just waiting to leave, I thought. Tomorrow to Florida and then to Germany! Sally, where are you? What are you doing? I scratched my balls. *I remember when I used to play in the Spanish moss, and I'd come home with chiggers on my balls, because I'd been scratching myself. Mommie would get out a can of turpentine and some cotton balls, and she'd swab the fire to those little red devils. I'd scream and beg her to stop, and she'd soothe me, telling me it just had to be done. And there was that poor kid at Vacation Bible School who peed his bed, and everybody made fun of him. I'm glad I didn't pee the bed. Then again, if I had, I bet it might have killed the chiggers. The born-again, born-never Christian brutes who were our counselors at that dreadful place should have been flushed away. Just because I was in the habit of saying,"gah" to everything that was fascinating, they threatened to make me wear a sign around my neck proclaiming, "I take the Lord's name in vain." I really didn't get what they were talking about. Every time I opened my mouth, they glared at me. And then Dad, my real dad, came to pick me up from that camp. He was wearing sunglasses. He almost never wore sunglasses. He asked me if I wanted to go to Miami with my mom and my sister. I said, "Okay," but I wanted to see my friends first. No. There would be no time for that. We had to leave immediately. The Mustang was packed and ready to go. Wasn't he going, I asked? "No," he said. And around the edge of his sunglasses, I could see that he was crying. My father never cried.*

I went downstairs to see what had happened to Sally. Andie was back on Skip's lap. Her bra was off, and he had his hand under her blouse. He was casually feeling her breasts while Andie laughed and talked to Sally. Sally was more than a little disgusted with Skip, and was trying to ignore him and what he was doing.

Skip said, "Why don't you guys quit fooling around and just go ball?"

Sally was appalled, and left the room.

"Great, Skip. Thanks a lot," I said as I scampered after Sally.

"You guys should use my mom's room," Andie shouted after us. "We're going to use my room."

I found Sally in the living room, staring out the window. I asked her what she wanted to do. She took my hand, said nothing, and led me back upstairs. We went into Andie's mom's room that was much darker because everything was blue. The walls were painted baby blue. The furniture was navy blue. The lampshades were daylight blue. And the bedspread was crazy blue. Sally lay down on the bedspread and told me to lie on top of her. What had changed her mind, I wondered? Did Andie and Skip's playing excite her, even though she had acted disgusted? She wasn't smiling when she told me to get on top of her, and she wasn't smiling when I crawled up close and did as she said. Immediately, I could feel myself growing between her legs. She pushed me off and jumped out of bed.

"Fuck," I groaned. Sally turned toward me and snarled. Then her expression turned willful and certain.

"Take off your clothes," she said. "I'll be right back."

I could hear her down the hall knocking on Andie's door. I heard Skip complain, and then, after a pause, I heard Andie and Sally go downstairs for yet another conference.

I took off my clothes and got back into bed. Maybe we were going to do it after all. I wondered if going all the way was a good idea, since I wouldn't be back for I didn't know how long. We might miss each other too much. I was scared and cold. I slipped under the protection of the covers. I wondered what she would look like completely naked. My dick began to grow again. *I had never seen a completely naked girl. Well, there was my sister. Boy, did I get yelled at for that. We hadn't been able to take showers together for a long time, and I wanted to know why not. So, one day when my sister was in there, I decided to investigate. I pulled open the shower door, and as my eyes bugged out, I stuttered my excuse, "Dad says to hurry up in there." She screamed and yelled at me to "get out." I thought she would croak.*

*I wondered how my sister was doing now. She had left so suddenly. I wanted to visit her and my Dad and my friends in St. Pete. I was so happy when Mom announced that she and Paw-paw were going there to pick up some things. I wanted to go, too, but they wouldn't let me. I wanted my things, too. "What about my toys?" I cried. Couldn't I at least have my toys? In the end, they promised they would let me go with them. But in the middle of the night, I heard the U-Haul pull up and drive away. And that was that.*

Sally came back into the room and saw me hiding under the covers.

"Did you take them off?" she asked.

"Yes," I said, and I felt the tingling heat race through me again.

And then, after all our struggling and fear, she simply dropped her loose clothes, and they relaxed to the floor. She seemed to enjoy me watching her. I wanted that moment to last forever. I gazed at her pale white skin, shining from out of the blue shadows. She was not a swan, or in that room a blue heron. Not a mermaid, either, but Sally. She approached and lay silently next to me. We kissed and hugged with me still under the covers, and she, naked on top of them. And I touched her softly, tentatively, admiring her, and amazed at this beautiful naked girl showing herself proudly to me. Her breasts were peaked with nipples much larger than mine. I loved the slight curve at her waist and her tender belly, her slender legs and the slight mound of brown hair between them! My heart pounded when I reached out to touch her, to kiss her breasts, and run my hand down to her...to her flower.

She whispered, "You can touch me there a little if you want to, but I'm having my period."

Sure enough, I could see the safety cord hiding in her pubic hair.

"Oh," I exclaimed. I was suspicious, but relieved. So that's what had allowed her to finally relax—no going all the way. I though about it, and then I offered, "We could lie on top of each other. Is that all right?"

"Yes," I barely heard her say.

And so I lay on top of Sally, and I moved around a bit.

"Does that feel good?" I asked.

"It's good," she said. "But I like it better when you don't move. Just lie here with me."

I wanted to cry. I still want to cry when I think of her. Sally, my cautiously gentle friend I never knew.

Mom flew ahead to meet her folks in Florida while I followed slowly behind on the Greyhound. She explained she needed to get there first to take care of a few things, besides, she could only afford one air fare. Down through the Susquehanna Valley past Harrisburg and eventually into DC, I waited out the miles and tried to sleep. But the driver woke everybody repeatedly, announcing the list of towns we could change to. It was tempting. Just disappear. The guy next to me offered to let me sit by the window.

"Have you ever seen our nation's capital?" He guided my attention toward the monuments, shining white in the summer sun. "We have a lot to be thankful for, Son," he beamed. "Just look at that."

I nodded, smiled politely, and fell back asleep.

Maw-maw and Paw-paw had moved from their old house in South Miami—the one with the big banyan tree out back and the coconut palms along the street—to Hollywood, Florida. I was disappointed. I used to have a friend who lived down the block. We would hide in her playhouse that she had long ago outgrown. All scrunched up inside, she told me how mean her parents were. That was true. They were mean as rattlers. Whenever they caught us kissing, they yelled harshly at her and sent me home. Maw-maw told me, when I asked about her, that she had run away to go live with the hippies out in Haight-Ashberry. I'd heard of "hippies". One day on the beach in Key West I saw some odd-looking people hanging out by the Martello towers. I described the men's long hair and pirate earrings to Mom. She told me what they were and that I should steer clear of those guys, but they seemed nice enough. To make cool sandals like theirs, I cut designs into my penny loafers with the Dive-bomber's double-edged blade. Mine didn't look as good, though, and I cut my fingers to shreds.

I don't know why Maw-maw and Paw-paw had moved to Hollywood. The place was awful. They lived in an ugly tan cinder-block house surrounded by nothing. There was nothing on all sides but fields of crab grass and sand spurs, and the ground was crawling with fire ants. The heat and the mosquitoes and the gnats were annoying, gnawing at us in our dull blank waiting. Every day, I watched and waited for the mailman to bring the news that we could finally leave. Day after day, nothing came. I often cursed the mailman, slammed the mailbox closed, and dragged myself back to the ugly house.

At last, they let me go exploring. "Be back two hours before dark." But I could only find a pitiful shopping center a two-mile trek across a sand-spur field from hell. The shopping center's only saving grace was a hobby store. I found a balsa wood airplane kit that used a gasoline engine, and it didn't cost too much. If I wanted it, I was told, I'd have to work for it. Paw-paw might let me do some weeding, they laughed.

I sat in the sandy grass next to the hibiscus and rubber plants. Fighting back the bugs and heat, I pulled at the damn weeds. After an hour, I was covered with dirt and bites and sweat. For my labors, Paw-paw gave me a quarter. A quarter! I demanded that he let me borrow the lawn mower, and I took off to find some reasonable customers.

I mowed the lawns of the wasteland to buy balsa struts, special fuselage paper, and lots of glue. And finally, I bought the engine. I worked feverishly, still listening for the mailman's jeep. No news. In a week, I had finished building my plane. I took it out to the driveway for its maiden flight. The engine started like a dream. I grabbed the controls with one hand, and let her go with the other. Up she went, and down she went, smashing to bits in the driveway. It didn't even complete a full circle.

After that, I didn't even care if the mailman or the whole damn post office had run away to the real Hollywood, never to deliver a single letter to our house again. Fuck it. I sat in front of the TV, watching nothing forever.

One day my real father interrupted. He called Mom and demanded to see me before we left for Germany. I hadn't seen him since the divorce. Not for three years. Ever since then, Mom and her camp couldn't stop criticizing him. Maw-maw, especially, repeated that he didn't care about me. She said he was "a no-count so and so." Dad must have struggled making that call. He reminded them that he had certain rights.

I took the bus up to Dade City, a Dixie town of groves and the moss of central Florida. Dad and my sister had moved there after the divorce. My sister, as I said, had no desire to live with Mom, and the court let her have her way, since she was "of age." When Dad asked Maw-maw how he was going to take care of a teenage girl, Maw-maw replied, "You made your bed, now lie in it." The court also decided that at age eleven, I was too young to know what I wanted. Twelve was the age of reason. Mom was pressuring Dad to get the divorce done. To make it easier, she arranged it so Dad wouldn't have to come to Miami. He could just sign the papers up in St. Pete. Although in another four months, I would have been twelve, "the age of reason," he signed the papers anyway.

While I was away, Dad had found a data-processing job at the local Lyke's citrus division. He had also found a young new wife. When I arrived at their simple house on the edge of downtown, my new step-mother greeted me. She was busy ironing in the sweltering heat. They had no air conditioning, and the fans turned loudly at full blast. Steam rose from the sprayed shirt before her.

The scene reminded me of when my mother took me to Knoxville, Tennessee. I was very young. Mom led me into a dry-cleaning plant where she introduced me to a tearful old man who had emerged from the steamy chemicals. Behind him, I could see large, sweating 'colored' folks, laboring at hissing and wildly gesticulating pressing machines. Each and every one of those workers smiled gently at me. Much later, when I was in my twenties, I was finally told that the owner, that tearful man, and not my paw-paw in Florida, was my real grandfather. But nobody liked to talk about it. Who were these people? For the first two years of my life, I was cuddled within the sweet warmth of my 'mammy'. She protected me from my mother until it was decided they'd have to let her go. Mammy, not Mommie. I cried for days, hoping my Cille would come home.

On my short visit to see my father, Dad did not know what to say. And my sister was preoccupied with her boyfriend and the obsessions of his domineering mother. My sister did try to visit with me, but, as with Dad, nobody could find the words. We were all blocked by the sorrow of the damn events. My new step-mother did her best to lessen the pain with kind words and her special tamale pie. We ate it for two days, and then it was time for me to go.

By the time I got back to Hollywood, word had finally come that Mom and I were to leave from Homestead Air Force Base on Capital airlines. We would be in Frankfurt by Labor Day.

At first, the flight was thrilling. I loved watching the endless dawn hatch and expire, over and over. The sky would brighten for a few minutes, then darken for a few more, then light up again. As we descended, the cabin pressure became so bad that I writhed in my seat and held my ears. The pain was so excruciating I thought my head would pop, or at the very least, I would go deaf. I cried out for help. I was given gum. I thought I was expected to put it in my ears, against those damn howling sirens.

# TWO

# An Inadequate Hug Upon Arrival

Mom's innocent Mustang, the color of mustard abandoned in the sun, carried our Dive-bomber faction from Rhein/Main airbase up into the hills of Schönberg, Germany. It *was* beautiful. As we made our final approach, little gardens peeked over the short walls and fences of Hermann Löns Weg. The pavement, made of interlocking blocks each the size of a hand pressed underneath, waved a curious "Hello."

"This is it," the Dive-bomber proudly announced as we turned into number 12. "But it's really bigger inside than it looks," he apologized.

A white square capped by a steep red tile roof awaited the un-likely event of containing us. Below each shutter-flanked window eye, the empty flower boxes were a blistered and faded brown. The enormous yard hosted a carpet of dandelions and plum trees, both purple and yellow. The tiny Hansel and Gretel *Wunderhaus* cowered there in the surrounding conspicuous space.

"We'll be the only American family living in Schönberg," the Dive-bomber beamed. Our little romantic house on "Beautiful Hill" was certainly protected, he said. It had survived the Allied forces who routinely dumped their excess ordinance northward after their Frankfurt sorties. That way they avoided blowing themselves to smithereens upon landing. Our charming home had been arbitrarily spared.

Around back was an unexpected hidden world. A large comforting tree shadowed a little patio. Slate steps curved up the rise to the porch and a polished wooden back door. The slight mound was grown over with weeds, and a lot of slate had cracked loose.

"I can see a project for the fall, can't you, Son?" said the Divebomber as he kicked away chunks of slate on his way to the garage. "Here's the hiding place for the back-door key." He reached into the darkness. "Always leave it on the hook." I could hear the key thumping against the wood as he twiddled it. "Okay, Son? You got that?" He reached in again and pulled the skeleton key off the nail. He held it in his hand for us to admire. "Isn't that something? Look at that old thing," he said, and then he laughed once. I didn't understand what he thought was so funny. The silver key rested in his outstretched hand. "I bet you wouldn't have to lock the doors around here, anyway. But, just in case." Then he clenched his fist around it and carefully returned the key to its hiding place.

The Bomber led us up the front steps and, for Mom, he ceremoniously opened the door. She squeaked like some kind of thumped rodent. "Oh, Honey, it's precious," she said. "I can't believe how cute it is. This is just perfect."

I followed in behind and smiled a lot. It was best to be politely silent.

The Bomber had time to decorate while we were in Hollywood, waiting for word of our flight. There were a few familiar objects from our days together in Key West, most notably for me, the model plane of the Dive-bomber's namesake. Throughout the living room, he had carefully arranged several things he had gotten out of storage. They were objects, mostly from his previous tours in Turkey and Greece—little dark metal oil lamps with the likeness of Medusa and Apollo molded into them; a javelin from Olympia; brass howitzer shells with designs beaten into the length of them, now empty, were made to hold umbrellas. And a *jambiya*, he called it,—a curved Turkish knife, bronzed, and decorated with costume jewelry glued to the handle and scabbard. Mom fixed her attention on the knife. It spooked her to her roots.

"Vic, I don't want that in here," she announced. "That's bad luck. 'Any knife given between those that is close, will surely cut them in twain,'" she recited.

"It's just a decoration, a letter opener," he sighed, struggling to stay light. "It can't hurt nobody."

"Well, I don't like it," she said.

The Dive-bomber smiled incredulously.

"I'm serious now," Mom insisted.

I watched the Dive-bomber's grin collapse into resignation. Mom coolly suggested we continue the tour.

Off the narrow hall that led to the front door, we saw a pull-chain
toilet, and next to it, the staircase swooped back on itself to the bedroom. "This is as close to a spiral staircase I could find," said the Dive-bomber. "I know how much you love them," he sighed.

"Oh, Honey," Mom said. "That's all right. I don't care about that. You have found a precious little home for us. It's almost perfect, excepting that knife."

The Dive-bomber forced another grin and led us upstairs.

The huge master feather bed was held up high by a chunky thick wooden cabinet. That, and a small dresser, crowded the room. At the foot of the bed, the Bomber had managed to squeeze in an old trunk he had covered with a *kilim* and a four-hose hookah, bought at an Istanbul bazaar. A double window looked over the patio below. From the window, you could also see through the branches to the garage. The Bomber pointed out how easy it would be to spot any intruders. Not that we had to worry.

We toured the cellar, too. The Dive-bomber had stocked it with what looked like a couple years' worth of canned food from the PX, just in case. If anything were to happen, *we* would survive, he said. The rows of Campbell Soup, Spaghetti-Os, Beef-a-roni, Chicken of the Sea, and so on, seemed to testify that we would.

Back on the main floor, was a dark living area, and just off the miniature kitchen was an even tinier room that was to be mine. The Bomber politely regretted its size. He said he hoped it would be all right for me. I told him I didn't care that it was small. I didn't tell him I was just relieved I didn't have to share a bed with Mom, anymore.

I could see that he had worked hard to get us started off on the right foot. I hoped we'd be okay. He promised that the next day we would see the best part, he said. We would take a hike out into the forest.

The next morning, the Dive-bomber was awfully grumpy. I figured he and Mom hadn't been able to stop talking about that damn knife. But when he was in the bathroom, Mom said the real reason the Dive-bomber was upset, was because he claimed she hadn't hugged him enthusiastically enough at the airport. "I hugged him real good," she defended herself. "I don't know," she said. "Just leave him alone." She smiled at me. Her crow's feet looked shiny like cracked fleshy glass.

"Are we still going for a walk?" I asked impatiently. "I gotta start school, tomorrow, you know?"

"Don't you worry about that, Honey. We'll go into the woods," she said. And Mom got busy making a few snacks, and the Dive-bomber gradually started to speak again.

The forest began where the stones of locking hands gave way to dirt, just 200 meters from our door. The forest was romantic. The canopy thick and dense, and the floor covered with pine and fir needles. The tree trunks were dark and ponderous in the occasional light. Several recently felled trees lay scattered about. Their limbs had been stripped off, leaving a kind of handle at the top where they had been attached to the trunk, making them perfect for walking sticks. The Bomber suggested we each search for a branch suited to our size and disposition. Then we could cut designs in them with his Swiss army knife. So, we playfully roamed around the waist-high trunks and limbs, looking for the perfect stick. The Bomber searched long and hard for a strong and sturdy straight staff, and helped pick out a curvier one for Mom.

The forest was exhilarating, and soothed the distance between us. I poked around the branches, looking for the right branch for me. I saw Mom and the Bomber lulled into hugs and kisses. He saw me watching them, and so he pulled away. He said, "When we get home, we'll shellac them." So, he and I took turns carving our designs. The bark peeled off nicely. On theirs, Mom and the Dive-bomber would later tack little metal shields, representing the places they hiked to on *Volksmarchen*, or 'People's Marches'. I wouldn't get any little shields, as it turned out.

We sat amidst the resinous tangle, enjoying the fresh scent of the cuttings. The Dive-bomber lit up a Winston. From who knows where, a forest ranger appeared. He had a very strict manner, yet explained politely, mostly in gestures, that the Dive-bomber was prohibited from smoking there. Yes, it was okay to take the already cut limbs for walking sticks, but only one for each of us. The Dive-bomber admired that man very much. He said he liked his discipline and "bearing." "He has the qualities of a fine soldier," he beamed. For me and Mom, though, our first encounter with a German person made us tense. In his uniform he looked a little too much like someone we might have seen in *The Dirty Dozen* or *The Great Escape*. We had felt we were in big trouble in the deep dark forest. But the *Förster* had been surprisingly kind. He saluted, then strutted away, and we laughed at our fear of him.

The Dive-bomber wanted me and him to attend to the yard. On weekends, I was supposed to help out. My first instructions were to pull up the dandelions, roots and all. They were beautiful against the green grass, so bright and eager. I just wanted to let them be. But my instructions were firm. So, I sat out in a field of dandelion remorse, plucking them one by one. At least there were no fire ants in Germany. From the patio mound, where he was terracing for the distant spring, the Dive-bomber saw me working reluctantly.

"You got to get 'em by the roots, Son, or they'll be back up in no time," he said. He yanked up a few to show me how it was done, and then walked back to his project.

I tried to get at the roots, but the flowers kept snapping off at the stem. I was working far too slowly for the Dive-bomber and he came back scowling.

"Put a little elbow grease into it," he said, "or you'll never get 'er done."

"I kinda like them," I said. "Why do we have to pull them up?" I asked, as politely as I could.

"Dammit. They'll spread and take over the whole damn yard. Just look at this," he said and pulled up a dandelion in its puff stage. He blew on it and the seeds flew. He looked at me with his brow furrowed. "Now, you see? They go everywhere. Now does it make sense to you?"

I smirked. He looked ridiculous blowing that dandelion, like a big fairy monster. He's just pretending, I thought.

He shouted, "If you're not going to do it right. . . . Just get in the house."

"Never mind. I'll do it your way," I said, resigning myself to his view of order.

"Get in the house," he bellowed.

I dragged myself inside. What a weasel, I thought. I complained to Mom, "I can't talk to him. He gets so mad over nothing."

"Now, honey...,"she started.

We heard the whirring push mower outside. I went out on the patio, as much to see what he was doing as to get away from my overly dramatic mother. I saw him mowing down the dandelions with a fevered vengeance, chopping them down as fast as he could. The sweat was drenching him and he huffed and puffed, paused, then huffed and puffed over the huge lawn. No, we didn't need no gas mower. I turned away from the fool. "What

53

an idiot," I said under my breath as I went back inside. "What's the point of that?" He never could relax in his orderly garden. He seemed to think gardening was a time for revenge.

Yet, it was through gardening that the Dive-bomber met Karl-Heinz *und* Herta. They were strolling through the village when they noticed the Bomber sprucing up around the plum trees. The Dive-bomber had been learning German rapidly, and successfully invited them over to visit that evening. They brought gifts of wine and flowers for the Bomber and Mom and chocolate for me. In fact, they brought gifts every time they visited, even though they lived only a few blocks away and we saw them often. Mom, especially, liked this gift-giving tradition, and so devoted a fair amount of her time to it. The gifts became more and more elaborate. I guess Karl-Heinz und Herta were delighted with our decision not to live on a military base the way 60,000 other American military personnel did.

Before long, Karl-Heinz encouraged the Dive-bomber to join the *Feuerwerk*, 'the volunteer fire department.' Nobody could remember the last time there was a fire in Schönberg. But membership meant, more than anything, a ticket to the *Hofhalle*, 'the community drinking hall.' I saw it from the inside only once. It was a long open room with just tables and chairs where everyone drank from steins, danced, and carried on, telling jokes until late. Since spouses were welcome, it wasn't long before Mom joined in the fun. Mom was a big hit. The *Hofhallers* said she was so charming and funny with her attempts at speaking German laced with an endearing southern accent. Later on, the guys at the *Hofhalle* said the Dive-bomber should join the men's choir, and he gratefully accepted. He became so popular that it was only half in jest that his fellow villagers suggested he run for mayor.

I couldn't believe what stars Mom and the Dive-bomber had become. The only problem was they had this son, me, who was not exactly part of the community. Instead, he moped about at home after school, and hid in the cellar playing the drums his real father had bought him. So it was suggested, I join the *Kappenklub*, 'a young folks club' that, in this case, was a *Fanfarenzug*, or, 'a drum and bugle corps.' I had mistakenly expressed my fascination with the Fanfarenzug when, very early one morning they woke me up, playing traditional military tunes as they marched through the streets.

I was certain to have problems in the Fanfarenzug. My German teacher at the junior high, with her dictatorial panics, had not helped engender a love for the language. And, despite my determination to play the drums like Spirit's Cassidy, I really wasn't making much progress. Nevertheless, the Dive-bomber insisted I join, probably to get me out of the house on weekends, so Mom and he could do it screaming out loud or whatever they did.

I was given a snare drum painted blue and white, and when we rehearsed I fumbled around trying not to play too loud while some guy shouted orders in a language I didn't understand. A few days into it, they gave me a blue tunic with the seal of Kronberg, our neighboring village, sewn on the front. And they gave me a floppy blue beret with a long white plume that was kind of cool. After several attempts they communicated to me that I was to start marching the next day at 5 a.m.

And so, I paraded around Deutschland, pretending to play the drums and waking up surprisingly receptive villagers at the crack of dawn.

It was a good idea to blend in to the community, I thought. We seemed to all silently agree, the best way to hide from ourselves was to escape into something foreign. The popular couple and their Kappenkluber Fanfarenzug son looked pretty good to the community, yet within our house, the Dive-bomber still drank into his dark moods, while Mom avoided any and all conflicts by constantly redecorating a la Deutschland.

The Dive-bomber worked on top of Feldberg at the radar site. Almost every day, he passed by Kamp King, one of 44 US military installations in the area. At Kamp King, I caught the bus to school 15 miles away in Frankfurt. It was convenient for the Dive-bomber to drop me off and pick me up at the base gate, and so we were supposed to establish a routine. But sometimes he wouldn't show up after school, and then I'd have to either take the *Straßenbahn* to Oberursel and then hitchhike, or would walk about three miles through the woods. In fact, he started coming home later and later and I eventually stopped waiting for him.

On weekends, he brought home a case of liter bottles of strong German beer, all for himself. He set to drinking the whole damn thing by Sunday afternoon. Man, did he ever look like Pablo, from "Streetcar". Sometimes, he even worked drunk in the yard. After ending my gardening apprenticeship, he established a protective territory blended with martyrdom, so the fenced-in yard became off-limits to me. It was his project, Mom declared, and I should just leave him alone.

More and more, it seemed to me that the Dive-bomber wanted to be left alone all the time. Well, except when he turned into a guest of the Germans. At home, his silences were long and brutal. I couldn't tell why he was so morose. Maybe, he and Mom were arguing when I wasn't around. Always silence. Sometimes, I came home and the house looked messed up, When I asked, "Mom, did anything happen?" She claimed nothing had, and told me not to worry about it. "Just go down in the cellar and play your drums," she'd say. But the violence was still there. I could feel it.

The junior high, a Department of Defense affair, was surrounded by walls five meters high. No student dared venture beyond them. During any break from the classrooms, the only thing most of us knew to do with ourselves was to walk clockwise around a large oval track. To walk counter-clockwise was unthinkable. We were also permitted to play ball games in the center of the oval, but only until we had been sufficiently exercised and made ready for more mind-crushing boredom. Our classes were taught factory-style inside this compound of a former women's prison. The military could not have picked a more secure place to manage us. Once the busses pulled in, that was it —droned algebra and screeched German without escape, at least until we discovered we could just walk out the front door, counter-clockwise! English was tolerable, I guess, since we got to have rap sessions. We rapped about the war, mostly. They taught us we couldn't do anything about that either. In any case, we were clearly theirs to mold, until the blessed busses came to take us home again where they could further protect us.

You can bet the administration wanted no pleasure, any-where. I fooled them though, stealing kisses from cute girls flut-tering through the halls and never tiring of playing try-to-pull-the-zipper-down on that girl's bumpy black dress. Her front zip-per had a big ring on the end of it, making it easy to grab. I pulled and she would catch it "just in time." She squealed, laughed and pretended to get mad. She wore that dress often, and when she didn't, I begged her to wear it again real soon. I doubt it got washed much. One day I got the zipper all the way down her front and I saw her underpants. That was a good day. The sight of the cotton-white prize, hanging loosely on her skin-ny hips, made me want to dedicate myself to her. But the game had gone too far for her, I guess, and afterwards, she safety-pinned her zipper dress forever closing it to me.

On the weekends, when I wasn't drumming for the Kappen-klub, I tried going over to Kamp King. I could have spent more time in Kronberg, I guess, that old beauty on the opposite hill, but I thought no one spoke English there. I didn't want to run into anybody who'd recognize me from the Kappenklub, or as the son of the Dive-bomber.

Like almost all American bases in Germany, Kamp King was ugly. The single GI grunts slept, whenever they could manage it, in olive-drab barracks. Meanwhile, the married enlisted men's families passed their time in stodgy gray apartment buildings. On a ridge, overlooking the whole installation, the officers and their families hid in larger characterless tan duplexes. The mili-tary is a caste system, someone told me, and the differences in housing made sure the ranks were clearly spelled out. The only way you could tell the base buildings apart was by the bland signs on them—K138-7 Officer's Mess; K 749-4 King's Kegelbahn. I spent most of my time at the *Kegelbahn* watching the troops bowl.

One day, I spotted a notice in the snack bar about roller-skating trips at another base. I thought I'd give it a try. The following weekend when we pulled up at the roller rink, some chicks were waiting to see who the bus would bring. No sooner had I gotten off the bus than a couple of cuties convinced me I could have more fun with them than skating with children. They were not at all ashamed or shy the way my zipper girl had been. In fact, one of them took me straight away to a loading dock, hidden from the street lights, and she encouraged me to forage around in her pants. It sure made kissing more exciting, and I loved her peppery smell. When it came time for the bus to take me away, I wracked my brain figuring out how I could stay. My hungry friend told me, "Don't worry about it, Sweetie, I'll see you in two weeks." With her promise ringing in me ears, I more willingly got back on the bus.

Two weeks later, as scheduled, she was waiting by the roller rink but with a couple of guys. She introduced me to them, and told me they could get us some beer. Who the hell were they, I wanted to know? But I didn't dare say anything. Had to be cool. Play along and don't piss her off. Soon they took off for the booze, and she and I went on to more intermediate groping. I had just managed to slip my finger deep inside her when the dudes came back with the booze. She slipped her pants back up, not caring that they could see her ass. Then all of us hid among the dark buildings, drinking as fast as we could. I guess we had fun, even though my girl didn't want to kiss me or fool around while the other guys were there.

I tried to sneak back on the bus without exhaling fumes. Our chaperone, who seemed to hate us, was guarding the door and taking a head count. I tried to be cool; I tried to make my foot reach the first step. It wouldn't go. The chaperone grabbed me by the scruff and launched me up the step well. "You see this, everyone? This is what happens when you stray, when you don't follow the rules and you play around with temptation," he said. "Thanks to. . . .What's your name boy?"

I gurgled something.

"Thanks to whatever his name is, we may not have any more trips like this."

I heard the moans swirl in a torment down the aisle.

"You just sit here in front with me," he snarled. "where everyone can get a good look at you."

After a while, nobody but him cared. Still, the whole trip back he made a point of frequently looking at me with disgust while shaking his concerned fat head. At least he didn't insist on lecturing me. I kept myself happy in the dark, sniffing my delicious finger.

"Who's picking you up," he asked.

"My step-dad," I slurred.

"Well, good," he said triumphantly. "Just wait until he gets a look at you. Of course, you know, you'll never again come on one of these trips," he said.

Bastard. That meant I would never see my girl again, whoever she was. I tried to think about how I might get back out there on my own, wherever it was. But thinking didn't come easily, nor did moving. In fact, I practically had to be carried inside the kegelbahn. I indicated which one of the bowlers was my step-dad, and the chaperone righteously dragged me over to him.

"Sergeant," he said. "Is this your son?"

The Dive-bomber cocked his head in a funny way, pausing for a moment while he seemed to ponder the question. "Yeah. I suppose he is," he slurred. He was smashed.

I laughed softly, and the chaperone scowled at me once more. He turned back to the Dive-bomber and chastised him. "Is this any example to make for your son?"

"Don't you worry yourself about it," the Dive-bomber frowned. He towered over the man. "I'll straighten him out," he said.

The Dive-bomber stumbled over the bright orange viewer seats, and tried to grab my arm in a show of repossession. The chaperone turned away in disgust and stormed out of the Kegel-bahn.

The Bomber said something under his breath like, "Uptight Army bastard." And then to the air, "Was he some kind of officer? OCS or something?"

The Dive-bomber put his arm around me. "You ever try this here 'Heiney-kin?'" He sniggered. "Better not now," he said. But it's good. It's Dutch. Nothing like a Dutch hiney. Ain't that right, Son?" With a smile he fell away to the bar. He left me alone, and somehow managed to bowl a couple more games while I struggled not to fall out of my pre-formed seat. I wanted to go home.

At last we got into the Mustang. He drove us the usual route through Oberursel and through the forest to Schönberg. He laughed about the "queer army bastard," about the look on his face when he told him to fuck off. Who did that guy think he was? He said I looked pretty fucking funny when the chaperone dragged me into the King's Kegelbahn. I told him he'd looked kind of funny, too. He started to laugh, but then just stared at me too long for safety with those howling mean raccoon eyes.

Winter had arrived, and the first snow fell on Mole. Who was this "Mole?" I say he was the first to walk the oval counter-clockwise at junior high. He said, "I am not the Mole. I am mere-ly wearing its skin." He did wear a shabby coat that looked like it was made of rat skin, or maybe brushed Chihuahua. Always hunched forward with his hands hooked in its pockets, he wore it like a harbor. His mom let me go inside their house. I went upstairs and found the window open. Mole was balled up under a sheet. His fuzzy halo hair, dimmed in the morning gloom, was dusted with snow. He looked as if he'd been sprinkled with powdered sugar.

"Mole, get up," I said, shaking him a little. He was so cold. He groaned and pulled away. I shook him again, and he peeked at me. "Man, you always sleep with the window open? It's snowing," I said.

Mole dragged himself out of bed and began to shiver. The snowflakes in his frizzy hair melted into sparkling droplets. He sent me to his older brother Leo's room while he got dressed.

Leo's walls were papered entirely with a collage of scenes from the war, John and Yoko in bed, a big black fist, and a giant poster about Jewish rye bread, which I didn't get. The floor and his desk had stacks of mimeographed pages ordered into neat piles. I picked up a copy. "Father, I want to kill you. — Jim Mor-rison," it said at the top.

This single page, copied hundreds of times, applauded the last scene in *The Graduate,* when Benjamin ran away with Elaine. Leo had written that our antiheroes had broken away from the plastic world and the hypocrisy of the church, and jumped on a bus going anywhere. It said something like, "They didn't know where the fuck they were going, man. They just got on a bus—two freaks riding off into the Amerikan nightmare. Happy forever? Hell, no. But they got out. Off to who knows where, flipping off the scene along the way."

"Wow! Who is this guy," I murmured.

There were a lot of angry-sounding books scattered about. Books about Cuba, and on one, a picture of a guy wearing a beret with the word "Che" written across the top in big red letters. There were also books whose covers had squiggly writing and simple paintings of squares and triangles and circles on them. I picked up one of them — *Zen Flesh, Zen Bones*, it teased.

"What's this?" I asked Mole when he came out of his bedroom.

"Put it back," he demanded. "It's some Eastern thing," he said absently.

Mole and I spent the day listening to music new to us. Black Sabbath was silly, but fun. It was simple and driving and rough, and very heavy. The album cover showed dudes of darkness, wearing big black crosses, and dressed up like demons. I knew what Maw-maw would do if she knew I was listening to "devil music." She would have filled me with shame. I was a bad boy to listen to "demon rock." For a moment or two, I thought of her trembling anger, but she was far away, and a fiery thrill ran through me.

I liked the *Led Zeppelin II* album better than *Black Sabbath*. I especially liked the "Lemon Song"— "Baby, when you squeeze my lemon, I'm gonna fall right outta bed . . . and the juice will run down my leg." That was hilarious. I liked Led Zeppelin so much, I decided to copy their first album cover that featured an exploding blimp. Mole got me some glossy paper and I spent a long time poking black dots like personal bombs going off. When it was all done, Mole laughed at me, because I had written "Led Zeplin" across the top of my picture, not bothering to check the spelling.

When I got home, I hung it on my wall anyway, right next to a weird brass-horn plaque the Dive-bomber had brought back from a military-sponsored, "morale-enhancing" field trip to Bastogne. It looked like it had been run over by a tank. I started to paste up some photos, too, plus all that Beatle's *White Album* stuff. I wanted it to look like Leo's room with its collage of torment. I draped a long string of beads onto wherever I could hook them, and also prominently displayed an incense-burner I had made in shop class. My room was starting to look pretty cool.

Meanwhile, for Christmas, I got some skis, a snowboard and a chemistry set. I liked to sit in the cellar with all the lights off and burn spoonfuls of sulphur over my alcohol lamp. The sulphur popped and gurgled and turned blue and yellow and green. It was just beautiful. One day, I burned spoonful after spoonful of sulphur until the whole cellar filled up with thick yellow smoke. I nearly choked to death. The Dive-bomber and Mom came home unexpectedly, and probably saved me from doing myself in. Anyway, on Christmas, Mom got a sled and a ring or something, (I forget what the Dive-bomber got). And we went frolicking *in der schnee*. It was a lot of fun, I guess.

I remember that Christmas break we three did a lot of things together. We went up to Feldberg, and toured the inside of the microwave site, with its banks of flashing lights and its orderly patch-cords. I attempted to snow-board down the mountain with Mom and the Bomber scooting behind me on the sled.

Another day, we hiked and sledded through the forest with Karl-Heinz und Herta to a couple of winter *Rasthausen*, a kind of rest stop for wanderers in the woods. Two Rasthausen were directly opposite one another. Each entrance was crowded with sleds and skis like colorful porcupine quills stuck in the snow-banks. Karl-Heinz und Herta led us into their favorite of the two places. Inside, was a vast wooden hall with long rows of picnic tables. As best I could tell, they served only four things: hot *Apfelsaft* 'apple juice,' *Glühwein* 'mulled wine,' hot *Apfelwein* 'apple wine,' and *Kaseküchen* 'cheesecake.' Steam rose from the hot drinks and our breath, and people talked loudly and, occasionally, burst into song. Ahh, to eat the world's most delicious cheesecake and sip sips of hot *Glühwein* on a winter's day in the forest in *Deutschland*! Yes, that was a happy day, too.

Nevertheless, I quit the Kappenklub Fanfahrenzug as soon as I could. That was the Dive-bomber's world and not mine. I had stopped going to practice, anyway. But the Dive-bomber insisted I join another civic organization, such as the Boy Scouts. I suppose he was looking for an escape, too, because joining meant a weekly trip over to Kamp King *at night*.

I didn't go to the scout meetings, instead, I found guys I'd met on the school bus, and, sometimes, a GI or two, to smoke some hashish. It was a lot better than the *kif* Skip had in Berwick. After a few months of that, I told the Dive-bomber through a stoned daze that, it was true, I hadn't been going to the scout meetings. He praised me for my honesty, and permitted me to drop out. Funny kind of permission, I thought, since I had never intended to go in the first place.

# Journal of an Attempted Break

---

**First Day** I called Paul Underhill. He suggested the trip. Don't know him very well. Smoked a couple of bowls together, that's all. At the last minute, Mom insisted she drive us to the *Hauptbahnhof*, 'the main train station'. Naturally, he was pissed. Afraid I'd blown our secret. Said he'd leave without me.

Convinced Mom that it was time I took some responsibility for myself—that kind of crap. She packed me off with a big bag of sandwiches. Told me to be good. Promised I'd call when we started our summer jobs in Sweden.

Met Paul downtown, and we walked past the train station and stuck out our thumbs for the first time, ever. "God, if she knew," I giggled.

Waited two hours for a ride.

Sprung, at last. 600 km on the autobahn in one jump—Frankfurt am Main to Kassel to Hannover to Hamburg.

Quick ride out of that city, then stuck outside of Lübeck for five hours! Jerks. Why didn't they pick us up? Heard they're more upright there.

Two sandwiches left.

By nightfall, hopped the islands through Denmark, riding with an American who said he'd just returned from working in the oilfields in Libya. Turned out to be a pervert. Endured a long night of leg grabbing. No way to escape — our backpacks locked in the trunk. By morning, he wouldn't talk to us. Disappointed we wouldn't suck him off or something. Drove us to Copenhagen, anyway. Angrily dumped in the suburbs at dawn.

**Second Day**. Tivoli Gardens. Tried to sleep. The stone slab benches in front of a glass pavilion ached our bones. Questioning tones in Danish hovered over us and passed by. No way to rest. Reluctantly, sat up. Exhausted. A swirl of joyful clean faces, like stirring tea.

$65 between us. Needed more money. A large chandelier hung over a craps table. A heated gambler looked up at us and scowled before rolling. I guess our road clothes didn't match his tie. Slots jingled all around. Felt like Pinocchio at Pleasure Island. Mom had told me to be good, but release tasted sweet. And I never wanted to go back.

I lost $10 at the slots. Knew I could win it back, but Paul said, "No."

He had to pull me out of there. Said we'd better leave before we went broke. He complained I'd lost that day's food money and then some. He decided *he* should hold the money. Said I couldn't be trusted with it.

What were we going to do for dinner? The lights strung along every edge of Tivoli's pavilions turned on in series, each blinking once against the glass roofs. We left hungry.

Sex shops opened onto the street, oozing red light. Women behind glass storefront cages. Looked like mannequins gesturing mechanically. "Come ball me." Creepy. Jumped into a shop. Saw troughs of monster-headed condoms, condoms with a clenched fist at the head, lion-headed condoms. Paul held up one shaped like a dragon, bulging with strategic ridges and scales. Knew I could score with that in my pocket. Big rubber dicks with straps made us laugh. Too weird. About to be thrown out. We fled.

Bought some cheese, bread and a hard salami chub and ate like kings.

Crossed the border to Landskrona, Sweden after midnight.

Customs official chose us two "hippie-types" over a vivacious couple who they happily whooshed along. Had to dump everything out of our backpacks. They poked and jabbed at our sleeping bags, tapped on the metal tubes of the backpack frames, listening for spaces that were no longer hollow. Even crumbs accumulated in the seams got the once over. Found nothing. Laughed at us when I gestured they should put our packs back together. Paul told me to shut up. They finally shooed us away.

Walked far to the outskirts of Landskrona. No shelter. Wandered exhausted into a field. Struggled to keep dry under a ratty army poncho. Woke up in the night to two aliens standing over us—dull silver and black. Units padded head to toe with quilted leather and polished steel. I saw a black visor open. *"Passaport,"* demanded the voice. We bumbled about sleepily. Luckily, a call came over the motorcycle radios. One robot gestured impatiently for us to get out of the field. Both hurried down a slope, mounted their motorcycles and were sucked away into a sick yellow street-lamp fog.

**Third Day**. At first light, we shook off the dew and then thumbed 250 km up the coast to Göteborg. It took a long time to find the farm house outside of town where we expected to work.

Parents of the Swedish guys who had invited Paul, greeted us with overwhelming hospitality. Our muddy, stinking pile of laundry was whisked away. Encouraged to freshen up, then treated to various breads and cured meats, herring and pastry, a little wine. Our hosts wanted to know all about us, what our opinions were about everything imaginable, and how long we could stay. Finally, acknowledged we were exhausted. Invited us to retire to the barn loft that had big fluffy feather beds, down comforters, fresh linen. Said they hoped we'd be comfortable. Said we should help ourselves to the snacks they had set out for us. Paul and I grinned at each other. Far out! This is heaven. All we lacked was some eager Swedish chicks.

**Fourth Day**. Agreed we should pass a restful day at the beach before starting to work at something the next day. Large smooth stones and chilly water. Hoped to see girls change right out in the open, after all, it *was* Sweden. But none did.

Back in the loft that night, Paul and I discussed what to do next. Kind of felt uncomfortable. They didn't even know us and they acted this way. Didn't have anything to give in return, except work. Bet they were going to work our butts off. So, announced at dinner we'd be leaving in the morning.

**Fifth Day**. Our hosts' farewell was chilly and distant. Couldn't figure out exactly why. I mean, they should have understood if we didn't want to hang out there all summer. Paul thought it was because I had shown up uninvited. Told him it didn't seem to matter. Said he would have stayed there and worked if it hadn't been for me.

Hungry on the boat back to Denmark. $40 left for the two of us. Paul said we had to wait to eat. I couldn't wait. Demanded he give me the money I'd given him. Began to scream at each other. Horrified touring adults watched us fight.

"You want your fucking money? Take it," Paul said. Gave me about $7. I demanded the rest. Called him a "son of a bitch." Told me to get fucked. Said I'd lost my share at Tivoli Gardens. Said he wasn't giving me anymore.

Screamed at him. Told him I was keeping all his shit. Maybe I could sell it. (We had divided the weight of our junk into two equal loads. I had some of his, he had some of mine).

Paul grabbed my pack. I caught the strap as it zipped by me. I pulled, and Paul pulled, and the pack popped open, and everything spilled out onto the deck.

Scrambled to our knees. The boat swayed and rolled our stuff —the mess kits, the poncho, the sewing kit slid across the deck toward the sea.

Paul grabbed his shit just in time and stomped away.

Three hours to go on the passage to Fredrickshafen. It was a small ship. Couldn't avoid each other. Eventually, we surrendered and agreed to split the money. After all, I had gambled for both of us. Besides, it was too scary to be alone, but neither of us said so.

Something meager to eat on shore—hard bread and tin-foil laughing-cow cheese, and then we whipped out our thumbs. Thought about when I was a kid. I found a big rubber thumb stuck onto a palm frond. I kept it in a secret place for several years, taking it out on occasion to practice in the front yard. Told Paul, but he thought it was a stupid story.

So. Denmark again. The mainland. Got a ride with a proud citizen who took us on a side trip to an old (Viking?) village with thatched roofs that looked like bowl-top haircuts.

Into Deutschland late at night. Dropped at an autobahn interchange outside Flensburg. Fell asleep under a sign.

"*Ausweis, bitte.*"

Opened my eyes in the dark.

"Ausweis," said the voice again. "You will show me your passport."

These units were more agitated than the silver streaks of
night who had hassled us in Sweden. Didn't like us sleeping under their freeway sign. Stood and watched while we packed, demanding, "You will hurry."

Once they'd left, we walked up to the on-ramp. Leaned
against our packs and waited for the sun to rise.

**Sixth Day**. By evening, finally, crossed into Holland. Near
the border, two Belgian guys with little motorcycles gave us a
slow and windy ride. Difficult to hold on wearing a backpack.
Found a place to camp together. One guy began cooking beef
stew on his *camping gaz* stove. Dinner smelled delicious. So
hungry. Smoked a bowl, waiting for the stew. Said I liked the big
peace symbol painted on the side of one of the motorcycles.

"They put her in the sea last night, because of that what you
like," one of them said.

I didn't quite understand. Then, realized he was talking about
his motorcycle.

"Yes. Some real fuckers rolled her away when we was sleeping," he said. "I think maybe the salt has made damage."

When the stew was ready Paul was given a modest portion,
and I, for some reason, was offered a single bite that I practically
had to beg for. They didn't like me. Would barely talk to me. I
felt branded—a shamed breaker of secret rules I had never
learned. Was never taught. Passed over. I was furious. Let me
out of here.

**Seventh Day**. Dropped off near Groningen, Holland. Waiting. Took turns sitting and resting while the other stood and thumbed.

Still waiting. Not talking much.

A bus pulled up. The door opened and, a perky American, holding a microphone, invited us inside. "Welcome to the Future Farmers of America's first tour of the Low Country," he beamed. "We are here to inspect the dikes," he joked. Hardly anyone laughed. Must have been an old joke. We piled in.

The passengers were "clean, friendly and proud," they told us. All dressed in blue FFA jackets, they recited their specialties—animal husbandry, agricultural engineering, and so forth. In the back of the bus, the more relaxed future farmers said they wished they could do what we were doing. The perkmeister with the microphone interrupted to lead everyone in patriotic songs, ironic songs—"This is *My* Country," and "This Land is your Land." The ride was brief. The ride was fun. It made Paul and I feel proud, too, mostly because of our courage to have escaped such a "future."

Amsterdam. Little hip villages had sprung up all over Vondelpark. Hippies were camped out everywhere. Heard drums and guitars and flutes, and the chorus of a Dylan tune hung in the trees. A stranger handed up his chimney-like *chillum* full of hashish, and we obligingly toked. A woman wearing a daisy-chain crown walked past us and smiled, as if to say, "I love you, whoever you are." "I love you, too," I wanted to say. But I just smiled, and she kept walking.

In the center of town was a sharpened white finger monument, at least that is what it looked like to me. In the middle of

Dam Square it was ringed by hippies sprawling about its steps. A place opened up for us to sit down, but we were still too intimidated to be drawn that deeply into the fold. We were of the marginally cool. We were in training—neophytes to a frightening, glorious new social order.

*The Woodstock Movie* was playing to sell-out crowds at a place that was more like a cabaret than any movie house I'd ever seen. Had a bar back behind the last row. Just before the show, an old guy came around selling ice cream the way they do with peanuts at the baseball games in the States. He'd holler out, "*Eis Krem*," or whatever it is in Dutch, and he'd throw one to a customer who was then supposed to pass the money back through the crowd to him. Ice cream sandwiches and Dutch Nuttie Buddies were not making it past a few stoned hippies. Ice cream fell mysteriously, landing in their laps. But not enough money was making it back to the old man. Some of the crowd protested loudly. The *Eis Krem* man just shrugged it off, and then he began tossing, willy-nilly, all of his cones and sandwiches into the delighted crowd. Not to be outdone, the movie goers started throwing coins in his general direction. Everyone was cheering and laughing. We tilted our heads back to watch the beautiful anarchic sky.

Well, Joe Cocker about bust a gut with "A Little Help from my Friends," as spastically tore the air apart. Alvin Lee from Ten Years After, streaming sweat, his fat lip hanging out, growling, screeching, "Goin' home, see my baby, goin' home." Crosby, Stills and Nash sang sweetly "Suite: Judy Blue Eyes," and I wanted to imitate them. Richie Havens ripped my heart, crying, "Sometimes, I Feel like a Motherless Child." Joan Baez's beautiful voice wooing the "Sweet Chariot" to swing low that night. It was wonderful. Yes. I was truly mesmerized with possibility once The Who's Townsend started jumping in his jumpsuit about a mile into the air. I quickly memorized his windmill-hammering stance and the look of him ripping every last bit of power out of his guitar. Then he smashed it and threw it to the crowd. Man, I would love to do that, I thought. Ecstatic. Stoned. Muddy and naked. Yes, I wanted more.

Sly & the Family Stone insisted, "I Want to Take You Higher." Carlos Santana grimaced his hot leads through "Soul Sacrifice," piercing my spine. And Hendrix, glorious Hendrix, waking it up with a most appropriate "Star Spangled Banner." Fantastic as Skip, back in Berwick, had insisted. Hendrix's anthem was cranked up so powerfully, cracking the seams. Just a wave of Hendrix's hand and the war would have to self-destruct.

If I had only known, not Mom, nor anything, would have stopped me from traveling those few miles from Berwick to Yasgur's farm. In love with it all. In love with the chicks, oh yeah. Happy and thrilled and defiant. What had been rumor had become personal. We were all a part of it, because we could feel its call to us. And wow, if Sha-Na-Na could do it, why couldn't we? Anybody could play, and everybody should play.

Called home collect. While waiting to connect, I watched a man pile condiments I could not identify onto herring, tilt his head back and slide the whole thing down his gullet the way a pelican would. Told Mom I wasn't working in Sweden, after all. I was in Amsterdam! Told her I wouldn't know when I'd be back. I hung up before she could protest.

To sleep that night, we threw our bags down in Vondelpark wherever we damn-well pleased. Slipped into the down with the delightful assurance that, at least for one night, no cop would demand to see our passports, man.

**Eighth Day**. The hordes, waiting in line for a breakfast, rubbed their eyes. A benevolent soul had decided that we should all get, at least, one decent meal a day. So, for one *guilder*, about a quarter, we were kindly served a plate of salad, a hard-boiled egg, and a vitamin pill.

Decided to head out to Bill Lyme's place in London. He was a far-out guitar player we'd met in junior high. His Dad had been transferred out just before the end of the semester.

On the ferry from Oostende, Belgium, Paul and I amused ourselves shelling peanuts. After the cost of passage, we didn't have any money left for food. Just enough for the ferry back to Belgium and maybe a little more for entertainment. Saw the white cliffs of Dover—dazzling. Reminded me of moldy cheesecake.

Arrived late in London, anticipating a bed and a big meal at Bill's folks' house. We had never met Bill's parents, but why should they care if we stayed a few nights?

Paul called, and Bill was busy. Said we should call back tomorrow night. Bill said maybe we should go to a show or something.

Hyde Park, we were told, was a dangerous place to sleep, and we shouldn't do it, and further, it was not permitted. Wandered around for an hour or two, hungry and exhausted, hoping to find some place hidden enough to crash. Desperate. Hopped over a fence into a little park surrounded by fancy buildings. Crawled under some trees and tried to ignore that it smelled like dog shit.

**Ninth Day**. Woke up and quickly stuffed our sleeping bags into our packs. A sign said that we had better hurry our vagrant asses out of their doggie park. In mid-leap over the fence, a bobby came around the corner.

"Good morrow, Lads," he said, talking and looking like something I'd probably seen on TV. I almost laughed. "Have a good rest?"

"Well, it could have been better, sir," I offered. "We didn't realize it was for dogs."

"Do your parents know where you are?"

"Yes," we mumbled. I pondered the question.

His tone changed. "If I were to take you to the station and ring them up, would they say they knew you were in London, sleeping on private property? And if I told them you had been jailed for vagrancy, how would they feel about that?" His smile had hardened into a block-faced seriousness.

We did the passport routine. He concluded with a strangely polite harangue, saying that fifteen-year-old boys had no business wandering around, and that we ought to get along home to a proper bed.

Speakers' Corner. Men, mostly, stood on soapboxes, all shouting their views simultaneously whether anyone was listening or not. "Join the Communist Party." "Stop the war." "Repent!" Only one man had drawn a crowd. He wooed passersby into stopping, showing them strange  signs, written on a chalkboard, that he said gave proof of the fast approaching Armageddon. He and the rest of the passionate shouted their convictions of no public consequence. I thought the whole mess was very funny.

Bill Lyme showed up, and he and Paul pitched in to get me into the Palladium. Paul admitted he had stashed some money away, in case of an emergency. We smoked a bowl. The band played, whoever they were. And the music faded away. Then we were really broke.

Took the tube out to Bill's house. He didn't know his parents would be home. Whispered in the dark kitchen that it was still out of the question for us to stay there. We should leave right away. Pleaded with Bill that we had just enough money for the ferry and none for food. At last, he agreed. Snuck us arms full of PX canned goods. I guess all military Dads were trained to make sure they had enough cling peaches come doomsday.

Stuffed the tuna, peaches, beef stew into our packs and caught the train-ferry back to Belgium in the middle of the night.

**Tenth Day**. Hit the mainland running, eating our meals cold as fast as we could, so as to fill our shrunken bellies and to get rid of the excess pack weight. Good rides. Made it back to Frankfurt that evening. Paul and I congratulated one another. Briefly, I took the train back to Kronberg.

Walked up the long incline to Hermann Löns Weg, got the key from the garage and let myself in. It was late. Mom was startled when I entered the living room. The Bomber was not around.

"Mom, I'm home," I said.

"Oh," she said, trying to appear cheerful. "I thought you'd be back much later." She passed by me and climbed the stairs. I stared at the place where she had been. I closed the door to my room and let myself fall hard into bed.

# Pizza Europa

---

The first time I met Evan White, we really hit it off. Together, he, Mole and I decided to start high school by forming a group we called Alvin Lipp and Ten Years Ago. We just had to make fun of Woodstock. Too many people were acting like they'd missed the Second Coming. I guess that included me.

So. The night of the rock festival at the high school gym, Evan slicked back his straight black hair. He wore a Daffy Duck t-shirt, and black jeans and Beatle boots. He was the bass player in our one-night-only no-practice-would-help-anyway band. Mole, who played the drums even worse than I did, took over my drum set. I had hauled into town piece by piece on the train. By now, Mole's electric hair curled crazily outward about a foot from his head. A techie, in on the joke, gave me a guitar he said I could destroy. He would be behind the speakers playing with about hundred effects he owned that he had plugged me into. I wasn't too sure what we were going to do. *Alvin Lipp* would just poke fun at a few sounds and images that everybody recognized, and we'd see what happened.

Just before we went on, a pushy, nervous sort of guy asked if he could put his light show panels on the Marshall stacks. He had sort of long hair, and he wore John Lennon wire rims, so we said okay, but hurry up. He told me I could help him with his "wet show" afterwards, if I wanted to. Although I didn't know what a "wet show" was, I said I'd do what I could.

79

Mole, Evan and me walked out onto the gym floor stage. The place was packed. I was dressed in my gray baggy sweat suit, the closest thing I could find to Townsend's jumpsuit. The mumbles and giggles from the crowd spooked me. I tried to ignore them.

I started off with a modified *Country Joe* "fish cheer." "Gimme an 'F,'" I shouted. And I got a roaring "F" back from the crowd. The chaperones winced and moved towards the stage. Quickly, I said, "Gimme an 'R,'" Damn if I didn't get an 'R' almost loud as the 'F'. However, after I asked for a 'Q' and then a 'P' and asked them to spell it, audience participation fell off. I cued the band and we jumped into a very loud, arrhythmic, atonal rendition of "Goin' home, see my baby. Goin' home." We played a broken rocking blues, babbling out a feedback wall of noisy fun.

The crowd, to our surprise, loved it. I was encouraged. I turned to do the dueling guitar thing, and Evan obliged me. Evan jived away in rapid, frantic paces like a yo-yo tied to his amp while Mole zealously banged away like a miniature Keith Moon. I managed to sloppily bring it down and cried, "See me," from the Who's *Tommy*, and the devoted fans screamed with glee. I went on with the rest, rubbing up against the mike stand, asking to be felt, and then touched, and, finally, healed. The techie must have turned me way up at that point, because my guitar screeched and wailed completely out of control. All I had to do was touch the damn thing and it went berserk. I leaped with each electronic squeal and hammered out the windmill. As we approached white noise, I took the guitar by the neck and smashed the fuck out of it. Unfortunately, Mole got into the act, too, and ripped my drum set to pieces — ramming the sticks through the heads, bending the cymbals, kicking the bass drum in with his army boots. And all the while, Evan kept a steady, Daffy bass line. He wobbled his head to the sound of his, "dum, dum, ti-dum," occasionally, throwing a grin my way. I felt great. The joker in me had come exploding out, and everyone liked me.

I left the stage more thrilled than I could have imagined. A girl who looked like a cheerleader — pink angora sweater, gold necklace holding a single pearl — ran up to me afterward and flopped her hand out to shake. "Hi. My name's Lainey Winter-green. I loved your show." Her limp hand hung there, waiting for a response. I grabbed it. It was a rock — a cold dead nothing. I took back my hand and kept moving.

I saw Mr. Rivette. He'd be my English teacher. He shook his head and smirked, "You don't have any idea how to play the guitar, do you?"

"No, of course not," I said.

"Well, that's what I thought. It sure sounded like you didn't. I had to ask," he said, "because just after your . . . spectacle, I heard a young man say that it was the best damn guitar playing he had ever heard.

I grinned. I thought it was pretty cool that Rivette had said, "damn" to me.

Later on, I didn't want any more attention. The thrill of my brief stardom had quickly turned into an isolating fear. Too many people wanting something. I escaped to the guy with the light show. He said his name was Sam Laszlo, and he immediately put me to work. I liked playing with his cool stuff, project-ing amoebic blobs — that was the wet show — onto a band called George & the Rockets, whose drummer punched out an impres-sive "Fire and Water" from the band Free. Sam, we called him Laszlo, also had several projectors that lit up the gym walls with freaky hand-made slides. I had fun, but Laszlo was real pushy and protective about how the show had to be done. I tried to get away from him, but he demanded I stay. After all, he said, I had promised I would help him. I helped a little while longer, and then I left, anyway.

A few weeks into the school year I was downtown with a couple of guys at the *Hauptwache*, an underground shopping district that connected all the major stores to the subway. On a poster, we saw a picture of Hendrix with multi-colored wires snaking Medusa-like from his head. He stared ecstatically and lovingly into space. He was going to play Frankfurt in a week.

"Man, let's get the tickets, now," I said, knowing I didn't have any money. "Can anybody lend me 20 marks till, uh — "

"Forget it, man," someone said. "He just croaked."

"Listen. That's what they're saying on the radio."

The German news was being broadcast throughout the Hauptwache. One of us could understand well enough to translate part of it. "They said they found him dead in his own vomit."

In my aching mind, I saw him soaked in it, stinking and sad. His kind, yet sometimes dismissive look was twisted and beaten into flaccid resignation. I took it personally. I felt cast out and forgotten, somehow.

A couple of days later, as if to try to soothe us, the promoters promised the performance of a new "Super Group" called ELP — Emerson, Lake & Palmer. They had premiered at Isle of Wight alongside Hendrix. Better than no music at all.

The night of the show, we smoked a lot of hash, again, and sat on the floor of the *Messegelande* watching Keith Emerson climb up on, and repeatedly stab his Hammond organ. I tried not to think of Hendrix. Wishing he was there, I couldn't help but feel betrayed.

The next day in the cafeteria, we agreed that ELP playing *Pictures at an Exhibition* was far out. But Laszlo, chomping on endless Fudgesicles, protested that the original was much better.

Ever since my return from my brief tour of Europe, I tried to stay away from Schönberg. I dragged myself home only when I ran out of places to stay, mostly at Laszlo's place, or just knew I'd better show up to avoid more problems. Often, there was nobody there, anyway. I'd grab the key from the garage and let myself in. I liked the pleasant surprise of finding no-one there, because it meant I could eat what I wanted, listen to loud music, and masturbate without getting caught. But, once when I jerked off in the bathtub, a damn vicious horror of myself attacked with its claws extended.

This is what happened. I put on Santana's *Abraxas,* and I turned on the water heater and waited the long 45 minutes for it to get hot. Mom had told me she really liked *Abraxas*. That was surprising. She said she even liked The Who's *Live at Leeds,* though it was usually too loud. Maybe, she was trying to find a way to talk to me. I didn't know.

In any case, I couldn't let myself think too soon about the girls I wanted to ball, so I distracted myself by rocking out to Santana. Anyway, when the water was hot, I started *Abraxas* again, and I made a hot sudsy froth and slipped into my fantasies. I thought about all the cute girls I had seen at school. I even thought about that Lainey Wintergreen chick, the cheerleader who had offered me her fish paw.

My immersion was very quickly a success. What smooth soothing deliciousness! It was kind of a sanctuary. I got out to drain the tub. I saw the little tapioca sperm globs still lingering, not wanting to die. But I worried that not all my goo would make it down the drain.

I waited anxiously, watching the watery scum slurp and suck itself downward. Still, my little jellyfish islands stuck tenaciously to the tub. I got back in, naked and began to scrub. Oh, my god, what if Mom was to come home and get in for a late bath and sperm swam inside her and got her pregnant! Sperm's so tiny. She'd never know what got into her. Surely, the heat of the tub could keep my stuff alive. I began to tremble. I scrubbed the tub hard, and I prayed no one would come home. Finally, I got dressed and went into my tiny room to hide. I did not know what to do. I fretted for a long time that she'd come home tired and want to soothe herself. How would I stop her? But hours passed, no one arrived, and, in time, I fell asleep.

One morning at Evan White's, I decided to have some hashish in my tea just to help make it easier to get through the school day. I put about a gram in my cup, thinking the hot water would dissolve it. But the damn thing kept bobbing to the surface. Evan's mom was busy in the kitchen, and I was afraid she'd come in and see the blob in my cup. She might get embarrassed at this strange shit she had missed while cleaning — oh, no, a humungous booger! She was such a nice gentle lady, and I didn't want to make her feel bad. My only exit was to hold the cup up to my mouth where she couldn't see it and refuse to put it down until it was cool enough to gulp.

Evan's mom came in.

Evan asked loudly, "What are you doing?"

"Oh, nothing," I said in a voice he knew was fake. "I just like to warm myself with some hot tea before going out into this cold morning fog."

"Yes," Mrs. White agreed, that was such a pleasant thing to do.

I grinned at Evan as he wondered what I was up to.

"Come on," he said. "Let's go. We're going to be late."

"I'd like to finish this," I said.

"Evan's right," said Mrs. White. "The two of you had better get along."

I aimed my lips at the teasing chunk and took a huge swallow of lava that scalded me from my teeth to belly pit. Did I scream? No. I just ran outside. I inhaled the slightly soothing fog.

Oh, the secrets we had to keep from the protecting world of our parents and teachers, a burden becoming every day more complex and more alienating. Just how could we ever hope to explain? What would they say to our need to eat from Laszlo's outstretched hand sprinkled with a selection of Purple Barrel and Windowpane acid?

I chose the Windowpane because I liked its tiny magical shape. It looked like a square bit of translucent mica. We no more than swallowed it, then the tingling excitement began.

Quickly, we escaped to the street, making our way to Pizza Europa in order to eat before the acid came on for real. We ordered their deluxe namesake pizza, the one with the surprise in the center, *das Große Ei* 'the big German Egg'.

It was taking an awful long time, it seemed, and the furniture was beginning to lose its supportive qualities. After much weird discussion — the shape of words blending into one another —

we decided we had better get our order to go. The waiter no longer had his original substance, and it took several snatches of elastic time before, as he walked across the room, his back caught up with his front.

When at last the box was plopped in front of us, Laszlo somehow paid. Meanwhile, Evan and I stared at the box. I asked Laszlo if we should open it right there? Seemed risky, Laszlo warned. We were already laughing more than could possibly be appropriate. We mustered up our collective courage and slowly lifted the lid. Oh, my! Pizza Atoll — a swimming dance of a bubbling red green saucy bits splashed at the brown sandy rim, whirling and pulled by the undertow, a grand whooshing overture, and right in the center, staring back at all three of us, The Grand Egg Eyeball knew us, said where we were headed, and what exactly we would do. Laszlo slammed down the lid and held the box tightly with both hands as we fled Pizza Europa.

# *Ei* of the Pizza

---

g. zan-pit painted his locker the colors of the North Vietnamese flag, and we covered the event in our new rag, *Davaii*. That's 'Right On' in Russian, or so we were told. In addition to zan-pit's bold attack with a paint brush, the first issue encouraged the boycott of the cafeteria because of its increase in the price of Fudgesicles and a review of *Revolution for the Hell* of *It,* which included "Fuck the System," a how-to for the budding Yippie.

zan-pit was threatened with suspension if he did not immediately "cease and desist" his "insubordinate acts." The people needed to know. *Davaii* reported that although g. had finally followed the administrations' command to "repaint his locker." The principal became furious that, instead of the regulation pale mint green, g. painted it a familiar war-time red. He had also attached a little piece of paper that read, "I bleed . . . ." He was given one week to return his locker to its original green or he'd be thrown out. Of course, he refused, and *Davaii* called on all students to paint their lockers red in support of g. zan-pit. What fun! What purpose!

More and more lockers began to bleed for free speech and against the war. Day by day, the tension built and the administration gave g. one more week, and then another. Meanwhile, many lockers turned red, and all zan-pit supporters were warned to repaint their lockers immediately of face suspension. No one did. In fact, we matched our lockers by wearing t-shirts with the red-fist image appearing everywhere in the States after the recent US invasion of Cambodia.

His nerves frayed and his position on a military base in jeopardy, the principal did suspend g. and threatened to expel him. And so, a new wave of lockers turned red. A dress code boycott was added to our grievances, and more students became attracted to our cause. Eventually, the principal smelled what he was helping to create, and allowed zan-pit to return. But still insisted, in a "friendly, reasonable" way, that zan-pit repaint his locker. To everyone's surprise, zan-pit said he would do what "the man" asked.

When we came to school the next Monday, we were relieved to see that g. zan-pit had done it again. A real poke in the eye this time. He had slathered his locker with a tank-tone olive-drab insult.

The administration, at last, left g. zan-pit alone. Fudgesicles suddenly came down a nickel. The administration stopped hassling us about what we wore to school. And it remained a pleasure to walk through the halls and admire the many blood-red lockers.

*Gruneburg* Park was next to the high school compound. We crawled through a hole in the fence and, for a while, avoided military eyes. It was in the park that I first heard the sliding bar chords of "Highway 61 Revisited" and first saw real Gypsies gather. I wrote poetry there, and I sprawled out on friendly blankets. In Gruneburg Park, so many of us, frustrated military brats, Frankfurt University students, and various travelers had a place to brew our many pleasures.

The park rolled luxuriantly over soft hills and hosted beautiful willows. It proved how ugly the adjacent military base really was. Across each field, and through every grove there was always more to explore. And, if you wandered far enough, a low fence marked Gruneburg's sister park, the *Palmengarten*. She was much more sculpted and manicured than Gruneburg. Inside ivy-covered walls, stood greenhouses of cactuses and tropical colors, with palms everywhere. Thousands of little candles marked the trees, paths and ponds come *Lichtenfest*. Huge lily pads bumped against each other when the rowboats glided by. It was a rich place to stretch out an acid-soaked brain.

One night after closing, I leapt the fence to frolic with some friends. I wanted to fondle the rubbery trees and kiss on elfin bridges. I kissed the lovely Sarah Christensen there, her lips trembled, and she tasted like sugarcane. Caressing one another inside a stucco cave, Sarah and I heard wooden collisions echoing toward us. We followed the sound to a fountain of colored lights. Someone had waded out to the rowboats and untied them for us to enjoy. A dozen or more delinquents floated through the wriggling colors on rippling black water. I waded out into the pond toward the fountain, encouraging my delicious friend to follow. I was hoping she would eventually take off her wet pants and show herself, the origin of life looking back at me. But the lights suddenly turned bright white and harsh and they were focused in my eyes. I saw frantic white lasers waving, searching.

Everybody ran. Some remembered to follow the brat route back to the relative safety of the American compound. Others didn't make it so far, and the *Polizei* arrested several.

They got Alex Jones that night. Polizei, wielding assault rifles, tracked him down with a spotlight and treated him like a dog.

The Polizei and the military community blamed the whole brat invasion on Alex, since he was a *Schwarze (Black Man),* so he said. It taught him how vulnerable he was because of his color, he said. It made him angry and ready, at last, to break off from all he'd been accepting, with few questions asked.

Yes, I began to understand the complaint.

It seems like wherever you go, something awful is bound to happen. Even in the Palmengarten.

Another day, that fall, Mole wandered into Gruneburg. He looked weird. He told us what he'd found. He was fooling around out by his house when he saw something hanging from a favorite tree of his. It was a big old oak that must have been there for a hundred years. He went up close to his tree. Someone had hanged a dummy from a branch to look like a hanged man. Why would someone do that, he wondered? Mole smacked it hard. "Good fake," he said, and the body let out what was left of its final breath. Mole looked at its face staring him down, and realized it was a guy from school.

None of us knew him very well. We didn't know his name. He was good-looking with a bright white face and white hair to match. We always thought he could get any girl he wanted, but he also seemed real shy. I had just seen him the week before at the bowling alley at Kamp King. He tried to talk to me, but I snubbed him. My excuse was that he looked like a guy back in Key West who used to beat me up for no good reason. Now this Frankfurt guy was dead, and I felt bad I hadn't been nicer to him.

I worried about Mole. He acted like nothing much had happened, but I could see he was shaken. I wondered how it would affect him the rest of his life.

In the towns, strings of white lights struggled to fight off the cold. In times gone by Germans built fires in the streets, but not now. The lights were meant to remind us of those blazing times. Christmas, or *Weihnachtsfest* was a pretty time in Germany, "reassuring and romantic." It had not yet started to snow. Instead, a thick fog hung in stasis in the streets of Oberursel.. With the insistence of that cold foggy night I sensed, not joy, but pain and suffering. I hoped there and then, the future would not unfold.

My body ached. From what? I knew what — the acid. But maybe it was the weariness of walking toward Schönberg in the dark. That bastard Dive-bomber drove right by me. Why couldn't I rely on him? Drunk and angry again, I bet. I could feel pain in my teeth — my dental work throbbed, and a piercing pain shot through my elbow joints. That continued to happen when I'd been tripping.

Nowhere to sleep that night — friends fed up, and no one new to ask a favor of. Another possibility? Gruneburg? Too scary at night. I took the streetcar out to Kamp King. Walked around there. Nobody. What to do?

Mom was getting increasingly depressed. I could tell from a phone call — she said she couldn't understand why I never came home anymore. What that really meant was, she could understand why I wanted to stay away from the Dive-bomber, but wasn't her love enough to keep me at home? So, I took the trolley back to Oberursel, and I walked to the edge of town to "home."

My teeth hurt. Somewhere in my memory I heard Frank Zappa's call to any vegetable. Hey, that's Mom and me — she, yearn-

91

ing and me, decrepit. Or something like that. "Call any vegetable and the chances are good — the vegetable will respond to you." Yeah, me returning home. Nonsensical. Surreal. God, my teeth hurt. And my elbows. Coming down. I sang the tune, "Call any Vegetable" over and over again, dodging the car lights on the road to Schönberg.

I remembered hanging out backstage and Zappa striding into the dressing room, zotzed from the power and excitement of yet another spectacular performance. He was surprised to see a bunch of little units — military brat muffins. We were smoking a chillum. He looked at us and said, "That shit will stunt your growth." So we put it away.

"Great show, Mr. Zappa," one of us said politely.

And just as politely and even gently, he thanked us and then teased, "So. You're sons of the service?"

We chuckled that we were.

The man was exhausted from the show, and we didn't want to impose, asking stupid questions about what his lyrics meant.

He towered above us. He was dark like the Dive-bomber, and I thought if the Bomber quit the stupid Air Force, grew out his hair and got a cool mustache, and that other chin-tuft thing, he would look all right. I laughed to myself, thinking of Zappa as my father. That would be great. Then I could eventually hang out with his daughter, Moon Unit. Maybe, I would eventually marry into the family. And what a family it must be, I dreamed.

Zappa had nothing more to say to us so, Zappa slipped away behind a divider.

But now, walking in the dark, I wished so fervently to go back, reconnect with Zappa, and invite myself along on the tour. Take me home, Mr. Zappa, if you please. When we get home I'll clean the litter box and wash the dishes, mow the dog and bake your muffins.

No. No father for me. Just another lonely, angry walk toward Schönberg. Then, like exhaling acid, I caught a ride.

In someone's car, I thought about the morning when I saw the Dive-bomber coming out of the bathroom, stuffing a semi-hard one back into his pants. He looked at me, smiled, and said something about waking up in the middle of the night with a stiffy, "Ha, ha, and you have to do something about it, right," he asked? "But your mother thinks I was dreaming about someone else, and she's kind of pissed off about it."

Sheesh! What was I supposed to do with that?

I want to be the father of myself.

As I came around the corner onto Hermann Löns Weg, I saw lights from cars parked in front of our cute little house. A lot of my parents' friends, all Germans, were out in the yard, speaking excitedly to one another. Either the Dive-bomber or Mom had finally done it, I thought. They had gotten drunk enough to greet the holidays with a loss of temper, and either Mom had smashed the fuck out of the bastard with something blunt, or maybe she had stabbed him. Or maybe the bastard had killed my Mom. I vowed to get him, the motherfucker.

But the Polizei let me in without resistance. I saw Mom sitting on the couch crying. Her friend, Herta, now playing Eunice, held Mom in her arms, a new Stella, rocking her like a little baby. The Dive-bomber was safely in the kitchen, talking to a cop who was trying to calm him down.

"*Was ist los, hier,*" I demanded. But no one paid attention to me.

Suddenly, a handsome young man with a bloody lip and a black eye pushed past the cops and made it into the living room. He shouted something in German at the Dive-bomber before the Polizei pulled him back. The Dive-bomber smiled drunkenly and called them *Schweinehunde.*

A short time later, the Dive-bomber disappeared, and so the Polizei went away, too, and Mom was left with Herta and me.

Mom explained, "Honey, he just blew up. You know how he gets."

"Tell me what happened, Mom," I said, slowly, darkly, hoping it would be the last time I had to ask, but knowing it wouldn't

"I was on the couch here, and that boy, Heinz, was sitting here, too, and we got to talking. We were very friendly and all. You know, celebrating the holidays. You know how the Germans get at the holidays. Well, he started to kissing on me and I let him." She started crying again.

I got up from the couch, without saying a word, and went to my room and closed the door — the father of myself.

Slowly dying. Show me the father of myself.

# The Importance of Being Eloquent

Kerouac's *The Dharma Bums* fell from the sky, and, at last, I knew I had found something I could be. More than an occasional singer in a goof band, and certainly more than a student. I could be part of the "rucksack revolution." In fact, I did not need to aspire to be anything, despite what the guidance counselor's interest inventory had told me — negative one in accountant to 87 in music educator. Why follow a sucking career when the adventure of the road promised "visions of eternal freedom?"

*The Dharma Bums* provided me a guidebook for me on how to live a poetic existence, a "Zen lunatic" existence, taking it all in, learning how to love, how to live cheaply. Transcendence. One main character, Ray (Kerouac) reminded me of the hobos along the Susquehanna, who had both frightened and intrigued me. Like him, I saw a way to confront myself in solitude. And as a bonus delight, the beat Zen bums practiced *yab-yum* — sitting naked in full lotus, facing a beautiful girl in silence for a few minutes to clear their minds, then making love to her. It sounded great. Yab-yum 'father-mother' was so cool because the woman wasn't uptight about it at all. She dug all those naked guys pleasing her, and saw herself as their nurturing mother. Why couldn't the girls we knew be as cool about sex? If we just balled over and over again, without having to struggle for it, maybe all of us could relax a little.

Yes. . . .Well.

Just before the *Traffic* concert at the Messegelande a girl told me Lainey Wintergreen wanted to talk. I was kind of annoyed, but curious. I went over to her and noticed she was looking a little more hip. Her hair wasn't pulled back, and she wasn't wearing makeup. Instead of a sweet little pastel sweater, she wore something loose and colorful that was probably made in India. She told me she had just turned 15 three days earlier, and she really wanted me to sit with her. She had a much better seat than me, so I agreed. She was very affectionate, smiling and touching my arm, and so I held her hard sweating hand for a little while. I didn't see her again until the *Ulysses* concert a few weeks later.

*Ulysses*, the former *George and the Rockets* with a new drummer, Alex Jones, was playing at Kamp King. To pass the time before the show, I went to the Rec. Center, and I spotted a Green Beret guy I'd met earlier. He made a point of telling me to make sure I didn't find myself shipped off to "the Nam." Surprisingly, he also told me to keep on protesting the war. I promised I would in the most immediate way I knew how. I told him about *Davaii*. Our protests were, I told him, against hypocrisy. We had learned that the educational system was an extension of the corrupt society that fed the war every day.

"I wouldn't know about that," he said." You just damn make sure that you don't get thrown out. Go to college and stay out of this stupid war."

When I saw him leaving the Rec. Center, I decided for fun to sneak up on him. I don't know why. Maybe it was out of affection. When I jumped out from behind a corner and yelled, he pivoted sharply in a sudden bursting animal-like scream with his hand positioned to yank out my heart. I melted before him into trembling goo. He relaxed his stance and heaved angrily.

"What the fuck, man! Don't ever do that to a Green Beret. You could get your ass seriously hurt," he shouted.

I apologized and swore I'd never do it again. I felt really stupid. I was pretty shaken up, and the guy calmed me down. He said he was sorry, that he'd been feeling jumpy ever since he got back from the Nam. I began to understand a little of what the bewildered sadness on the faces of GIs must have meant.

Anyway, I wandered away from him and found a quiet place near the PX to finish reading *The Dharma Bums* and wait for *Ulysses* to begin playing.

Whew! It was difficult to concentrate. Looking up from the book, I thought about going back to Amsterdam. The military crap was too much. If only I could find some sort of Zen refuge in Amsterdam. That would be the perfect escape. I didn't really need to worry about the draft. Not yet. I'd be okay. I didn't even need a place to practice Zen lunacy. I could do that anywhere — just have to watch for the cops. God would protect me.

What's that? That voice. Always that tyrannical God voice hovering above me, watching me, making me feel afraid, making me feel guilty. Zen wasn't like that, I thought. No Zen-god cops. The voice was in my head, man. When I was about three years old in Tampa, I took a big spoon out to the vacant lot next to our house, and I began to dig with purpose. I wanted to find out what was down there. Soon, I thought I heard someone calling me, and looked up to the neighbor's house across the street. It had a rainbow painted across it. No one was there. Mommie wasn't there. I went back to digging. When I had dug about six inches down, I became very frightened. I looked into the darkness before me, and I saw the Red Devil reach out his hand to pull me under. I screamed and ran into the house trembling. I watched out the window. Oh, no. I had forgotten to cover up the hole. The Devil could get out and come after me. A dozen years later, and I was still afraid, and it made me mad. If there was a god, I wanted it to liberate me.

I saw Lainey Wintergreen coming toward me. I was finishing the last page of *The Dharma Bums*. Kerouac prayed for us all to be taken care of, and then followed the path off of Desolation Peak, leaving his cathartic solitude to rejoin the world.

I closed the book and Lainey began to jabber on about something or other, and I interrupted her.

"Look, chick," I said. "If you want to talk to me, read this first." I handed her the book and got up and walked away.

Later that night *Ulysses* entertained us all. Alex Jones' imitation of Neil Young's "Southern Man" was hilarious, since he was Black. But he really meant it, when he sang that the southern bigots had better "remember what [their] good book said," because "Southern change gonna come at last."

Ulysses also covered Traffic's "40,000 Headmen," Crosby, Stills & Nash's "Wooden Ships" and their "Almost Cut my Hair." They even did a couple Sly Stone songs.

The singer of the band was cool — way cool beyond what I hoped to be. He didn't give a fuck about what "The Man" was trying to shove down his and all our throats. His hair was real long and straight blonde. He, too, looked kind of like John Lennon. During the break, he decided to rest by lying down on the sidewalk. Before long Unit Police Lively — yes, that's UP Lively — saw the singer lying there and decided to arrest him for "stoned behavior" or some such crap. We knew you couldn't get arrested for being stoned. Luckily, he wasn't carrying. Just because he was lying on the sidewalk he got pissed upon. I mean, "The Man" tried to make it look like UP Lively had found a "marble-sized piece of hashish" on the singer. It was probably all a frame-up.

After the show, the band played the second half without its singer, the Camp Commander came down to straighten everything out. The Colonel raged against his son, Jimmy Delighter, the band's guitar player, for getting mixed up in all this "hish-hash" business, he called it. Evan White reported the whole damn mess in *Davaii*. He warned us that, "The pigs are out to get you. They are not fictional characters in hip movies. They're very real."

A couple of weeks after the so-called "hishhash" difficulty, Lainey came up to me at my shining red locker and told me she had read the book, liked it very much. Although she didn't mention yab-yum, I was still, I impressed. She asked if I was going to see Ulysses play out in Bad Vilbel? I said I would, especially if she was going to be there. She was really cute, I decided. She smiled, and what remained of my resistance to her affection softened. With absolute co-operation, my heart became hers to play with.

Lainey and I were to meet outside before the show. I saw her standing under a tree, and as I approached, I could feel the two of us yearning for love. Her body was open and relaxed, her head tilted back slightly, her nostrils flared, and her eyes glinting. Her lips parted, and we kissed. At last, someone really loved me. From that moment, I knew we would be together always. We held each other close in a tight embrace, rubbing slowly against each other. We had to find some place to make love, and quick. We searched for what seemed like forever, pushing to re-fuel with more deep kisses.

"Why can't we just do it here," I joked, pointing to anywhere. And Lainey began to sing it from *The White Album*.

"Why don't we do it in the road?" she sang, and I joined in.

I thought, maybe she meant it, but I, at least, did not have the guts to pull off my clothes in the middle of an army base. So we crawled into the driver's pit of a World War II half-track that stood watch at the entrance to the compound. Our groping was pretty cramped in there. We felt silly. Every time I tried to get into her pants, I would bang an elbow, or she'd smack her head. We couldn't stop laughing. I feared the attention of the UPs. Clearly, we'd have to postpone the consummation of our love forever flowing.

From that night on, we spent most of our time together. I would go over to her house and she would sing folk songs — songs like James Taylor's "Fire and Rain" or something off of Carole King's *Tapestry*. I joined in on harmonies. She showed me how to make "sparkies," she called them. You take a winter-green Lifesaver, cup your hand in front of your mouth, or better yet, darken the lights, and bite down on the candy sharply and watch the sparks fly. Then kiss. She and I shared a pleasant gen-tleness that made me very happy. I showed genuine affection with every act and word I had to carve my way out of my bewil-derment with the world. I needed to take our love as far as it could go. I wanted her so badly. I wanted to be inside of her al-ways. But when I suggested the inevitable, to my surprise, Lainey said she wasn't ready. After that first time in the half-track, she wouldn't even let me touch her breasts. I became con-fused. You couldn't fake the kisses we shared, but she still didn't want to ball me. I was dying. Hadn't she read the book? I asked her what she thought of yab-yum in order to test her, and she said it seemed kind of weird, but maybe it would be fun. I understood. She was asking me to wait indefinitely in a kind of splash-pool of coquettishness. She needed proof. A sign. Still, she was mine.

Laszlo said we were dealing with two kinds of chicks, the goddesses and the munchkins. All the chicks we hung out with, were definitely munchkins. They were playful fun-loving chicks our age or younger. They got stoned with us and went to concerts with us, but, Laszlo said, they weren't all that intelligent. Therefore, we shouldn't expect much of them. Laszlo's munchkin group included most of the girls at school I felt I could talk to. People like Sharon Worley, Lainey's best friend, and smiling Sarah Christensen who I loved to kiss, and several others. They flirted around us more like girls than women, Laszlo said, but were too scared to ball us. Nevertheless, it was our job, our duty even, to deflower as many of them as we could, as a kind of benevolent, elevating service. Someone should start with Lainey, he said, since she appeared to be the queen of all the munchkins.

I cringed. "You leave her alone," I said.

"I don't want her," he said. "But you should do it to her quick."

I began to worry. I hated what he was saying.

"On the other hand," he said, "there are the Goddesses, and they are the real women."

The Goddesses were about a year or two older than us. What separated them from the munchkins, according to Laszlo, was, first of all, their beauty. Every last one of the goddesses was strikingly beautiful. They were, we agreed, very intelligent, creative women who were graceful and fascinating, superior in all ways, and absolutely inaccessible to us. Laszlo longed for Sonya Sorenitch. He even wrote a slightly mocking song describing his fantasies about making love to her. He called it "Soft Fields of Sonya." Evan yearned for Mary Applegate, a tall woman who wore her hair in long braids and spoke in a soothing, gentle voice. I knew they were all too far above me, and the thought of even talking to them filled me with dread, so I didn't care that much what Laszlo was saying. Besides, I was happy with Lainey.

On less romantic days, Laszlo made pronouncements such as, "You know, guys, we should all just castrate ourselves. That's the source of all of our problems. We suffer because of this ridiculous biological insistence. If we cut off balls, we could get more done without always having to worry about scoring. Come on. We should do it," he said to me, Evan and Mole.

From the school steps, my friends started to walk away from him, saying he should go right ahead. I stayed at his side, though. I guess, I owed him my allegiance for letting me stay over at his place all the time.

"Come on, man," Laszlo said to me. "You're probably worse off than any of us."

He was probably right, and my balls ached to hear him say it.

As a more practical solution to our torment, Laszlo suggested the two of us build a fort out in the fields near his house. That way we would have a place to ball girls. We agreed that not having a place to take them was a serious obstacle. Although, some girls let you finger them, even with everybody watching them at parties, nobody actually fucked in front of you. We thought that all we probably lacked was a comfortable, private place.

Ours was another fortress, built out of railroad ties and brush. This one looked remarkably like the one I had helped build along the Susquehanna, except our Bad Vilbel fort was much lower to the ground, and there was no river, no hobos. To my surprised anger, once it was finished, Laszlo would not let me go inside. He said he wanted to christen the fort with his own love making first, and then we could take turns using it. What a stupid selfish thing to do, but I respected his desire for romantic privacy. Besides, it didn't look like Lainey would be willing to go out there with me anytime soon.

Laszlo made only one exception to his fortress rule. In the spring we saw Gentle Giant backing up Colosseum. After the show, Frank, the head roadie, gave us a tour of the equipment. He even opened up their Mellotron to show us how it worked with all its pre-recorded tapes triggered to a keyboard. To show our gratitude, Laszlo invited Frank to come hang out with us at his fort. It had not yet been christened, but Laszlo felt he could be willing to temporarily compromise its sanctity for such an honored guest. Frank gently laughed and politely declined.

Laszlo finally did do his thing with someone out there in the fort, I don't remember who, and I don't care. It had been a magical night, he said. But he still wouldn't let me go inside. He said I should build my own fort. It wasn't right that I should want to even see the inside after he had had sex in it.

I was getting sick of his bullshit, but I still needed to be able to crash at his parents' house, a least until it warmed up outside. I resolved to spend even more time with Lainey, or somewhere else. Besides, I was beginning to prefer the company of girls. There wasn't as much struggle if you forgot about having sex.

Okay, that was impossible, especially when it came to Lainey Wintergreen.

Unfortunately, Lainey was no longer trying very hard to find me. I didn't know what had happened. It got to where I usually had to ask her if it was okay to come see her. Then I made the mistake of telling her I believed we would be together forever. She agreed that, yes, we would always be together in some way. Those last words cut through me. "Some way"? What did that mean? Instead of running like I should have, I chose to painfully accept her qualified declaration of love as good enough for the time being. I didn't push it. I didn't dare risk knowing any more of the truth.

Still it went on, and one miserable day, in a military housing stairwell, Lainey and I were stuck in a discussion of when or whether we should make love. I was emphasizing the "when" while sadly realizing she was thinking of the "whether." It was then that I understood the importance of being eloquent. I kept scrambling my words of love and devotion and, meanwhile, backing myself into a silent pit, alone. I knew I was never going to get the love I craved unless I learned how to speak more smoothly, more seductively. Jack Nicholson had been great at it in *Five Easy Pieces*. He could choose whoever he wanted, because he was in control with his words. I couldn't just be a silent admirer of women, or feebly plead for their attention. I had to express what I felt in a way that would woo her, soothe her, and show her how wonderful I was.

But soon a creeping sense of doom slipped in between my love for Lainey Wintergreen and the need to be loved by her. She was fickle and much more than a charming bit dishonest.

I heard about it in the alley by the teen club. I was stopped by one of Lainey's friends who was bursting to tell me.

"Lainey lost her virginity last night."

"With who?" I demanded to know.

It was the drummer that had been with George and the Rockets at the rock fest. Him? That little shit. We called him "Lunchmeat." I didn't think he was very good-looking. He was two years older than me, and had kind of a soft, low way of talking. So, that's it, I thought. He had convinced her. He didn't give a damn about her. He had talked her into it. Fucked her because he could convince her she should. I couldn't accept that my Lainey wanted to do it with someone who didn't love her. Why? She knew deep inside we were meant to be together. We should have lost our virginity together. The bitch! Maybe I should cut my fucking balls off like Laszlo said. But you know, I loved her. But why did she do that? "Lainey," I cried out to anyone who would listen. "You've destroyed me."

When I saw her next, I tried to be cool, but I was trembling. I told her about my theory of eloquence, and she assured me that "Lunchmeat" hadn't talked her into it, that she had really wanted to make love to him. Everything she said cut me more deeply. I kept telling myself to shut up, to not ask any more questions. I tried to remember that we should all love one another, that all we needed was love, that we had to rise above our petty possessiveness. But I hated her. I hated her. I hated all women. And I wanted her to be mine.

So. My words must have meant something. Lainey must have understood how cruel she had been, because, soon after, Sharon Worley delivered the message that I was to go over to Sharon's house right then, and Lainey would let me do everything I want-

ed except fuck. I was on my way. But it crept into me, as I gal-
loped over to Sharon's, that I was about to receive the consola-
tion prize. Why had she done it with that guy? I told myself I
didn't care anymore if she loved me. I just wanted my hand in
her pants. I wanted to smell her. I wanted her to submit.

There were a couple of chicks hanging out at Sharon's, and
when I saw Lainey I didn't even stop to concede their presence. I
just went up to Lainey and began kissing her aggressively. She
unbuttoned her shirt, just like that, and the other girls kind of
gasped and giggled. I briefly felt up Lainey's tits, but what I
wanted was her cake. I grabbed at her pants and tried to hur-
riedly pull them down. She helped me a little bit, and the other
girls in the room tried not to watch too much. I forced my hand
into her underwear and tried to ram my middle finger inside
her. She was not at all excited, and after a few more angry attempts, we pushed each other away. She buttoned up her jeans,
and I left.

Almost everyone at school knew what had happened, and
when the guys asked me how it had been, I said, "She was too
dry."

Laszlo said, "Well, she said you were too rough."

"I guess that about sums it up," observed Evan.

So what?


On my sixteenth birthday I got a green moped. The Dive-
bomber joked that in the States most young men get a car for
their sixteenth birthday, but in Germany, a moped was the best
they could do. I was completely astonished. Still, it was just a
thing. A possession. And I was suspicious. Was this a peace of-

fering? I thought they had completely given up on me. I certainly felt that way about them.

Now, I had the mobility I needed. I could really come and go as I pleased.

But Mom said, "This is just to get you back and forth from Kamp King. I don't want you riding this to Frankfurt."

I obeyed her for about a week, but Laszlo now had a Honda 50, and he convinced me how much fun we could have if I brought my moped into the city. Besides, what good was it going to do me out in Schönberg, when I was mostly staying with him, anyway?

Laszlo said he had found some old bunkers and tank emplacements that were used for military exercises, and we should ride out there with Evan and play war. To us, playing war meant, of course, a parody of war, or so we believed. We could smoke some shit and act out silly para-militaristic maneuvers. He said that Lainey wanted to go, too. I didn't know how I felt about seeing her again. I was still pretty angry, but agreed.

On the battlefield, I sulked around, not knowing how to control my emotions around Lainey. She seemed to take it all in stride, ignoring me. And, she played at war. She said she would be "Nancy Nurse," and heal wounded soldiers on their way back from the front. The others joked and laughed a lot, but I felt increasingly sad and distant. I wished she would really heal me. I went a little ways off on my own, hoping Lainey would follow. But before long, I noticed all of them were gone.

I didn't dare leave, since three couldn't ride on the Honda. They would be stranded, and Laszlo would give me hell. Eventually, Evan came back without the other two.

"Where's Laszlo and Lainey?" I asked.

"I think they went off to play Nancy Nurse," he teased.

I didn't think it was funny. My soul was rotting. "Let's go, Evan," I said.

"Get over it, man. They'll be back soon."

We waited for a long time before the two of them returned. Their clothes were rumpled and their faces were red. Lainey glanced at me, and she smiled.

# Lifting the Needle

Alex Johnson always managed to get what he wanted. And he wanted to go to Amsterdam, but on his terms. Paul Underhill and I agreed. Alex felt hitching would be too much of a hassle with three. Two of us should take the train as far as the Dutch border (I had a bit of dough I'd saved from a job as a camp counselor), and then hitch the rest of the way into Amsterdam. Paul decided he would rather hitch the whole trip alone and save some money. Besides, he and I didn't want to risk another lousy trip together, like the one that fell apart when we crossed into Denmark.

As it turned out, Alex was fun to hang out with. We talked about music — jazz and classical, mostly. He knew a lot. The whole time we talked, he practiced his drum rudiments. He beat them out on the little slide-out table by the train window.

Just before the border, a damn good-looking girl got on the train and sat down next to us. She was cool. She smoked hand-rolled shag cigarettes that made you kind of high, because the tobacco was so strong. To mellow them, she showed us how to add dried peppermint tea leaves for a cool refreshing smoke. I was eager to share. But Alex didn't smoke! That didn't matter much. This chick told Alex he looked a lot like Jimi Hendrix. He did; but he was a shorter version. Whereas I looked like Don Knotts, but more ragged and probably goofier. Alex was smooth, whereas I was just confused. So, the pretty girl flirted and snuggled with Alex. Meanwhile, I wished, and dreamed and wondered why not me? After our brief ride together, in honor of her, I smoked nothing but hand-rolled cigarettes with a pinch of peppermint leaves.

Alex and I got off the train near Roermond. He said the many dark-skinned people we saw walking around the station were Indonesians. I wondered how they had all gotten there. Alex tried to explain to me about the old Dutch colonies and the history of the idea of race. He seemed to have learned more at school than me. He told me he wanted to stop in that little town of Roermond, and experience a sort of "non-Anglo environment" for a change. We wandered around the marketplace, trying hard not to stare. "Their hair is like mine," Alex whispered. "It's softer. Not as kinky as the American blacks." He was half-Japanese. He said he felt, in a way, like he had come home. "I've got to talk to them," he said. But in a café where he tried to share his enthusiasm, he found there wasn't much to say. He confessed to me that maybe his only connection with them was complexion, and it made him wonder who he really was.

I did not know how to come to terms with the racism everywhere around and within me. I watched black GIs at the PX going through their elaborate soul handshakes, and yearned to be part of their secret society. I read Eldridge Cleaver's introduction to Jerry Rubin's *Do it! Scenarios of the Revolution*. Eldridge Cleaver said that we, the white folks, the children of the conquerors, are the children of blood spilled. I knew that the FBI had killed some and imprisoned many more Black Panthers. Blacks were up against something more deadly and disgusting than what the white student movement had to face. I remembered the day I burnt a dollar bill in front of the high school annex just as Abbie and Jerry and the Yippees had instructed.

110

The scowls and ashes were blowing away when I said to a black guy who had stopped to stare, "I wish I were like you, man. I mean, as a white guy, it's hard to make a statement that people will understand. But if you're black, any act of protest will be understood, because people will feel guilty about the years of slavery and suffering that white people have inflicted on Blacks."

At first he looked at me like I was nuts, then he looked defiant, and then seemed uncertain. Finally, he shook my hand and walked away. He never said a word, and I felt better for a while.

It was an easy hitch the rest of the way into Amsterdam. We caught a ride crowded with a Dutch family. Alex and I sang, "Happy Birthday" and whatever else we could think of, to try and soothe their crying kid.

When we arrived, Alex talked me into staying at the youth hostel instead of the park like I suggested. He decided he didn't want to sleep in Vondelpark, because when I took him there to show him how cool it was, one of the first people we saw was a guy whose head crawled with lice. "Ee-yew," Alex shuddered. "Ain't no way I'm staying here," he laughed. "You go right ahead, but Mr. Alex is staying in a clean place."

The next day he made arrangements for us to bike 40 kilometers to Scheveningen near The Hague. I don't know why he was set on going for such a long bike ride, but it was hard to challenge Alex. He was right about so many things. So I rode, painfully, on a dumpy one-speed down the coast to nothing, and then we turned around and came back. Okay. That's not exactly true. We did visit Madurodam, a miniature replication of Amsterdam. Very strange. You could walk through the tiny city while watching other tourists looking like we polite human monsters. There were little versions of us, too. Most people thought it was hilarious to see the miniature hippies sprawled around a replica of Dam Square.

That night we were supposed to meet up with Paul Underhill, but I ended up going on my own. I decided I'd rather sleep in the park and leave Alex to the expense of hot showers and protection. I spotted Paul in Vondelpark in front of the kiosk where we had planned to meet. He was counting a wad of money, and then I saw him shove it into his wallet and then into his jeans, and then he started to walk away. I shouted for him, but he couldn't hear me. I didn't care. It was kind of fun spying on him. A couple hundred hippies were gathered around in front of a concession stand/bar, drinking and smoking. Paul was headed that way. The park was thrilling and I felt right at home. Everybody was talking and laughing. You could talk to anybody. No one shunned you or made you feel stupid or too young. It was one big community of perfect strangers. I made my way through the crowd to catch up with Paul. He had stopped to talk with four African guys that he must have just met. Maybe he wanted to score some shit. I went up to them and was about to say, "Hello" when I saw Paul's face tense up. He was white as bone in the outdoor bar light. His eyes glistened and they nervously caught mine. His hands began to reach reflexively for the sky.

"Keep ya fuckin' hands down, man," one of the Africans said.

Paul began to whimper. He was shoved a little forward, and he quickly shut up. I realized they were holding a knife to him. The men went through his pockets and found what they were after. Paul pleaded with the four of them to give back his wallet. It was all the money he had, he explained. But I doubt they believed him. Surely, the white American had more money at home, they laughed. The wallet fell to the middle of the circle we had formed, and Paul thanked them for what he thought was a change of heart. He picked up the wallet and saw it was empty. He begged them to give the money back. But they just stared hatefully at Paul and maybe pitied him a little in spite of this show of force and entitlement. None of the four guys said anything to me. They merely glanced at me, threateningly, before fading back to the crowded night.

The next morning, Paul and I walked around the park looking for them. We didn't know what we were going to do if we found them. We were just mad. Maybe we wanted them to apologize for being uncool. Just that, forget the money. We found them sitting on a blanket, hanging out with some white people.

"You think they're going to rob them, too?" I said, "Maybe we should say something."

"That's stupid. Remember, *you* didn't have a knife to your back."

We thought of reporting them to the cops, but then we changed our minds. I mean, how could we do that? The cops were the true enemy. Still, we resented that our most blissful communal sleep spot was about to be surrendered to erupting fear.

Paul and I met Alex down by Dam Square. We were telling Alex about the robbery when a bunch of singing, finger cymbal-clinging guys dressed in orange robes, came dancing down the street. White two-pronged forks were painted on their foreheads. They were bald except for a little tuft of hair at the back of the crown. Over and over they chanted the same song, accompanied by little cymbals — ching, ching-ching, ching — and a couple of long orange drums that looked like Indian *tablas*, Alex said, except they were about four-feet long. A few hippies climbed down from the Square and started dancing with them. I wanted to join in, too, but a glare from Underhill and Alex said, "Forget it. Don't embarrass us." A dancer handed me a card with an address and map on it. On the other side, was an invitation in English for a free lunch. I wanted to go straight away. Paul said he was hungry, too. But Alex insisted we go to the Rijk's Museum to see Rembrandt's *Nightwatch*. If we agreed to go to the museum, Alex said, he'd consider visiting the Hare Krishna temple. Their poly-rhythms appealed to him, he said. It might be interesting.

I'd never heard of Rembrandt, but was glad I went. I liked the way the soldiers' metal helmets reflected light made of nothing but paint.

At the temple, we sat on the floor passing delicious curried pastes, some made of garbanzos, some of lentils, others of potatoes, that you put onto pita bread and then topped it with strange sauces and seeds. We silently ate with our fingers. It was fun digging up big handfuls of spicy potato stuff and plopping it onto hot bread. We couldn't believe it was all free. Even Alex was impressed. We three exchanged the comrade look of, "Hey man, this is really cool." And we were offered seconds! After the second go around, someone rang a little bell. The food was quickly snatched away, while another person began singing what I guessed were a few prayers. They sang softly and solemn-like. And then they broke into the more fun chant we had heard them singing on the street. After a couple of cycles, they stopped and asked if we knew the Hare Krishna chant. They explained that, according to their main guru guy, singing and dancing was the best way to communicate their message. Words alone, they said, could not adequately convey the message of "Krishna Consciousness." I could dig that. "Let's do it," I said. So we sang over and over again —

*Hare Krishna, hare Krishna*
*Krishna, Krishna*
*Hare, hare.*
*Hare Rama, hare Rama*
*Rama, Rama*
*Hare, hare*

The more we sang, the more exuberant and entranced they seemed to become. I really enjoyed the singing, but didn't feel like I could let loose with Paul and Alex around. The two of them seemed uncomfortable about having to sing for their lunch. After about a half an hour of it, they stopped and asked if we had any questions. Alex wanted to know about Eastern rhythm patterns, and he demonstrated with some taps on the low table what he meant. No one responded to what he was talking about, so he quickly shut up. I wanted to show I readily accepted their "odd" behavior. I asked what the words of the chant meant. They told me it was something like "Hail to Krishna, Hail to Rama." Not too exciting, I guess.

I noticed that some teenagers were living there, and some of the girls were pretty cute. I began to wonder if maybe I could stay there and not go back to Frankfurt at all. It wasn't Zen, but was a start. When I told them what I was thinking, they told me I should come back the next day and talk about it with the head temple guy, or whatever he was called.

That night, we went to the *Milkweg* nightclub — it was so dreamy, it was a hulking moated castle strewn with hundreds of tiny lights. Inside, was a wonderful maze of musical venues. Through a narrow hall and under a low arch, Charlie Chaplin films flickered. There were pillows for seats. And just about everywhere you looked, many niches promised places to make love. The chillums smoked like fumaroles, and we got blissfully stoned.

Afterwards, we wandered into the opera house, paid about a quarter to get in, and were swept away into a happy fervor. From way up in the last balcony, amidst a thick cloud of "hish-hash" smoke the crowd was exuberantly appreciative. All the way down the layered balconies — with the audience dressed more formally the further down I looked — a great twinkling funnel of our delight and gratitude poured onto the stage. From high above, we watched as little figures twisted and leapt to the music that Alex said was Mozart.

The next day, Alex insisted that he definitely did not want to go back to the Krishna temple, even for a free lunch. He said he liked the music, but didn't trust the people there. Paul reluctantly agreed to return with me, perhaps he thought he needed to protect me from myself. He probably said as much.

When we arrived, the atmosphere of the temple felt more serious — no one was chanting. Lunch was not as ceremonious, and the devotees seemed a bit agitated. After we all ate a meal in silence, followed by a few minutes of lackluster chanting, I asked about staying on for a while. They told me that they did not want to discourage me, but staying would require a permission slip from my parents. My heart hit the floor. My enthusiastic smile slacked into a pout. Yet, they assured me, if I could show I was truly dedicated to Krishna consciousness, they might waive the parental consent requirement. To show that I was in earnest, I got a hardbound copy of KRSNA: The Supreme Personality of Godhead which was full of pictures of a blue Krishna in various poses. I bowed to them, I said I would study the book. But I never read it.

One Saturday morning, after wondering all night in the streets of Frankfurt, I called home and said I'd be there, as if they cared. When I got up the hill, I found a note on the kitchen table. It read something like — "You will not go to Kamp King or anywhere else today. You will stay home and help out around the house. Signed, Vic." Well, that sucks, I thought. I had made plans to go to Kamp King that afternoon, after I got some sleep. I resented that the Dive-bomber suddenly wanted to wrestle his way into parental domination, and since no one was home to stop me from leaving, I wrote my response. "Vic," it said, "I've gone to Kamp King to do what I want. You are not my father. Do not try to restrict my freedom — Steve"

I had to hitch to get there. My moped had broken down permanently in Frankfurt. When I got to Kamp King I couldn't find anybody. I hung out for a few hours — long enough for the Dive-bomber to get home and read the note. Then I hitched home. When I got there, Mom told me that the Bomber had left in a rage. She looked at me hatefully and asked why I had written such a note. I told her because that's the way I felt. And so she retired, weeping back upstairs to their bedroom.

Since eating macrobiotic food at the Krishna temple, I had decided to become a vegetarian. I declared I would forever oppose the violence and barbarism of meat. While waiting for the

Bomber to hit home, I sat down to a meal of eggs and rice and tomatoes. I heard him at the door.

He didn't hit me, but I could see he wanted to. He seemed far too shattered over something else to be moved to violence. His eyes were watery. He said nothing for a while, but I could feel it coming. I slowly ate my food trying to remember to chew each bite forty-nine times so as to digest properly. Then he burst out, "No meat, huh?" He had found his strategy.

"That's right," I said. "I've become a vegetarian."

"Oh, you have, have you? Isn't the food I provide good enough for you?"

I stared at him, wondering what I could possibly say.

"I work hard so that you can eat. And the food I buy, you think is shit."

"Brown rice is the perfect food," I began foolishly. "It has all the nutrients we need to sustain us. In Asia, most people eat rice because they know this," I said with great superiority.

"You ever met anybody from Asia?" The Dive-bomber had begun to shout. "Well, *I've* been there. And why do you think they are so skinny?"

I didn't dare say a word.

"Those people are starving over there while you think you're too good to eat the meat that you don't have to lift a finger for. All you have to do is come and go as . . . ."

He stopped short, his forehead was about to explode. Suddenly, he turned away and walked out of the room.

We didn't speak to each other for months. It didn't help that one time I was hitching back from Kamp King, and he refused to pick me up.

From then on, I redoubled my efforts to never go home again, at least not while they were there. I stayed where I could, which usually meant at Laszlo's, despite his stealing my girlfriend. Or, occasionally, I slept at Mole's, and once in a while stayed at Paul Underhill's, until he moved away to Luxembourg. When I couldn't find a place to stay, or was fed up with Laszlo, I stayed in Gruneburg park or on our high school football field. Both were pretty scary. I dragged a big dull-silver bag around with me. It held my sleeping bag, whatever I was reading, a little camp stove, and any food I had managed to scrounge. Several times, I stole canned goods from our quaint *Wunderhaus* out in Schönberg. My method was to call before catching the train, to make sure no one was home. Then, once at the station, I'd call again and hope to get to the house before anyone arrived. With the coast clear, I filled my bag with cans from the Bomber's survivalist cellar to last a week or two, and then split. But I got sick of canned vegetables real quick, and it became increasingly difficult to bum meatless food. I had to admit that my vegetarianism had quickly become impractical, and so I gave it up.

By the spring of 1944, the allied forces had destroyed 80% of the center of Frankfurt with their incendiary bombs. The fiery mess included a direct hit on the opera house. In 1971, what had once been a neoclassical plume for Kaiser Wilhelm the first, was now a gray shell surrounded by a chain-link fence. Standing outside in the dark with Laszlo, I thought I saw the broken statue bodies of famous heroes balanced at the top of a wall. Was it Mozart? Probably Bach? Or, maybe those were the half-cracked heads of gargoyles way up there. We crawled through the fence with a few other people and met a guide with a flashlight. He showed us the way to the party, saying in both English and German that it was too dangerous to go alone, and that the party was a great success.

By his dim flashlight, shining too far ahead, our guide led us down dirty hallways and into broken rooms. Occasionally, he shined his light towards the ceiling and walls where the swirling peeling painted flourishes reminded me of a decayed circus. Were we in what was once an opulent parlor, a lounge for in between acts? Through a passageway, a rotting wooden spiral staircase was missing several steps. Our guide had to help each of us separately. We didn't dare go. But one at a time could make it, he said, as he pulled us up to the next level. At the top of the staircase, we saw stars shining through a huge hole in the ceiling. In front of us, a narrow dirt path, that must have been the top of a wall at one time, led to the sounds of the party. The path extended above a murky pool on one side, and the tops of a few stunted trees on the other. Down below was what had once been the back of the stage. I was terrified to cross, but I was told if I didn't cross then, between muck and impalement, I would have to sit and wait in the dark until a guide felt like returning. One at a time, as best we could, we followed the erratic beam of his flashlight.

Safely across, Laszlo and I were led into the first party room, and the guide disappeared. A fire blazed inside the room and we could see the expected chillum being passed around. Some folks were singing a heavily accented Cat Stevens' song, "Oh, baby, baby, it's a *vild vorld.*" We recognized a few people, but most of the crowd were University of Frankfurt students, we decided, and no one we could really talk to. Our German was limited and lifeless, and besides, many of them seemed to be debating the

American military presence again. It was no fun being the enemy. And we could never convince them otherwise. After a few
polite tokes, Laszlo and I decided to explore on our own. We
snagged a loose flashlight, and then we headed out.

In the dark we found a room with a few old props and cos-
tumes — tattered golden shoes and fragments of something lacy.
A pedestal painted white and gold looked like a lion's perch. A
couple of times Laszlo and I almost fell. We groped along the
damp crumbly walls, straining to see where the floors had rotted
through. At last, we found the old stage itself where the bombs
must have hit hardest. Below, where once the audience had
cheered, was now a flooded swamp. The trees were taller there,
since the roof had been completely blown away in a storm of
sucking fiery horror. Only a few of arched walls remained. The
walls rose two stories above the stage floor making an angular
higher space where the fake gods resided, waiting to descend
upon the troubled singers on stage. Laszlo and I were admiring
the rounded room around us, up against the hard edges of the
stage area, when we saw that someone was standing above us on
the ledge of the highest wall. Laszlo said he thought he recognized him from school, but it was too dark to tell for sure. Still,
we heard him singing in what was clearly an American accent.
He was dancing along the wall edge, singing, "Light my Fire." I
was horrified for him. I wanted to get up there somehow and
help him down. Laszlo thought the guy must be tripping, and
there was nothing we could do about it. I shouted upwards. Laszlo told me to shut up, or I'd attract the cops, or maybe make
him lose his footing.

Shouldn't we get help, I wondered? Laszlo said he thought the
dude would be okay, and that we should continue on our own

journey. But I was distracted. I could hear him hollering and singing up there. If I managed to get to the top of the wall, and I didn't want to do that, it might freak him out — a gargoyle come alive. He might jump. Laszlo was right, there was nothing we could do about it, but it hurt that I couldn't help him. Laszlo told me to not be so paranoid, that the dude was having a good time, and I should leave him alone. The tripper was shouting something I couldn't understand. And    I pointed to some words carved in huge letters just below him. In the city-light glow I read, *Dem Wahren Schoenen Gutten.* I wondered what it meant and told myself to look it up later. I took one last look, and Laszlo and I turned our backs on the acrobat above us.

The next day, I listened for rumors about the young man who had surely fallen to his death at the opera house, but heard nothing. I did read in *The Stars and Stripes* that the Polizei had arrested several people for trespassing that night and that some of them were Frankfurt American High students. The article reported that the German community was furious about the fire that had been lit. How could people be so careless and mean-spirited when plans were underway to restore the opera house? The article called for renewed efforts in Cold War co-operation and a crackdown on drug use among military dependents and others. It did not say how the sight of flames coming from the *Alteoper* must have sent a shudder of recognition through the older Germans that night. And the report neglected to mention Dem Wahren Schoenen Guten — '(Dedicated to the) True, (the) Beautiful (and the) Good'.

The Dive-bomber informed me over the phone that he was fed up with my absence. He said I was very disrespectful to my mother who was worried sick about me. From then on, I was going to do as he said, or there would be hell to pay. I had better be home by midnight that night, he told me. He was too pissed off for it to seem like a bluff, and, anyway, I was getting stinky from sleeping out in the park. I figure I'd better spend more time in the Wunderhaus or else.

I caught the last train home. By the time I was walking up Hermann Löns Weg, it was after 2 a.m.

All the lights were off, and the doors were locked, so I went to the garage for the key. I reached my hand into the darkness, but the key wasn't there. I stood on the patio and looked up to Mom and the Dive-bomber's window. Maybe they were getting it on and didn't want me to disturb them. I didn't know what to do. I thought of taking the last train back to Frankfurt, but there was no way I'd make it to the station in time. I could always sleep in our yard, but that seemed ridiculous. I wanted to sleep in my bed. I deserved to. But I sure didn't want to deal with the Bomber past this new curfew. Ah, fuck him. I called out his name, "Vic, it's me." No answer. I called out over and over. "Somebody let me in." I knew they could hear me.

I was about to pull out my sleeping bag when the door creaked open about a foot. I went towards it and repeated, "Vic, it's me, Steve." The lights were still out, but I could see the shadow of  someone in the darkness. I pushed the door slightly. "Vic?" I said. I took a step inside, and there he was, hiding behind the door holding a butcher knife high in the air. He was poised to plunge it into me. Poised to strike, at last, at the heart of his jealousy and rage. "Vic," I said sharply looking directly into those shadowy eyes. He let his arm fall limply to his side.

Without a word, he put the knife back into the kitchen and disappeared upstairs.

# *Ich kann mein Haus nicht finden*

I slept with a knife under my pillow. There would be only one reason for the Dive-bomber to come into my room. If he did, I wouldn't be able to get out the window fast enough — not enough time to jump out and run. If he dared open my bedroom door, I swore I was going to kill him. And yet, I was afraid *not* to come home at night. If I didn't obey him and "stop coming and going as I pleased," he might take it out on Mom. I'd watch over her and she would look after me.

Or, maybe she secretly wanted him to hit me. She used to beat the shit out of me when I was a little boy. She made me pull down my pants and then she whupped me with a switch. Just like her mother used to beat her. Mom would always say to sister and me, "Now, if you kids don't behave, I'm gonna cut me a switch." One time when Sis and I were watching cartoons, Mom cut her a switch and placed it right on top of the TV, as a reminder, she said. That switch stared back at us, stripped of all but a few withered leaves, the bark rubbed away to the sappy tan stem beneath. The threat of it, drooping over the screen, ruined *The Huckleberry Hound Show* forever.

My sister was strong. She faced Mom one day and told her enough was enough. Then there were no more whippings for her. But I didn't know how to make Mommy stop. One time she caught me going through her dresser drawers. I was playing with her bra and falsies, when she snuck up on me. She thought it was pretty funny, her little boy prancing about, pretending.

But she told my dad. He said he reckoned I should be punished. Mom told me to go back to her room and wait for her there. She came in and closed the door. She made me pick out a belt — a wide white  patent leather belt, and then commenced to lightly swing it at me. It didn't hurt at all; she was barely hitting me. Just little pats on my butt. She'd never hit me so softly before; she'd never swung so playfully before. She said, "Now you don't have to tell your father. This is our little secret." I figure, for her satisfaction, I had better cry, anyway. That was the deal. I thought I had to cry, or it didn't count. I had to, at least, pretend I was suffering. And then it became a habit. Real pain or not, I had to suffer.

I felt claustrophobic in my little German room. I had taken most of the crap off the wall to simplify it, make it more stark in a non-attached Zen kind of way, but the room was still a cell to me. I'd sit at my desk and wait for another day to end. I could hear the Dive-bomber devil clanging around in the kitchen, starting the water heater, sterilizing the blade, preparing for, or, at least hoping for, my death. I'd be no more competition to him. No more usurper. Ball-less. But try as he might to castrate me, I decided that the sacrifice — the cruel and magnificent necessity that had always haunted the Wunderhaus — would not mean my death, but theirs. Maybe I would not kill him with my pillow knife, nor kill her with my hatred. My sacrifice, the death of my mother and my step-father would be . . . a *transmogrification* (yes, that's it) into a dedication to endless yearning love, to a life filled with longing just as my "parents" ceased to exist. I alone would watch over me. No castrators and no emotional manipulators would surface. I would be my own father and my own mother. My mother. . . would never love me the way I desired,

126

unconditionally and certainly without the threat of abandonment.

And yet.

If I didn't love Mom, it would have meant I was a mean person — a very bad boy. Terrible guilty love. As best I could I tell, according to Mom, we are receptors of pain, a secret sexual pain. And women are the source of comfort from pain received, yet women are also the inflictors of grave, eternal pain. They just can't help what they do. They are innocent, though, and deserve forgiveness, as does everyone, just as the Bible teaches us.

In the meantime, the hammer of history went tock, tock, tock. Mom wallowed in her woe, and the Dive-bomber got drunk. His usual case of liter  bottle beers was no longer reserved for the weekend. He drank continuously. According to him, women, at least the one he had, were lunatics to be suffered. Men should work hard, be self-sacrificing, and then do as they god-damned pleased. I figured Mom thought that even if men beat you, they were necessary for support. As a bonus, men could be used for pleasure and for occasional comfort. Any talents a woman possessed were better used as weapons for emotional blackmail than as expressions of joy. I remembered once, Mom got mad at my real dad and refused to make any more of her beautiful flower arrangements, because she felt he had complained too much about the expense of  her shop in the carport. And he had complained. Then there was the time my sister and I woke up to find the generic Roman ruins she had been painting — copied from a scrap of wall-paper — transformed into an abstract swirl of white and gold. Mom used a cloth to smear the oil paints into chaos after Dad insulted her talent. She hung the painting over the living room couch and refused to ever paint again. My sister and I loved the swirling abstractions. Day after day we set our imaginations loose on that painting, but Dad brooded under it for months until Mom relented and finally took it down.

RE: Andie Carnelian in Berwick. A couple of times, Grandma Dive-bomber's letters mentioned that she had seen Andy Carnelian's aunt, and she had asked after me. I had written to no one in Berwick since I left, and the talk of Andie made me feel curious and a bit remorseful that I had neglected to send my address to her and Sally.

As part of my junior year school orientation, we were assembled to hear yet another lecture about the evils of drugs. In the fall of '71 the school administration and the military community decided to get hip and have a "rap session" about what was on students' minds regarding drug use. Spies were everywhere. No one was stupid enough to "rap" with the fuzz. Time to slip into the natural depressant of glazed mindlessness. Yet, amongst the panel perched up onstage was the head of V. Corps' psychiatric division, and this doctor seemed pretty cool. He could tell where we were at with drugs, and he had the courage to express it. I sat up and listened when he took a bite out of our idiotic vice principal who was acting the cop again. He asked him:

"Did you ever stop to ask yourself why these students want to take drugs?" the doctor wanted to know. "Maybe they're bored, or in pain, or angry, or maybe they hope to see the world in a different way than you do."

A great slice of the student body tittered, then we remembered the spies, and we hushed ourselves.

The doctor assured us he did not condone the use of drugs, but if the community ever hoped to come to terms with the problem, the first step was understanding. Yes, but he has to say that. But maybe this is someone I can talk to, I thought. I didn't want to risk losing him. I told my friends I wanted to speak to him — kind of asking for permission. My friends reminded me of what had happened in *One Flew Over the Cuckoo's Nest*.

"What's he called," they asked, playing with the sound of his name? "Dr. Armcleavage?" they laughed.

The doctor told me he was a very busy man, and so he asked if I wouldn't agree to consult with someone else? I insisted it was going to be him or no one. He reluctantly told me to make an appointment and that he must interview my parents before the appointment.

The Dive-bomber refused to go. He would not offer any explanation. I pressed him a little, but his rage began to brew, and so I backed off. Mom explained that no one in his family had ever been to a psychiatrist. More importantly, he was pissed off because my going to a shrink might negatively affect his chances for promotion. He had already decided I was the reason he didn't make master sergeant.

At the doctor's office, the chief underling to Dr. Armcleavage instructed me to wait on a bench while he and my mother talked about my "situation." He told me they would be back within 20 minutes, and not to worry, they just needed some family history.

I knew it would take longer. Mom needed attention more than I did. At least that's the way she would play it. She had a way of demanding affection and attention that made the listener feel guilty if he tried to escape. I wasn't as good at it as she was, but I was learning. The world is truly a cruel place, and all we can ever hope for is a weeping hug. Unfortunately, my hugs for her were becoming more and more artificial. I guessed I wanted to help her, but she seemed to cultivate ignorance. So, education wouldn't save her. Sympathy wouldn't help either, since she took deep pleasure in it. Confrontations with her only ended in my being chastised for not following the Christian law of honoring thy mom, etc., and indifference was strictly forbidden. They had been in there for forty-five minutes so far.

I had begun to give up on her in my mind, but not quite in my heart. Not yet. She taught me not to lie, and to "be good." She said if I put my mind to it, I could do whatever I wanted. I wondered if that included leaving. She had her own problems, so didn't notice what I was about. Once, she told me she thought I'd make a good preacher! How could I ever get her to understand? I desperately needed her to, but on my terms, about me, not her, for once. It had been over an hour since they went in there.

It occurred to me that Mom's implicit instruction to me was, "You are on your own, because I don't know what the fuck I'm doing. I love you, but I don't know how to express it without screaming for my own needs. I'm sorry. I wish I could have done better."

After an hour and twenty minutes the underling psychiatrist came out of his office and apologized. He said, "I'm sure it's your mother who needs help, not you." And with that dismissal he turned my sobbing mother over to me. She was desperately in need of a hug, so I put my arms around her — rubbery lies.

Evan came back to Deutschland on his own, just as he said he would. He had left for a while because his dad was rotating back to The States and, "All military dependents must depart on or before the rotation date of the enlisted parent or guardian." Now he was staying a Laszlo's.

I persuaded Laszlo to let me stay at his house, again. "Okay, but you'll have to swear you'll obey the rules," he said. That meant not talking to his folks and indulging Laszlo in all of his new experiments, including those with Lainey. For our accommodation, Laszlo had his parents install bunk beds in the basement. There was also a new guy from Barbados, Sam Apricot, who started sleeping there, too.

Sam seemed a disoriented surfer type whose tan was fading fast and whose blonde curly hair was awaiting adjustment to the Frankfurt fog. He said he was relieved to find his kind of people, he said. To prove himself, Laszlo, Evan and I invited him to help us lug a bag of potatoes around Frankfurt to perform psychological experiments on the populace.

We placed potatoes on the sidewalk in front of the *Kaufhaus* department store to see what people would do to them. Hardly anyone noticed the potatoes at their feet. So, they accidentally launched the spuds down the street. After studying the situation, we agreed that to refine our experiment, to determine will and intention, we needed to concentrate the pedestrians' attention downward. The foot of an escalator to the *Ubahn* 'the subway' proved the perfect spot. One potato was placed to roll at the edge of the smoothly meshing, disappearing steps. Meanwhile, we tried to make ourselves inconspicuous. Each rolling spud was a universe unto itself, vulnerable and inconsequential. What would humankind do to an unsuspecting, spinning world at their feet? Some kicked it, and we laughed. Some scooted it aside, or poked at it with a toe. Most tried to ignore the lost potato, yet, once in a while, someone picked it up, looked around to see if anyone was watching, and then put it in her bag. We howled at our success  and imitated the dances of each person. We decided to call ourselves the *Kartoffel* Brigade, and we marched back to the high school compound to cram potatoes into every orifice we could find. We dropped a potato into the library book return, rammed one into the principal's mail slot, several into the Idle Hour Theater box office; we hid them under mats and placed them in the crooks of trees. We emptied the bag. Our assault was complete. Thus, Sam became one of us.

Sam Apricot played the guitar, too, and he invited Evan and I out to his parents' house to listen to the kind of folksy stuff he liked. His best treat for us was an album called *Blue* by Joni Mitchell. He swooned when he played it.

Ahh, hashish and Joni. Sam played, "All I Want," and my emotions swirled, my heart beat faster, and her smooth lilting, soothing voice thrilled me with the possibility, with the freedom of the mutual love I craved. That love could exist. In her lyrics, I could hear my hope unfolding.

Oh, Joni. Where is my Joni? If I loved Lainey as strongly, as deeply as this Joni feeling, how could Lainey fail to respond to me? I lay back on Sam's bed and let myself dream.

The tone arm lifted and waved, and we were impatient for the album to be turned over. "Oh, hurry Sam; don't let her fade."

I had never really cared about visiting California until I heard Joni sing about it. One day I'd have to go there. Meet her, maybe. She sounded young enough. She couldn't be too much older than me. Yes, she was better than all the goddesses at high school. Every note convinced me of her entrancing sadness, of a gentle understanding in the face of all the impossible political pain, the home pain, the distance between me and everyone. When she sang "The Last Time I Saw Richard," her penetrant voice brought me to tears.

As the second side's resonance faded into a revolving crackle and darkness, we three guys lay stunned on the bed. It wasn't just me who had fallen. It looked as if I'd to have to share her, of course. There was nothing left to do but play it again. And again and again. As it played, I rehearsed in my heart how to approach Lainey.

Once we recovered, Evan and Sam and I decided, without hesitation, to form a group that played acoustic music. We called ourselves Wit, White and Apricot.

Whenever we got the chance, we sang "Two of Us" from *Let it Be* and "No Expectations" from *Beggar's Banquet*. We did Spirit's "Nature's Way," and Crosby, Stills & Nash's "Suite: Judy Blue Eyes." But the song that always caused the most ruckus, and that I enjoyed performing the most, was John Lennon's "Working Class Hero." The night we played it for the officers' wives, I stuck little American flags out from my cracked granny glasses, and I sang Lennon's words with feeling about how I felt robbed, and bullied and abused into citizenship. As a concession to our gentle audience, or just to protect our butts, I mumbled the words "fucking crazy" and changed "you're still fucking peasants" to "you're still plucking pheasants." Unlike their standing invitation to the school choir, the Melloteens of which I was a part, Wit, White and Apricot were never asked to perform for the wives again.

Eventually, I was accepted for counseling. However, Dr. Armcleavage believed I should do all the talking. He rarely said more than a few words in our sessions and he usually seemed bored, but I did not know what else to do but keep talking. Our sessions were supposed to be an hour long, but he always arrived late. Once I complained, and he corrected me that we were only scheduled to meet for a fifty-minute-hour. It was more like forty minutes or less, but I kept talking. The only things I discovered with his help was, vaguely, that I had some problems, and that I was indeed "neurotic." So now it had a name. A flimsy name, but a name, nevertheless.

Evan said that he, too, doubted my Armcleavage visits were really helping. He said I was acting even weirder and getting more and more paranoid. I guess I proved him right one day when he, I, Laszlo and Mole were walking across a field to Laz-lo's house. I was dragging along feeling lonesome and misunderstood. They were cracking jokes about me and galloping across the field, and I begged them to slow down. "Wait up," I screamed.

"Fuck off, man," Laszlo said. "If you want to come over, you've got to keep up."

I decided I would not tolerate their disrespect, and so I began to cry. I screamed that they were cold mean fuck-heads, and why couldn't they wait? What kind of friendship was this, I demanded? I said they disgusted me. I got some attention, but it didn't feel very good. They said I should stop going to the fucking shrink, that I was a mess, that I had some *real* problems, that I was never going to get a chick acting like that. They left me slumped in a sobbing pile of cultivated sorrow. But not for long. I imagined what the story would be about me at school. I picked myself up and slouched toward Laszlo's.

Once, after a visit with myself in the shrink's office, I was bouncing back into the school when I saw Lisa Marascino. She had a hall pass to go pee or something, and I gave her a big hug for the hell of it. She liked the hug, but as we gently embraced, our fascist vice-principal, Pig-man came around the corner.

"Where's your hall pass?" He shouted. "Get into my office. *Now*." He sent Lisa on her way, then he turned to me and said, "I've got you now."

I explained to the moron that I didn't need a hall pass, since I was on my way back from my shrink. He decided he was "tired of my antics," and so he suspended me for "displaying amorous conduct." He informed me that I would not be allowed back into school for at least a week, and then, only after my mother came in for a conference.

Mom thought the whole thing was pretty ridiculous, but she came in anyway to support me. After her private interview with the less volatile principal, Mr. Harken, she told me the administration was thinking of forcing me to go to school 30 kilometers away in Wiesbaden "if my behavior didn't improve." Harken said, that nearly every day after school, he had seen me making out on the lawn in front of his office, putting some young ladies in "very compromising positions." It was true I had copped a feel or two out there, but what confused me was that they mentioned Lainey Wintergreen by name. How did they know I was in love with her? She would hardly ever let me kiss her. My mother asked me about Lainey, and I had to tell Mom that Lainey was the love of my life, and yes, I made out with her on the lawn, but not like the principal said.

After some lengthy discussion and sufficient contrition, Harken let me stay in Frankfurt. "Consider this a warning," he told me. He smiled. And Mom smiled, too. When we were out of the office, she said  I should try to calm myself down, and that none of this was a surprise to her. She knew already that I had "hot blood," she said.

The Dive-bomber freaked out so badly at Thanksgiving dinner that Mom and I fled, just for old time's sake. The difference between Key West and Frankfurt was, Where the fuck did she think we were going to go?

"How about I take you to your girlfriend's house?" she asked.

Mom said she thought she ought to talk to Lainey's mom first and that I should wait in the car. This should be interesting, I thought.

After a few minutes, Lainey came running outside. She wrapped her arms around me and hugged me so tenderly; we both began to cry.

"I am so sorry," she said.

I didn't know if she was sorry about having done me wrong, or  because she felt bad that the Dive-bomber was on the attack again. Either way, I didn't dare interrupt the feel of her warm body pressed so hard against mine. She kissed me passionately, and I was even grateful to the dear Bomber. Because of his violence, I was going to live with Lainey. Yes. But no. Lainey's mom thought it entirely inappropriate for me to stay with the Wintergreens. And she was sorry, but we would have to go elsewhere.

Mom and I got back into the car, and I persuaded her to let me off anywhere. I told her not to worry, that I could fend for myself. After all, I had a lot of practice at it.

I could see it clearly. Once again, I was the peas on the floor in Key West. My globe had exploded into thousands of little green orbs scattered chaotically. "I am peas," I exclaimed to my friends.

They paused to consider my bizarre observation, then Evan joined in playfully. "Yes, that's it. Of course," he said. "You know what you have? You have Nutritional Neurosis!"

Oh, thank you, Evan, for naming it, for completing the thought.

I understood that I had much work to do. I needed to write about my recent Thanksgiving. I called it:

## *Fantastic Fatal Foods and other Forced Feces*

*I finally blew up my entire house today, with my parents inside. It was really neat — flaming high with brilliant satisfaction; the roof's nice little German tiles projecting themselves out of comprehension. Sheets of glass sliding onto the charcoal lawn; the platinum mailbox melting never to receive senseless meat-market propaganda again; manicured trees announcing their radiance. Flowers in highly varnished boxes launching themselves, searching for freedom.*

*The roof divided and crashed downward while wasted leftovers, sorted appliances, movie magazines, and the household wastes chaotically replaced it, the walls crumbling down to the flaming ground on which my parents lay smoldering in a stifling stench.*

*I felt at first a bit of guilt and reluctance but easily thought otherwise when I realized their lack of intelligence and their* great ability to disease my mind. It was as if I had finally been relieved of my main source of oppression. I was free. Free of all worries and . . . Oh, wait a minute. I've just murdered two people! I had better worry about law and order and all that crap. The islands — the blue crisp Caribbean waters — Ah, that's it. Escape to a nice tropical island with all kinds of delicious nourishment and —

"Son, wash up and come to dinner."

"What? Oh."

"Come on now, quit daydreaming. Your dinner's getting cold."

I stumble out of my little bedroom into the fragrant dining area.

*Delicate edibles steam in the candle lit air. I rise with their emissions as they sing of vitality. My eyes take notice of fresh peas melting with a butter topping. Texture plays with my mind, as the deep greens frolic like nymphs on lush lawns. They are very seductive. They sit cunningly waiting for oral ecstasy to capture their existence. Walking towards them with passive intent, I sense their gratification as I admire them by the plush velvet couch. With sensual movement they lure me to their bubbling fantasy of sensitivity. Into the foam I slide as my harem follows. Down, down into smooth curving flesh pressed to mine as we copulate in the dulcet foam.*

"Are you going to stand there all night? Sit down and eat your dinner."

While I sit at the table with my elders, the food is passed.

"Would you care for some meat? How about some mashed potatoes?"

"I must say, honey, these peas are delicious. What did you put in them? Why don't you try some, son? They're really good tonight."

"Yeah, sure."

The meal commenced with all kinds of fascinating things to eat or, in the case of a loss of hunger, to contemplate. I chose the latter.

With thought games of food I avoided mental intercourse with my secretly not so amiable masters.

Wow, look at those potatoes with all that gravy — plateaued mountains of mashed potatoes surrounding a fresh pond. I stand naked on the edge, preparing to dive to its depth.

"Quit playing with your food."

"Sit up straight, young man, and finish your meal."

"May I be excused? I'm not very hungry."

"Well. . . I suppose."

To my bedroom I hobble — "Take two aspirin and you'll feel like a new man." I do, but I still feel like shit. What's wrong? Lack of entertainment? I guess. You should try a book. Oh, yes. Let's see, what would be interesting at this time of mental crisis? The Gospel According to Zen? No, no. Revolution for the Hell of It? No. Hmm. What about Das Kapital? or The Bible? The. . . . My cheeks puff unexpectedly as I catch the upheaval. Running to the miniature bathroom, splat. Ah, just in time — ugh, again. My body is convulsed with nausea. The wavering feeling surges through me like an explosion. Pulling my life out of my intestine, it spills onto the toilet seat. The stench flares my nostrils as I reluctantly, but immediately clean up the mess.

"What's wrong, don't you feel well? Did you take that aspirin like I told you to?" inquires my mother.

*I walk back to my room, still feeling a little queasy.*

*"Now get in bed, and I'll take your temperature," she persists. The cylindrical glass toothpick is shoved painfully into my mouth.*

*Sleep well.*

*Farther and farther to Florida. Singing songs of freedom. Singing songs of life. Farther off to Florida, to end my discouraging plight.*

*Wow, I suppose that would be neat. Would you like to come?*

*Yes, definitely. I've got to get out of here.*

*Ah, just think of those blue crisp waters.*

*My drooping eyes remind me of the long, hard night, as I lift myself out of bed. The room is hot and dreary and my mind feels its potency as I stand, my head whirling with memories of the night.*

*Ahh, breakfast — my growling stomach screams, "food." Gurgle. Buzz. We walk to the kitchen in search of victuals. Hmm eggs, bacon,toast, milk, no vegetables; frying pans, pots and utensils clank out of their abode. Shining brightly, they humbly greet the heat.*

*Premature chickens flip into the pan, careful not to break their sunshine. They become white-hot and sizzle harmoniously with strips of pig. Bread anxiously becomes toast, as slabs of butter prepare to melt themselves into a short life.*

*The table is set in an exotic fashion as the heralders announce the fanfare. The dining Haus has been decorated with fringed velvet banners bearing the victual emblem. High fashion carpet and famous oil paintings add to the aristocratic setting. The oregano-colored table linen accentuates the sparkling goblets and soft china which soon will overflow with their fragrant delicacies.*

*A record flops.*

*A rumble is heard above. A terrible storm is approaching. The rulers of the castle are about to enforce their law.*

*"Turn down that stereo. Don't you have any consideration for anybody?"*

*Avoiding a confrontation, I wander off to the household waters of complacency. The red and blue dials are turned and the liquid flows down to the cold porcelain. Steam rises with the liquid water and tingles my deserving face. I peel off my clothing, carefully, as I think of myself as a crouton about to be dunked to its soggy death.*

*The toast slides into the aromatic soup and soothes my filthy body. The storm persists and curdles the soup with its obstinate thunder. Lightening cracks through the doors. I can hear the rain falling on the hard porch as the wind blows furiously. The wind is blowing away my life, and I just sit in the bathtub.*

*"I don't know what to do about him. He's so stubborn. He won't do anything around here."*

*"Yeah, except sit on his skinny ass."*

*Zotz of light flash through the fog of the bathroom, just long enough for me to catch a glimpse of my life — a huge rock rolls down through the desert. It's a very angry rock. Nothing gets in its way. It just keeps rolling until it is electrically overpowered. The storm rumbles on with duteous anger (a very stupid storm). It reaches out into the tub of soup with its electric paws. Zot — fried soup with charcoal croutons.*

My creative writing teacher, Mrs. Blotter, did know what to do with my little story. I bet she felt it her responsibility to report what she had read to certain administrators, who in turn would be well-advised to keep a closer watch on me. My friends enjoyed the story as an excursion into my nutritional neurosis; it was a much more effective and flavorful manner than Dr. Arm-cleavage could ever entertain. He wasn't helping me a damn bit. He, sitting there, stone silent was even less of a father than the Dive-bomber.

One evening I hauled myself up the hill to *mein* Haus, stopping for as long as I could to admire the light snow and fog, and brace myself for more fun with the family. As soon as I walked in the door, I could smell the smoke. I rushed through the hall to the living room where the Dive-bomber sat in his easy chair, staring into his most opaque funk yet.

"Vic," I shouted. "Don't you smell that smoke?"

He chose not to hear me. I raced into the kitchen. The smoke was coming from my room. I looked back at the Dive-bomber. Was this his strange way of finding his vengeance, to burn my room down and kill himself and all of us in the process?

I opened the room and there was Mom. No. It wasn't Mom. I couldn't accept that. A creature so horrible and frightening? Her eyes red and glazed over. Her bleached hair frizzed and tangled around her pale wrinkled face, pink lipstick stains on her yellow teeth. I heard a siren stop outside our house in Florida. My sister and I were sitting on the cold terrazzo floor, watching *Deputy Dawg*. Two men in uniform burst through the front door and went straight to the back of the house. A minute later they carried her out, wrapped in a blanket. And then the siren wailed again. Dad came out of the bedroom. He said Mom had to go away for a while.

Much later in the hospital, we were told she had a "pinched nerve."

The flames were confined. Mom was tearing the pages out of my books, one by one, and burning them in a trash can that she had put on my bed. I could see how she might not have taken to *The Student as Nigger*, but why was she burning my copy of *The Boy Scout Manual* which I had kept for entertainment.

"Mom, what the hell are you doing?" I screamed.

"You think we're stupid?" she asked. And then I knew she had found my story.

"Get out of here," she said in a low, quiet voice as malevolent as I have ever heard. Her eyes tore at me with every venomous sword her mind could sharpen. I looked at her and saw how de-monically "pinched" her nerves really were. My mother, the fire witch. Remember when she panicked out in the front yard? She was screaming and crying for us to get inside because the whole yard was crawling with snakes, and little me and sister had to calm her down and show her they weren't snakes. They were lit-tle pine cones, mommy. Do you remember that?

I thought she might claw me, or burn me, or do whatever she could to harm me. I backed away from her and felt no sorrow or remorse, only fear and disgust. As I moved away from the door, the Dive-bomber jumped up from his chair and pushed me aside. Heroically, he grabbed the flaming metal can with his bare hands and tossed it into the bathtub. Like nothing had happened, he sat back down in his chair and resumed his brood. He never said a word to me. He didn't even look up when I stood in front of him and stared at him for a long time. Finally, I turned away and thought about where I might sleep.

Another Christmas was just around the bend. All I wanted was to never go back to that fucking house. I was really afraid of who might do what next.

I had been hanging out with Mole over at Berkersheim housing, but he had to help his parents prepare for their move out to Ockstadt. Mole told me Evan was going to move in with him. I asked, half jokingly, if they had room for one more. I hoped for it, but Mole ignored the question. He said he had to get back to his chores, so I left.

Right outside the housing gate, I saw a little girl a ways ahead of me drop something. I found her change purse which had about 16 or 17 dollars' worth of Deutsche marks in it. Is it true that you can only understand the evil around you by becoming it yourself? Is that the only way to liberation? Maw-maw sent me a letter once, saying she prayed for me every day. Her prayer was from the First Psalm, she said. She prayed that I "[should] be like a tree planted by the rivers of water, that bringeth forth fruit in His season." Yeah, well, my fruit was rotten, and I wanted it to fall. I saw the little girl ahead of me begin to panic. I saw her clutch her face, probably crying, as she searched the ground. Her mouth moved, but I could not hear the words over the traffic. She had probably been going into town to secretly buy her family presents. I hated her little life. Why should she be any happier than me? I'd keep the money for myself. I had found it. I convinced myself it was meant for a different purpose. It was meant to buy a little train set. Something symbolic. A vengeful toy. The little girl had probably been saving a long time to make her mommy and daddy happy. Mom and Paw-paw hadn't let me get my stuff from Dad's house in St. Pete when they left in the middle of the night without me. That wasn't fair. I wanted my train set. Out of spite, I'd buy a train for me for Christmas. And to go with it, I'd buy a little plastic train station, and I'd call it "Schönberg."

When I got out to the Wunderhaus, I worked quickly. I didn't want to get caught should anyone come home. I pasted my "Schönberg" sign on the miniature station and stuffed it with an m-80. I let the train go round and round, and then I lit the fuse.

# Big Bear Harbor

I bought my big bear harbor coat on a second trip to London. Laszlo bought one, too. They were a bargain for so much oversized wool. I also bought a sailor's shirt because it was tough, durable and it was red. I could tell people it was from the Russian navy. That would poke fun at the commie searchers. Laszlo said the shirt made me look like a little kid. I wore it, anyway.

Laszlo's mom had invited me to join her family on a short getaway. I think she felt sorry for me. I believe Laszlo had leaked the bad news of what I was suffering at home.

We had a few hours to shop and sightsee, Laszlo's mom said, so I took him to Speakers' Corner. The shouting was much more raucous than the last time I was there. Lots of people were speaking out against the war — the increased bombing — and I felt ashamed to admit I was American. On the other hand, out on the streets of London, amidst the competing voices, I could apparently say whatever I wanted. On American military bases in Germany I always felt like I was being watched. I could even buy a copy of *The Quotations of Chairman Mao* right out in the open and no one would hassle me. At Speakers' Corner all conflicting voices were part of the same soup.

*The Quotations* was so cheap and compact and handy. Holding it made me feel like a rebel. Truth was, whenever I tried to read it, I fell asleep. Maybe it was the translation, but I couldn't get much out of it. I liked *The Communist Manifesto* better, (I got it for 10 pence) even though, everything Marx and Engels wrote about seemed self-evident. I don't mean to fault them; besides, they had really cool beards.

Laszlo wanted to listen to the speakers some more. I think he wanted to get up on a soapbox, himself. Meanwhile, I wandered around looking at the street vendors' wares. I didn't dare tell him I was searching for a gift for my new friend. Her name was Helen Ljungbe, and I liked her a lot. She was Swedish or Norwegian, I'm not sure which, and was very smart. Just before Christmas break we had kissed by the school annex. I thought it would just be a casual kiss, but the way she moved her hips made me think she would want to give more. I knew I had better bring her something back for Christmas.

Most stuff on the sidewalks looked like junk, but one person had mounted copies of old paintings onto wood, and I saw a most beautiful picture. It was very dark and hazy except for a golden mysterious light that shown on weirdly shaped rocks with moss and ferns growing out of them. By those rocks a gentle woman sat with a couple of babies and an older girl at her feet. I craved the love and warmth showing on that woman's face. I wanted to enter that painting and sit at her feet with the rest of her family and adore her as she loved me.

I was impatient to buy the painting, as if the possibility of giving Helen the perfect gift would vanish if I did not possess it without a moment's delay.

"Ah, yes, *The Virgin of the Rocks*," said the vendor and I shoved the money into his hand. I asked him to repeat the title. When he did I wished I'd never heard it. I wanted a woman, that woman of the rocks, any woman, to make endless love to me. I wanted Helen, or anyone to find loving understanding and bliss

147

in bed with me. I wanted nothing further to do with virgins and virginity.

The vendor wrapped my purchase in brown paper. I carried it away, and it pulsed in my hands. Of course, Laszlo wanted to know what I had bought, but I stood up to him this time. I insisted I didn't have to tell him everything.

Late in the day, Laszlo's dad drove us back toward the continent. He suggested that we stop to see the white cheesecake cliffs. That was cool, but as a consequence of our detour, we arrived in Oostende, Belgium past ten-o-clock. We were all starving. Laszlo's dad insisted he take us to one of his favorite restaurants as a kind of Christmas present, so we rode another 30 kms to Brugge. The trouble was, the place had already closed for the evening. Laszlo's dad, the Colonel, said it didn't matter, and so he banged on the door until they opened up and let us in. To my surprise, the owner greeted us warmly — old friends? Deference to a US colonel? The proprietor said he would prepare whatever we wanted.

Looking over the menu, I liked the sound of a few words. Whatever it was, it was damn expensive. But the Colonel had promised to buy whatever we desired, so I ordered it. The owner warned it would take extra time to prepare, and was asked if I still wanted it. I said yes. The headwaiter warned me that what I was asking for was quite large, but, glancing at the Colonel, added that he did not want to dissuade me. I said I still wanted it.

We could barely keep from falling asleep while we waited for the meal to arrive. Laszlo was grumpy with me, and I could see his dad was pissed, although he said nothing. He just kept drinking. Only Laszlo's mom maintained her protective smile. At last, the food was served. At my place they plopped down a huge stingray, its fins flying out well beyond the edges of the plate. The extraordinary fish was dripping in a sea foam caper sauce. It was some of the most delicious food I'd ever eaten.

By the time everyone else finished their meal, I had only worked through about a third of my fantastic stingray. I was too sleepy to chew anymore. I wanted to take it with me, but didn't know where I would be able to heat it up later. It didn't seem like I was going to be allowed to stay at Laszlo's any time soon — not after this fiasco. So, sadly, I had to leave my scrumptious friend behind. It would have been so nice to have flown away on its back to sandy beaches, to some place where I could be protected without this heavy wool coat.

In the Taunus Mountains, north of Frankfurt, a ragged shadow hung about the sun. Occasional snowflakes whispered their way down. I walked up the same mountain path our fledgling family had taken into the woods two-and-a-half years before this day. I stopped at the big oak tree where, back then, we had picnicked on Mom's southern-style fried chicken. We ate more than we should have, and Mom and I wanted to nap, but the Divebomber had insisted we continue hiking. Because of that stubborn will to power and our incongruous desires, our happy feeling quickly faded. And so, in anger, we turned around and went back home. Don't worry. No need to pout. We'd continue up that mountain together another day. But we never did. Today, the sky was flat and grey as I trudged past our special oak, dragging a sled behind me. I was gong to make it to the top, no matter what.

The Sunday crowd, dressed in their best walking clothes, were strolling in the forest. I hurried past them. Higher up, above the *Spazierstüken* 'walking sticks' and *Lederhosen*, the snow was falling steadily, and the wind whipped kicking flakes into my face. But I was warm. Onward.

As soon as I crested the mountaintop, the snow reached my waist, and I had to use the sled to lift myself up and out to inch forward, like on an old man's walker. Suddenly, the wind howled around me. I saw nothing but a white blur lashing the dark gray shapes ahead that I guessed were trees. I searched them through the violent white confusion. Something ahead of me moved. To get a better look, I struggled towards it, flapping around with the sled. As I got closer, the dark blur hurried away. I hoped it was human. Where the hell was I? I began to yell and wave my arms; isn't that what you're supposed to do? "*Achtung, achtung,*" I shouted. It turned around and began to make its way towards me. Coming into view, I realized it was on snowshoes. I saw the shape stop and point a rifle at me. I shouted again. The rifle rested, and I heard laughter. He shouted something into the wind, but I only recognized the word *Bär*. He gestured with outstretched arms, his ski poles dangling. Bär, he laughed. My oversized wool coat, snug like a harbor, made me look so ferocious on the outside, — a bear in Royal Air Force blue.

I yelled back, "*Wo ist Schönberg*?" several times before he lifted his ski pole and pointed the way out. "*Gib acht!*" he shouted over the wind. At first I didn't understand. "*Vorsichtig!*" he said as he gestured to his gun. I pulled myself toward the path he had pointed to. As I reached a spot where the snow wasn't so deep, I pushed myself off and began to fly.

# Jiggling

The snowy wind rushed over me as my breath froze into my scarf. My eyes felt cold and clean, and my ears began to throb. When I came upon the Sunday hikers again, I had to crash the sled into a snowbank to avoid hitting them. Someone helped me up. I assured her I was fine. I was at a crossroads of mountain paths. I hopped back on, chose a direction, and fled down the mountainside. Whoosh! I floated for a long time. When I landed at the bottom, exhilarated and happy, I looked around and did not know where I was. It wasn't Schönberg.

# Tenderizing an Octopus

It would be so easy to escape forever into the folds of Europe. I could deliver myself into her twisting streets where every memory of me would erode. Maybe I'd go back to Amsterdam, but not to the Hare Krishnas — too constraining. Oh, it didn't matter where, just away.

At the entrance to the high school I tried to read through the list of spring semester electives.

"I can't do it Laszlo," I said. "I have to go. I can't stand it anymore. This is no place for me."

Laszlo was bummed. He told everybody they had to find a way to keep me from leaving. I was grateful for his attention. And the effort to keep me close at hand caressed me. I drank it up, shitting out my paranoia and loneliness.

Helen loved the painting. She already knew its title. I emphasized the beautiful woman's sensuality, her fecundity, even. I told Helen of the desire resting in my heart's cave. I renamed Helen "Crea," after a Great Mother I had read about in a book of mythology. I wrote Crea poems about Nature, love and suffering. She drank them up, kissed me, and she encouraged me to write more.

Within a few weeks of our first kiss, Crea invited me to meet her parents. She lived in Darmstadt, 40 km south of Frankfurt. Since it was so far away, her parents invited me to spend the night. I hoped that Crea and I, following some beautiful Scandinavian tradition, would have to share a bed with one of those dividers that no one realistically expected you to heed. But, alas, if the tradition did exist, the Ljungbe family didn't follow it; Crea was locked away at the far end of the house. Regrettably, she thought it outrageous when I suggested she slip into my room once everyone had gone to bed. But the food was good, and her family treated me warmly and with respect.

Deliciously, on the cold winter school bus back from Darm-stadt, we kissed until our ears caught fire. The blanket over our legs concealed our rubbing, rubbing. Rubbing each other with such warm determination that, I'm sure, worn spots began to appear between the legs of our corduroys.

Crea was never allowed to stay in town and play. We could never go anywhere together. She always had to catch the bus shortly after school, and she was whisked away from me. We usually passed the little time we spent together hiding from Crea's younger sister, so she couldn't witness Crea pinned against a Quonset hut slowly gyrating her hips, pressing harder and harder, pulling me closer. But that was all we did. To my amazement, Crea would go no further. She would not let me un-zip her, and I began to doubt our future together.

Unfortunately, I couldn't spend much time at Laszlo's and not just because of the incident in Brugge. Things had gotten bad out at his house. His dad was drinking a lot and going into rages. Yeah, his dad, too. It was too cold to sleep outside, so I stayed in Schönberg for a while. No more avoiding it, I had to finally de-cide what to do.

And then one day, to my surprise, Mom announced to me, "You know, Son, if it ever gets real bad, you can always go back to Florida."

The way out settled onto my ears like fairy dust. "I'll have to think about that," I said and quickly turned away, embarrassed by the hurt I was sure to cause.

Immediately, I began to plan my escape. How could I possibly get back across the ocean to Florida without any money? And then what? Did my father want me to move back home? He had never said as much. Although I had longed for Florida, I never believed it would be possible to move back there. I thought separation from Florida was just part of the terms for divorce. I could imagine escaping into Europe, but nowhere else. I knew many guys were evading the draft. I'd have to start thinking about that, too. There was no question what I'd do if called. Maybe Mom and the Dive-bomber wanted me to leave. In any case, it was toward the US and not within Europe that the path began to pull me.

But I did not dare announce right away that I wanted to leave. I was afraid of something ugly and insistent coming to pass. Something told me that no matter what I did, I would have to descend. So I kept my desire a secret for a while.

My decision to eventually act made it easier to enjoy school. I was getting a lot out of my music composition class and my English teachers no longer seemed to mind too much when I told them which assignments I wanted to do and which ones I didn't. Mr Rivette (Remember him from the Alvin Lipp spectacle) helped me along with "Howl" and "The Love Song of J. Alfred Prufrock." I got into Ferlinghetti, too, especially "The Junkman's Obligato." Rivette had us listen to a lot of Paul Simon songs: "I am a Rock," "The Sounds of Silence," because Rivette hoped, at the very least, Paul Simon would be fairly easy to understand.

He didn't expect us to read Ezra Pound and only a few William Carlos Williams' poems.

I didn't try to tell anybody at school that I was still thinking of leaving, that I certainly would leave as soon as I got up the nerve. Reaching out in several directions, I knew I'd miss my friends.

Then I came home one night to find Mom drunk and falling over herself. The Bomber sat hunched in his cloud, pretending he couldn't hear us. From the bathroom, I heard a sudden loud "bonk," and the house shuddered. I rushed in to see if Mom was all right. There was water all over the floor, and she lay there like a stunned fish. She stank so badly of alcohol that my eyes began to water. As I moved to help her up, I saw several empty pill bottles in the sink. I couldn't hold her, so I had to let her slide back to the floor. I rushed to tell the Dive-bomber.

"Vic," I said calmly. "She's taken a lot of downers, uhm, barbiturates." He did not move, "Vic," I shouted. I stared in disbelief at the disgusting child of a man sulking before me. I envisioned having to knock him out and steal the keys to the Mustang. I'd somehow drag Mom out to the car and then find a hospital. I guess there might have been an easier way, but I didn't think of it. I knew it would be the last thing I ever did in Schönberg.

"Vic," I shouted as loud as I could.

He again pretended not to hear, then glared at me, suddenly jumped up from his chair, pushed past me, and strode into the bathroom. Mom was clinging to the sink. The water was running and she was fumbling around, splashing in the sink. The Dive-bomber pushed her aside, and she fell back to the floor. He picked up a pill bottle from the swirling collection. He turned off the tap and nudged the rest of the bottles aside. In the sink trap he could see Mom's pills, her colorful potpourri of deception. The Dive-bomber threw the bottle back into the sink. And as if nothing had happened, as if nothing were crumbling, sinking, he went back to the living room to resume his chair.

I followed him. "Vic," I said angrily and about to panic. "What should we do?" I asked.

"Nothing. There's nothing wrong with her."

"Vic, please," I begged.

"There's nothing wrong," he thundered.

I went back to the bathroom to look. Mom was trying to quickly poke the pills down the drain. She hadn't swallowed them. It seems, she, too, was struggling to make up her mind. Get a little more attention. Again. But, this was an unnecessary push.

I was nearly gone.

I liked Helen a lot. I liked her, and the yearning, and the possibility, and the certainty that all would be well if I could just rest. Oh, but it didn't matter that we had nowhere to go, she didn't want to do it, anyway. To justify my feelings, I asked myself, What else can I possibly learn from her? And so I broke it off. I decided to end it because I had to find a way to escape her refusal and her concerns for me. I had to rid myself of guilt and flee unmolested.

I saw her walking toward me with the farewell letter I'd written her clutched, or more likely, crumpled in her hand. She found me slouched  down on the floor wedged between two lockers. "Get up. I want to speak to you," she demanded.

Like a sorry mule I refused to move. Surely, that would make her go away. And finally, she did. I heard her angry cries echoing off the polished floor and fading down the hall.

A few days later she gave me this poem. It was written on onion skin paper and sealed with burgundy-colored wax:

*Rainbow of Rainbows*
*My father worked for days of nights in summers of*
*winters. My mother kept house for Wednesdays of*
*Sundays at birthdays of Christmases. My sister studied for*
*Septembers of Junes at Algebras and Englishes.*
*And they only knew wrongs of rights.*

*Come with me to the*
*house of houses in the woods of woods by the water of*
*waters. Our love will be the love of loves welling in the*
*heart of hearts through the rains of rains and (though*
*harder) the sunshine of sunshines in the spring of springs*
*and the winters of winters. Although sorrow may come, it*
*will be the SORROW of sorrows as the happiness of*
*happinesses. Our life will be the life of lives knowing the*
*wrongs of wrongs even as the right of right. Come with*
*me?*

My emotions rippled. Still, I said nothing to her. What she had offered was impossible, and, I had to protect her from me and my future. And, I insisted, secretly, I needed Lainey. Now.

157

Visits to Armcleavage had become an unbearable bore. More and more often, he wouldn't even show up. When he did, it was so dull to have to carefully drone the particulars of my changing moods. I had to choose my words carefully so they would not offend or alarm him. We sat in silence whenever I refused to play. So one cloudy day, there I was again, waiting for him to say something, even though I knew he wouldn't help me. Oh, fuck him, I thought. If he doesn't a conversation, and is not really interested in what I have to say, anyway, then I'll say whatever pops into my head. I'll have a genuine conversation with myself, not one tailored to his expectations.

I listened to the wind flapping in the leaves, and then spinning in the nothingness, trapped in the hospital air shafts. I said, "Okay. Pull me inside out, ride on your back and zip around dark out there in the middle of the day. Give me a chance to hide and scream and roar. Teach me how you make that sound so smooth and haunting and hypnotic like Donna, Betsy, Cleo — the hurricane girls. I'm looking for a whooping kiss right down my spine and out my butt." I paused and turned from the window to see that Armcleavage was sitting up. Indeed, he had moved to the edge of his seat.

"Go on," he said. At last he was entertained.

I said, "Ahhh, darker now. Is that a flute? Pied Piper rat-fink fun, call me out to play. Back home to the other side of the levies, to the inside of drains, circling down, tidal pools, *Journey to the Center of the Earth*. Sucked down and spat out. Mommamomma, pop me out of here."

I played with him like that, even past our allotted time, giving him some Freudian meat to chew on. He was so excited, I thought he might wet his pants. He wanted to know from where my thought associations originated. I admitted that I had been able to think like that ever since I started taking acid.

His face dropped, and he advised me that he could not, and would not see me as his patient if I persisted in taking drugs. I told him that the following week, Easter-break week, had been set aside as an acid-fest week for our new band, Mantas, and that we hoped to find, via acid, the inspiration to write more songs.

"I must warn you, sir, that if you take any drugs at this party, I will be forced to discontinue our association," he said.

So it had come down to that. The decision was easy to make. I could certainly learn far more taking LSD than listening to his ignorant silences.

Laszlo named us Mantas with the hope that a menacing name might help us to get gigs. Even with our new drummer, Vince, and our difficult set with songs like "21st Century Schizoid Man" featuring Sam Apricot on sax and Evan on guitar playing King Crimson's insane melodies more and more rapidly a third apart, and even though I was ready to pretend to be Jagger pretending to be the devil in "Sympathy for the Devil," Mantas never played in public. Our only gig, at the Teen Club, was stopped short by a bomb scare just as we were going on stage. Was it because someone did not want to see what I would do dressed in a ratty poncho, wearing a bread basket on my head with a yellow squash sticking out the top?

Anyway, for our long trip together, preparing for gigs that would never come, Laszlo had a handful of Micro Dot and a few hits of Orange Barrel. He warned us that the Micro Dot was very heavy and a full tab would knock our socks off. Each of us took a hit of the Micro Dot and Laszlo also took a hit of the Barrel. Our plan was that once we felt ourselves coming down, we would take another hit, then another, and coast all the way through to Easter.

Waiting for the show to kick in, I prepared some Dirty Moore beef stew for the troops. I wanted to make it special, so I added several spices and sauces to perk it up. Lo and behold, miracle of miracles, I achieved the first canned beef stew treat that tasted exactly like bananas! Every spoonful of what was supposed to have been beefy potato did not smell like bananas, yet each bite was a tropical paradise. All of us were astounded by this event which provided a perfect entry into the land of hyper-sensual reality.

Each of us were off to any number of softly popping bubbles. My hard-edged secure substances faded and crumbled as I swung the refrigerator door wide open. On the other side, I saw large-curd cottage cheese. I shoved my hand into the family-size tub. The curds gushed against my fingers, separating into bright sweetbreads, glowing under a little 15-watt sun. Cold white pebbles on my lips, dissolving on my tongue. Mammawmamaw, mushing it against the roof of my mouth. Some pickles. Off with the lid, but eww, pungent knife wounds to my eyes. I closed it and set the jar aside. I sat down on the cool floor. Much easier to see. Oh, the vegetable bin. I pulled, but it seemed stuck. Some greens, maybe, mucking up the works. I yanked. The glue gave way, and the whole full drawer slid onto my lap.

"God, man, what are you doing?" I heard. "If my parents . . . ." Someone stood behind, laughing, then floated away. I went back to my studies. "Bonk!" Something on my head. What's that? No apple. Damn bludgeoning gravity. Yes, the guy under the mechanical tree. That was me. Aluminum foil from heaven. Nutritional Neurosis is an industrial disease. Armageddon shall come upon us, not in the shape of dragon beasts, but as sheets of industrial foil. I jumped to spread the word. But everyone was involved in their own separate epiphanies, so I grabbed a piece of paper and crayon, set aside for exactly moments like this, and, for posterity, I wrote it down in my electro-cardiogram acid-style, writing as best I could. Then I went onto something else. I found a box of frozen crab legs. I yanked them from their frosty half-way house. I would make another very special treat. Yes. So much is in the presentation, you know. Everyone would love the long pink and white black-spotted creatures served on a bed of red-flamed chard. *Preheat oven to 375 degrees. Place legs on greaseless tray.* Serve myself up, *her* up. *Her* legs on a platter. *Sprinkle with bread crumbs.* Home to Progress(o). *Preheat oven to . . .* to make it hot in here. Oh, forgot the freezer. Closed the freezer door. Shoved the legs into the oven. And in no time at all, browned and scrumptious juicy treats. I gathered everyone together. Had them sit by candlelight, by fancy place settings. They clamored for the surprise. I sang the legs to the table and served them up with chomping tongs. Each of us tried to come to terms with the split, spindly sizzles in front of us. "Is it hot?" someone asked. "I can't tell." We poked and struggled. "The top is hot." But beneath the surface it burned differently. It hurt, too. What is that?

"I know what it is," Sam cried triumphantly. "They're frozen down under."

"Ah, man," said Evan. "Fro-zen."

Laszlo's eyes rolled and he looked stunned as he kept gnawing on a leg, trying to decide.

Laughter. My friends drifted away from the table.

Enough of the kitchen.

My red navy shirt brought out my color, I thought. *Very* red in the mirror. My eyes and cheeks shouted a bit of acne. Avoid the mirror, they always say. In the horror of anti-drug films at school, someone always looked into a mirror and, seeing a monster, collapsed into a bad trip. I wanted to see if I could turn myself into a monster. Whoa! Undulant monster man deeper firedevil red, flaming and knotty forehead caved in. My hair screaming. Jee-sus. I got out of there quick.

Time had flattened out. Or, this was *real* time. Two minutes, a moment; all night, an hour. Events passed and blended. Sequences occurred and doubled back, and the future became memorable: Industrial foil hatchlings in Key West; Moma Clause divorces Satan; What a treat/flossing my teeth/in bare feet!

In the basement, the instruments waited in our beatnik cellar — dark and bongo poetic. Vince behind his drums mixing with the shadows. Laszlo opposite him on a high stool in the corner — his eyes bulged in perpetual shock. No one spoke. It was too loud without speaking — that roaring silence. Laszlo put his hands over his ears. He whispered, cutting through the crowded sounds. "They are liquid. B flat liquid." I didn't understand. "D minor," said Laszlo. Vince stared at his cymbal. Laszlo looked up toward the plumbing. "They can't hold it all," he said. My attention slipped to a flash popping light by the stairs. Vince shouted, "Fid-dle." I didn't recognize the word. He  was pointing behind me. I turned to look. The violin I'd borrowed from school separated from Laszlo's hand — slow tumble across the room. End over sweet end, rolling like a 2001 bone-spaceship-bone toward the wall, then "Crack." It fell, shocked back into "real" time and splintered onto the floor. Laszlo was groaning. He hopped off the stool onto Evan's clear acrylic guitar and began stomping on it.

"Go get help," yelled Vince.

No one else was in the house. I tried to concentrate. Which world? Outside. The helicopters were beginning to land, and I had to hurry. I found the friends in the apple orchard. Sam and Evan were each different electronic components — resistors, capacitors, relays, diodes. They sat across from each other, and when the "initiator," they called him, sent a charge of electricity through them, each jolted into play. I heard:

"Resist, resist."

"Ca-pa-ci-tate . . . ca-pa-ci-tate."

"Reeee-lay."

I could not stop them from laughing.

"What's a diode do?"

"Laszlo's going nut, guys," I screamed. "And . . . and helicopters are landing, I think. It's gotta be the MPs."

"Go away, schizoid man."

"No, really. Come quick," I shouted. "He's walking on your Ampeg, Evan."

The helicopters were hovering, and I ran back to the house and upstairs. They had landed on the roof outside Laszlo's upstairs bedroom. The window was open. If only I could get close enough, I could close that window and we'd have a fighting chance. I counted four choppers on the roof, and I saw several others waiting to land. The sirens were deafening, and the pulsating red lights made my heart pound. The troopers were dressed in black weaponry; the first one came swinging in through the window on a rope. I managed to escape out the bedroom, just in time. I ran down the stairs to warn the others to evacuate, evacuate. The others were sitting bewildered at the dining room table. The crab legs had been pushed aside. I convinced the guys of the threat on the roof, and we all rushed upstairs, but the police had departed, thank god.

Laszlo sat silently at the table, staring off into space. The guys tried to calm him. "Keep an eye on him." Someone might have been speaking to me.

I moved to the living room floor. Was there music playing? Where was it coming from? Or, I'd put some on; too complicated. Better not add to the mix, anyway. Laszlo is hearing too much. I listened to me. The surfaces of daily reality were even less tangible. No senses were connected to the mundane. No thought fixed. Each thought, a sensation like a puff, no longer manageable. Nothing to manage. But which smell held the greatest fix? I heard images sift into the adjacent ones. The night had been long past for days now. How could any of us begin to speak of it? The drug was over. And it had never stopped. Permanently altered into acute impermanence. No ox to capture; it had slipped through my fingers. I could, maybe someday, ride the gentle ox home. To home. Sitting on the floor. Home at last. Free as a breeze.

Yet, no one will understand this: my mind flailing. This is the way I'll forever be. They'll not understand, and they might catch me up; trick me into divulgence. I'll be doing laundry, for example, and they'll spot that I am not of this world. And they will take me away. I could not support much more suffering. Not to a hospital. No pinched nerve. No arbitrary scalpel up the nose, jiggling in my brain. I had to find a way to cope. Convince them that I was normal, though forever I would see things, hear things, taste, and smell and touch harsher realities than they could ever know. I felt so sorry for them. But, I needed to practice. Okay. Imagine you are at the laundromat. Now how do you do laundry? Do nothing unusual. They'll be watching your every move. Your whites from tub-fasts. So hard to concentrate.

I fell asleep.

When I woke up, sprawled on the living room floor, Laszlo was still dazed, sitting at the table. It seemed lighter outside, but I wasn't sure. My elbow joints ached, and my dental work ached, and my jaw ached. I could feel the acid swirling traces, rumbling colors all around me. Was I still tripping?

The world began to encroach and painfully solidify. You're back to suffering. Daily and predictable. They won't lock you up. You have not lost your grasp on it, nor it on you.

The fellows compared notes in a collective groan. No one felt like taking another hit to keep the journey going. Especially not Laszlo. He was really fried. It was Good Friday, I remembered, and the thought made me chuckle. We had just a few days to recuperate until it was time to go back to school.

The next day Laszlo told me what happened to him in the basement. He said all potential sounds in the room emanating from the instruments, especially my violin, were made manifest simultaneously and were liquefying into drowning colors. The basement was flooding with sound and color, and he had to stop it. And, by the way, even though I was responsible to the school for the violin, he refused to have it repaired. I could not understand his attitude, and we argued until I was hoarse.

I dropped in on Armcleavage at the regularly scheduled time and reported that, yes, I sure had been tripping. And so, Armcleavage excused himself from any further responsibility.

There was no way I was going back to school so soon after that night of my mind impaled. My new traveling companion, David Jordan, and I decided to take another week off; we headed to Corsica. It was easy to hitch out of town. By nightfall we were at the youth hostel at Constance.

At first light, we saw the jagged triumphant peaks across the Bodensee. Those were mountains, as I had yearned for back in Berwick — I saw the Alps breaking through the flat, dull crust. We waited outside Vaduz, Lichtenstein, major export: false teeth. Waiting, I wailed on my new blues harp while David clapped and jumped about. At last, a playboy in a red Triumph convertible with the top down told us to squeeze in. We zipped through the Alps. He told us not to miss St. Moritz, but no one would talk to us in St. Moritz. Nor could we find any grocery stores, only expensive restaurants. We splurged on a bar of chocolate, then found some potatoes and carrots someone had left at the hostel.

David and I hitched through to Como where we met a guy who asked, "Are you wanderers or meanderers?" He explained, "If you meander, you have no particular direction; you just go where you heart takes you. But if you wander, you add purpose to your travels." I guess we were both.

Eventually, we made it to Milan and stayed in the Milan hostel. It was one of the most militaristic places I had ever been. They woke us with bells and sirens. The fascist director told us, every five minutes, to hurry and clean the area before moving our butts outside. What a jerk! We wanted to be out and away from there.

So we took the train to Genoa; and the next morning ventured further down the coast to the promenade at La Spezia, wondering about Rapallo and Ezra Pound in a cage. A ride persuaded us to stop and see how much the tower at Pisa really leaned. We gawked at three sides of the beautiful plaza and at the fourth side, a wall of plastic Pisa-tower gewgaws. Then we scrambled back up the coast to sail for Corsica late that afternoon.

We were beat when the ferry docked in Bastia. It was decided that for our first night we'd eat well. Afterwards, we'd be full and happy and it wouldn't matter where we slept.

The meal was an amazing feast of several glorious courses. We ate fresh bread, rich cheeses with strange names, and fresh fruits and salad, followed by a delicious bouillabaisse. And it was all washed down with a great red wine — there was no label, just the bottle embossed with the map of Corsica and a pirate on it. We took what wine was left in the bottle with us. A churchyard down by the harbor beckoned. Sprawled next to a couple of broken tombstones, we finished the wine and fell into an exhausted slumber.

The next day we hitched down the coast to the first good-looking sand we could find. We decided that the best landscape is where glorious ragged mountains crashing down to a deserted beach. We camped out there for the next few days; we just snorkeled, hung out and slept in the sunshine. David  and I speculated on what it would take to live there forever, evading the onslaught of the old work-a-doom. Maybe it could be done: living cheaply, asking for little. We decided to put the hope to the test. Poking around the coral, we spotted an octopus and determined to catch it and sell it to a  restaurant down the road. It was surprising how fast it could undulate away from us to its refuge in the rocks. Every time we got close, the bulbous thing turned from brown to porcelain white. At one point it inked up the water and turned its body into a surprising cranberry red. We gave up trying to catch it with our hands, and so I shot the poor thing with a cheap spear gun I had brought along.

The spear clumsily lobbed into its sack head and it was ours. I wondered if its head would pop. Poor thing. It was a victim of the confused. We put it into a plastic bag and it oozed around the way a snake squirms after it has been clubbed or shot. Its suckers stared up at me when I checked to see if it was dead yet.

No restaurant wanted to buy it. We'd have to prepare it and eat it ourselves. One guy told us, to make it more edible we would have to slam it against the rocks many times to tenderize it. Sure, we were tired of eating canned sardines, but neither of us could bring himself to beat up on that creature. It was bad enough that I'd shot it. I reluctantly tossed its gooey mass back into the sea. It floated for a while, and then it sank.

The next morning we needed to leave; we were hungry and we had run out of money. It took all day to hitch the few miles back to Bastia. When we arrived, we were tired and frustrated. The first chairs we saw begged for us to rest. Too soon a waiter came out to greet us.

"Oh, shit," I said. "Maybe he won't hassle us. I mean nobody needs these chairs. Nobody is sitting here."

We told the waiter in our best collective French that we didn't care to have anything, thank you. We hoped to just rest for a moment. The waiter bowed nicely to us and retreated.

A minute later he came back and set down two glasses and a little bottle of water; he poured out some strange green liquid.

"*Deux Pernod, Messieurs,*" he said. He bowed again and then went back inside.

There was nothing we could do except to relax over our drinks at this nice café overlooking a fleet of brightly painted boats in the harbor. Real postcard stuff. When the time came to move on, we fished out the few extra coins we had left, tossed them onto the table and split before anyone could tell us how much we really owed.

# Coitus

---

The draft was getting too close to ignore. What to do? While *Davaii* had fallen apart due to lack of momentum, Laszlo said we should not let ourselves be dragged down by apathy. The war against the war had to be fought on many fronts, and we, too, were responsible for the continuance of their war if we pretended it did not exist. He insisted that we start another newspaper that would express our disgust in a more serious and engaged confrontation. Each issue would be named after a book in the Bible, starting with Genesis and continuing if necessary, all the way to Revelations until the draft expired and the Vietnam war stopped.

*Genesis* was published in April of '72; it encouraged our readers to participate in Frankfurt University's May Day march against the exploits of the United States.

I wasn't sure how I felt about this. Yes, I had learned that extraordinary times required extraordinary measures, but advocating violent revolution made me squeamish. After reading Camus' play "The Just Assassins" in English class, I doubted more violence would get us anywhere.

Yet as soon as *Genesis* was distributed, several students expressed an interest in working on *Exodus*. My rage, together with the enthusiastic response to our little paper, allowed me to temporarily put aside my doubts. Sure, I'd be at the planning meeting for *Exodus*.

On the day of the meeting, Mr. g. zan-pit, our lead anarchist and student locker saboteur, stormed in, making it clear he was ready to rip whatever to shreds. We were pleased with the turnout. Even John Waterford, an avowed Marxist who was well-connected with the Frankfurt communists, quietly appeared.

Waterford was impressive. He had something on his mind that he wanted to share with us. First, he calmly told us about the hard-won successes of Allende's Marxist coalition government in Chile. But, he said, Kissinger and the CIA were at it again, robbing and terrorizing the world with the excuse that the "free and democratic nations of the world had to prevent any more dominoes from falling." And, Waterford warned us, if the US leaders were not stopped, they would certainly find a way to assassinate Allende. Was this the kind of world we wanted to live in? The kind of country we wanted to pledge allegiance to? Would we continue to allow the US to meddle in other countries' affairs, acting out a world-wide policy of domination? How much longer would we sit back and watch, as US foreign policy engaged in a systemic, pathological horror show?

I was stunned. Unable to respond. I did not know where I belonged.

After the meeting, I remarked to Laszlo how intense everyone had been, especially the ironically soft-spoken John Waterford.

"That's nothing," Laszlo said. "You should see him alongside the University Marxists. He comes off as a real lightweight compared to them."

"They scare the shit out of me," I said.

And just like our PE coach, Laszlo warned me, "Don't be such a pussy."

171

The two of us walked out of the high school's main entrance. On the little patch of grass in front of the principal's office, the spot where I had been sighted "expressing amorous conduct," sat Kaye Brumley; Laszlo's new ball of convenience. She was nearly drooling for Laszlo to come make out with her. I'd hoped Laszlo and I could take the new momentum of the meeting and spend the rest of the day working on *Exodus*. But Laszlo stopped to reestablish his territory by copping a feel. Maybe they'd be done soon.

I sat down on the curb away from the zealous gropers and waited. I'd just bought Yes's new album, *Fragile,* and if we weren't going to work on the paper, I wished Laszlo would hurry up so we could go out to his place and listen to Yes. After several minutes, he came over and told me that Kaye was getting pretty hot and she really wanted to do it again. He was going over to her house for a while.

"So what am I supposed to do?" I whimpered.

"I don't know," he said as he walked away with his hungry catch.

I went to the library. Sarah Christensen, my Palmengarten kissing buddy, was studying at one of the tables. She smiled at me with that wide beautiful friendship. Suddenly, I couldn't have cared less about the *Exodus* meeting. "Peace" would have to wait. I told Sarah how happy I was to see her. She closed her lips to that wry, crooked smile, cracked open at one end. Her long blonde hair crisscrossed the horizontal stripes of her shirt. Her breasts pressed outward, making the stripes curve like ascending-descending highways.

I told her I had Yes's new album, and she suggested we listen to it in the private study room. I didn't know they had one.

The two of us were placed in a brightly lit room with a turntable and a couple of sets of headphones. We each pinched our heads with the heavy padded phones and I turned up the stereo.

"Roundabout" teased us with a few bars of gentle acoustic guitar before rumbling into a seat-shaking bass. We both tingled together. I could see the delight in her eyes, squinting happily. We danced in our chair to the syncopated backbeat, rolled with the organ riffs, and pumped our bodies, imitating fat buffoons to the heavy punching bass guitar. I saw her laugh without sound, and wondered why we didn't yank off the headphones, crank up the music, throw open the study room door, and dance up and down the stacks. That would be our statement to the world. No. It was better alone, we two digging it.

The last chord of the song faded and we could hear each other's sighs muffled. Sarah was looking right at me. I took off my headphones and motioned for her to do the same, but she shook her head, no. She moved closer to me. What I had to say could wait. I understood by her eyes, by her parting lips, that she wanted me to kiss her. Ah, Sarah. We kissed in a long wonderful embrace of friendly love. She kissed me with all the passion and love and sincerity of mutual appreciation and respect—the tender recognition of like-minded beasts.

The music propelled us along through "South Side of the Sky"gently singing and marked with little kissing punctuations. But I began to want her for more than kisses. I could feel the semen begin to wet my pants. I craved the next move, but Sarah did not want me to touch her breasts. Was it because someone could have looked in and seen us? I didn't dare turn off the light. That would have been far too suspicious. I surely didn't want to break the beauty of this exquisite kissing. Would there be more? A future of lovemaking? Would we be more than playful friends? She pulled away, feeling my distraction. Side one was over, and I had an excuse for my lapse of attention, and a chance to start again.

"I think you are wonderful, Sarah." I rubbed her shoulder and she closed her eyes and floated her head backward. I wanted to kiss her neck, but I knew I shouldn't risk it. I placed my cheek next to hers and stroked her hair. We began to kiss again and Sarah and I floated over one another, tumbling softly through the blissful room I imagined darkening. We were our own stars, kissing to blind the fluorescent light. Our moods shifted and mingled freely, tasting a moment of guiltless hermaphroditic release. "Mood for a Day" startled us with its frenzied attack, and we pulled away from each other for a moment. Then we learned to kiss to even that shaking frenzy. And we held each other, squeezing, yearning for something explosive. And just as quickly the music settled under a tree by a stream: "Heart of the Sunrise." We were sung to about finding love, dreaming, hoping, "How can the wind with its arms all around me?" Jon Anderson sang. We didn't know what it meant. We didn't care. We kissed, and we never wanted it to end.

But, of course, it did end. Sarah took off her headphones and placed them on top of the stereo. I watched her movements; my mind slowed her down to prolong her presence. Then, happily, she took off my headphones and kissed me on each of my two reddened ears. She said, "Thank you," opened the door, and long afterwards, her presence painfully faded away.

A couple of nights later, Laszlo suggested we pay Lainey a late night visit. Her parents had moved in right next door to his parents' house. I couldn't believe his luck. Now he could see her all of the time.But I didn't mind too much, I convinced myself. I was now confidant of being loved by Sarah.

The only way to accost Lainey, Laszlo said, would be to dress as outrageously as we could and spook her in the middle of night; then she could only laugh. She'd have no way to be pissed at us for waking her up. We dressed a cross between *Gyrorabs* and Musketeers spiced with nutritionally neurotic accou-trements. That is, we found dark capes to drape over our white-belted long underwear; I dragged out my knee-high sneakers and Laszlo found us a couple of berets. We each carried a baggie full of pickle chips, and I snatched Laszlo's mom's eggbeater, my only defense, to tuck into my orange, spangly belt. The pickles were for pelting Lainey's window. We called ourselves, "The Pickle Patrol," and set out to accomplish our mission.

Far from angry, Lainey was delighted by the soft "plaffs" against her bedroom window. She said I looked "cute," but was waiting for Laszlo. They had planned their little rendezvous ear-lier that afternoon, Laszlo admitted. So why did he have to drag me along? And worse, as soon as I saw Lainey, my Sarah-love foundation of self-esteem and confidence dribbled away. It was Lainey again.

What could I do? I had to have her. I insisted she be mine. It was only right that she love me. We had started in love together and would finish together. I would tell her of her righteous des-tiny, of the two us forever united, but she still didn't want me. She would prove that over and over. Yet, I remained undaunted. When I tried to win her again, I thought my buddies were just helping the love wheel along for *me,* when all of us stuffed an orange with marshmallow fluff, and then sewed it up again; we set it by her front door with a log cabin made of Graham crackers. This was my domain. *My* nutritional neurosis. Wasn't the large cauliflower bouquet enough to attract her to me? But every time, it had been Laszlo she wanted. On again, off again, a kiss here, a little sexual rummaging down there, but she always ended up with Laszlo. Even though he was balling Kaye Brumley and Lainey knew it, Lainey insisted she wanted Laszlo, too. Not me. Maybe that was because I wasn't balling anybody, never had. I wished Sarah would do it with me, but I knew, for some reason, she never would. Helen wouldn't do it either. Rub kiss rub. Nothing else. But it wasn't their fault; there had to be something wrong with me.

Meanwhile, Laszlo alone continued to throw his pickle chips, or turds, or whatever to Lainey to announce he had come a-calling, and she climbed down from her roof onto his. He told me they would sip white wine and roll around and play at their sexual fantasies. Both sets of parents, as usual, were completely oblivious to what was going on. I felt like telling on them. Fuck them. Every one.

All of this meant that, even if I wanted to, I couldn't stay at Laszlo's anymore. I clearly had to face up to facts and let Mom know I was leaving. Not with anybody else. Just me alone.

It was okay to sleep in the park, but I thought it would be better if I hung around Schönberg for a few days to search for the right time to tell her. I knew Mom would take it hard. I sure as hell didn't want the Dive-bomber around when I said it. I had to take care of myself, love myself. God, I was scared.

It could only be done casually, I decided. She was cleaning up around the house. I remember, it was a weekend. I would tell her, and then go for a walk, and then later, I'd check on her and make sure she was all right. Poor Mom. I stopped her sweeping in the kitchen.

"Mom," I said. "I want to go back to Florida." The words were out of my mouth, and they hung in the room like acrid smoke. She looked pale. She said nothing. She just stared at me with that kind of hurt I had seen so many times, flushing over her face.

"I need to go out for a little while, but I'll be right back," I assured her. I was quickly out the door.

I didn't know where I was going. Out of habit, I wandered over to Kronberg toward the train station. I stopped in to check the schedule. A train was leaving for Frankfurt in a few minutes. I was tempted to take it, but knew I had better go back and check on Mom. I waited the few minutes and then watched the same old train zip away on its electric runner. I walked up the hill toward the ancient part of Kronberg. At the peak, I could see the castle. A cobblestone road led the way. I stared down at the dirt packed between the stones. After tearing up the cobblestone roads for repairs, the Germans painstakingly replaced each stone instead of paving it over the way we did it in The States. I admired that. It was the Dive-bomber who had pointed that out to me. The thought froze my mind. I turned around and headed back down to the central square. The Dive-bomber had said, "Did you ever notice that there are no junk yards in Germany? Where does all their trash go? In The States people have got trash strewn all over their yards. Old cars, rusted refrigerators. Not here. Why can't we get it together in The States?"

I bought some *Gummi Bären* and "chocolate dudes" and an Apfelsaft at a green tubular *Trinkhalle*. I sat in the square and

177

ate silently. Nobody came up to me. Nobody asked me anything or gave me any advice.

I guessed a couple of hours passed. I walked down into the valley and back up the Schönberg side to quiet Hermann Löns Weg. The Mustang sat poised in the driveway. That meant the Dive-bomber was home. I wanted to turn away, but there couldn't be too much more of this. Soon, I would be gone forever.

Inside, the house was silent. Something had changed. Something about the furniture. At first I thought Mom had redecorated as she often did to soothe herself. I went in the kitchen and found the sink filled with white rags floating in a murky red soup. Someone was coming downstairs. I noticed red spots that trailed into the bathroom.

In there, more rags glowed brighter, not diluted. Fresh. Shouting. Hulking, behind me. It yelled, "You bastard." I turned to see the awful bulging head, its mouth widening. "Get your little ass down in the cellar. Now," it shouted.

No. Not that. Not down there. That would be my end. I tried to position myself so he could not corner me.

"I found your mother crawling on the floor," he grunted. "On the floor. . . . On all fours." His ogre voice rolled into my spine. "Chewing on the furniture like an animal."

And the blood? I tried to slide past him. If I could make it to the door, I'd run. Yell out to the neighbors, *Hilfe mich, Hilfe mich*, until he was too ashamed to pursue me anymore. The *Feuerwehr* would come to my rescue. But the Dive-Bomber grabbed me by the hair and hurled me across the room.

"I had to hit her," he shouted. "She wouldn't stop."

My body smashed into a bookshelf near the cellar door. I scrambled to my feet and ran. "Get down there," I heard vaguely. I made it as far as the narrow hall where the stairs and toilet and the front door were all tightly packed together. The Dive-bomber tangled his fingers into my hair again, my long defiant hair; he slammed me to the ground. A skein of it remained in his hand. Over and over he kicked me in the ribs: Someone is screaming. I could no longer listen. I wanted away. Outside. I cried out for Mom to help me. He kept  kicking. "Mom," I cried again. I lifted my head toward the stairs. And there, she still sits, calmly watching. I don't know how long she'd been there. "Mom," I pleaded. "Help me." Her eyes were bloodshot and her face was puckered and white. Her lips curved slightly upwards at the tips, like a scythe, a sickle. A jambiya, the Turkish knife. Smiling. I had seen that look before. Chasing me around my bed, my little underpants pulled down to show her the target. Not satisfied with the welts she had already scored; she waved her switch above her head. Shouting: "I'll tan that hide. Beat the tar out of. . . . The living daylights." I don't remember my father ever hitting me. Yet, here, now, my new father and mother in one body sat on the stairs. She was championing her brutal helpmate, grinning through a mask of born-again evil. Of betrayal, thick and complete. Disowning, yet clinging forever to my heart, my dick, all hope. And then suddenly, the Dive-bomber ceased. The kicking stopped. There was a terrible pause of sanity. I got up and ran out the door.

Andie Carnelian wrote me an affectionate letter from Berwick. She said she heard I was coming back and that she couldn't wait to see me again. She said she had missed me a lot over the years, that she had always enjoyed my company. I showed the letter to Laszlo. He said it sounded like Andie wanted me bad, and he started to call her "Oatmeal Mouth" for her "sweet, mushy" way of expressing herself. He teased me how good it was going to feel having her having me for breakfast. It was funny, maybe, but I wanted to protect her affection for me from Laszlo's hammer. I didn't want him crushing the future far away, too. Though I hadn't planned on going back to Berwick first, I decided I kind of liked the idea. Andie hadn't said anything about beautiful Sally Chesterfield in the letter. I wondered if Sally missed me, too.

Mom told me the Dive-bomber agreed to pay my fare, a $79 military flight, back to The States as their present for my 17th birthday. How generous!

Although the Dive-bomber and I weren't speaking, Mom quickly switched back to presuming we were allies against him. She said to me, "I might be following right after you, Son." I asked what she meant.

"Let's just say I've got some information on him," she said. "Something I've always suspected, but couldn't prove."

"What are you talking about? I don't get any of this."

"Don't say anything, but I know he was married before, to that blonde."

"Who?" I asked. She dismissed my question with a flick of her hand. "And so what if he was? You were married before, too."

"But he never told me. He swore he wasn't. He probably has kids somewhere. You can't do that. You can't lie like that. I'll be right behind you. I'm gonna get out of here as fast I can."

I didn't like her trying to be my friend and confidant. I couldn't trust her anymore. I have to admit, it was a relief to hear she had decided to leave the Dive-bomber. At least she knew she had to do that much. I supposed she would go back to Miami to live with Maw-maw. I knew I sure as hell wouldn't follow her. Not this time.

I ran into Helen Ljungbe in the hall and she told me she heard I was leaving. She just wanted to let me know she had been accepted to a selective school called New College in Florida and she would be there by August. I had never seen her so happy. New College was in Sarasota, Florida, she said. And I wouldn't be too far away, would I? We should write and visit each other, she said.

New College sounded cool. There you could do what you wanted. No grades or ridiculous requirements. But I didn't have any interest in college. They would never admit me, anyway. Besides, who would pay for it? It made me uncomfortable that Helen wanted to exchange addresses. I agreed to do it, but what was the point?

Laszlo asked me if I had gotten laid yet.

"No," I reported.

"Well, you can't have Lainey, but I bet Brumley will do it with you."

"I don't want to do it with her, I don't even like her."

"Look," Laszlo said. "You're 17, and you're still a virgin. You can't go on like that. You need to be initiated. You can't expect to get chicks when you're still a virgin."

"Well, then give me Lainey."

"You can't have Lainey." He was starting to get mad; I could see he wanted to hit me. "You want Brumley?" he said impatiently.

I stared back into his eyes. I wanted to cry. I guessed he was right. It had to be done with someone. "Okay," I said.

"After her, you know, like after the first time, it'll be easier," he repeated. I hoped he was right.

The next day, the arrangements were made among the three of us on the lawn outside the principal's office. The same old sex spot. Once, in that semester, Principal Harken called me into his office to congratulate me for managing to keep my hands off the girls. I thanked him and left feeling like I had really failed. I sat away from Brumley and Laszlo as he whispered shit into her ear. His words made her giggle and beg to be kissed. And then, I could see her resisting what he was saying. Laszlo suggested that I come closer and try kissing Brumley to ease us into it. The kiss was all right. We both felt some tingling, I guess. We couldn't help but be polite. It was decided we would do it at her house near the school. Her parents would be out that evening between six and eight.

Laszlo slipped me a condom. "You might need this," he whispered.

"How do I know?" I whispered back to him.

"Ask her."

"How?"

"I just say, 'Should I take precautions?'"

The guys had been calling Brumley, "Squishy Tennis Shoes" because she had said, making love was like that. The jokes began, trying to imagine what she had meant. I guessed I'd soon find out. At seven she took me up to her room and immediately started taking off her clothes. The light shone brightly in her room. I asked if we could turn it off, but she insisted we leave it on. Soon, she was lying naked on the bed, and I wished I could just sit on the edge there and stare at her for a while.

"Come on," she said in a thin, high voice. She had a tight smile that never completely relaxed into abandon. Her lips just bent slightly when she thought something was funny or she felt kind of good. I didn't dare ask her which. I took off my clothes in front of her as she propped herself onto her elbows and watched. As I undressed, I stared at the patch of hair ruffling around what looked like two side-by-side blanched almonds. My goal was between them. It was my mission. The source of completion.

Something creaked outside, and I found myself wishing I could leave. I dutifully crawled onto the bed and tried kissing her a little, but she seemed impatient. I pulled back, and there it still was, waiting for me, the only route to silence the clamor. She spread her legs further and I could see her pinkness, moist. I hesitated. "Should I take precautions?" I asked. Her "Yes," sounded muffled somehow as if it had been layered with a dampened giggle. The condom looked ridiculous stretched over my dick. The "special reservoir tip" looked like a fool's cap. I climbed up and aimed as best I could, but needed help understanding the angle; and she guided the rubber tube inside her.

Something vaguely warm cradled me. It felt all right, but not great. I didn't feel like moving, but I knew I should. I started to pump myself into her. One, two, three, four and then I slipped by me. There was no shudder of ecstasy, just a dribbling surprise that it was already over. I lifted myself up, and the glistening wrinkled mess, so resignedly attached to me, hung stupidly between my legs. For her part, she looked almost the same as when we had started to fuck. Her secret had opened a little wider, but was the only thing different about her. There was nothing about tennis shoes that I could tell. I went to the bathroom, still in full view of her, and I tried to flush the rubber down the toilet. But the commode wouldn't flush very well, and the condom just spun around and around in the bowl. I looked behind me and saw her still lying on the bed propped up on her elbows, silently watching me. I felt I should hurry and go back and kiss her or do something. Maybe I could rub her breasts or stroke her hair.

"What are you doing?" she asked.

"It won't flush," I said, and I heard laughter outside the window. I saw bodies moving on her rooftop in the twilight. The window opened and in came Laszlo and Mole and I don't remember who else. They couldn't stop laughing. Brumley lay on the bed with that crazy smile pasted on her face, and she hardly moved. Some of the guys were drinking up the sight of the naked her. And so Laszlo grabbed a sheet and protectively covered her up. I turned away, wilted and humiliated. I gathered up my clothes and slammed the bathroom door.

The toilet was still running, and I resigned myself to fishing the condom out of the bowl. I hid it in a bunch of used tissues where I hoped her parents would never find it.

Mole's colonel dad worked at the I. G. Farben building. A couple of times I walked over there after school and sat with Mole while he waited for his dad. The best thing about the building was the *pater noster*. I'd never seen one before; I enjoyed the way it clanked and shuddered, looping over and over. I wondered what it looked like before the US military painted it an ugly maroon. I imagined it had gleamed with a highly polished wood finish as it escorted Nazis round and around. Nowadays, the khaki and olive-drab bodies did not glisten, but slipped out of sight below the floor all the same. And then, they popped up again, just like the vanquished had done, riding in those upright coffin boxes.

The only other thing to do while waiting in that echoing lobby was to check out the glass display cases. I read: "Built in the 1930s, the I. G. Farben building was the corporate headquarters for the chemical conglomerate of the same name." The sign didn't tell us that those were the same folks who had developed nerve gas for the Nazis, or that the US had supported the enterprise. "In 1945 it was occupied by US forces and became Eisenhower's first post-war European headquarters," it reported. Yeah, and although the allies had no qualms about smashing the opera house, Eisenhower specifically ordered that the I. G. Farben building be spared because he had designs on it. "Today it houses the headquarters of V Corps, here to protect and serve our American interests overseas."

Apparently, some other people had a different idea about what should happen to that building, because on the morning of May 11th, we learned over the Armed Forces Network Radio that the I. G. Farben building had been bombed. Several people were injured and at least one person had died. The windows of the officers' mess had exploded, sending a shard of glass into the throat of a decorated Vietnam veteran. He bled to death on the freshly buffed floor.

Later in the day, a group calling itself the Petra Schelm Commando claimed responsibility, They demanded that the US stop mining North Vietnamese harbors immediately.

The Petra Schelm Commando turned out to be another name for the Baader/Meinhof Group which had been "fighting imperialism" for a long time. It was probably because of them that bomb scares at school had become routine. We treated the scares like fire drills, and were happy to be free for maybe an hour. Now, after the real bombing, every time we got close to the American compound we were met by MPs with M-16s who nuzzled the barrels of their weapons with those of *der Polizei*. Those partners in security checked our IDs and carefully searched each of us for armaments and the all-inclusive "paraphernalia."

Over the next couple of days bombs blew up in Munich, Augsburg, Karlsruhe and Hamburg. Some of us figured we knew why. You had to "destroy what destroys you," some of us had thought. It was the final act: "the opening of the European front of the Vietnam war." Anti-fascist resistance had to be provided, not just through talk, but through action.

I was frightened to the extent that I thought that way. Just when I thought I could ignore what bothered me, the game had become too real. Our screaming and shouting protests, at least in me, had been effectively silenced. Now I hid in the horror of understanding.

The local war escalated. On May 24, a parking lot outside a US army barracks in Heidelberg was bombed. One Vietnam veteran was blown in two. The upper half of his body remained by his brand new Ford Capri, The Stars and Stripes reported, while the rest of him hung like dripping "meaty leaves" in a nearby tree. Another soldier was crushed by a Coca-Cola machine, when the wall it stood against was blown outside in. The Baader/Meinhof group were precisely hitting their targets. I had a plane reservation for June 19th, and worried I might not make it out alive.

After we balled that once, Kaye Brumley and I met in the bushes of Gruneburg park a couple of times, but it never went very far. Also, Lainey's best friend, Sharon Worley and I almost got caught by her Dad when we were about to get it on. I had to hide in her closet until the coast was clear. Still, on the last day of school, when Lainey asked me to call her, every other desire faded away.

Her request thrilled me with fear mixed with the pleasure of her acknowledgement. She was the eventual antidote to all pain and yearning. I still believed in her. And her simple request was enough to convince me that, at last — her final opportunity before I left — she had found the truth in her heart: She was sick of Laszlo, and it was my name that burned deeply inside her.

I went to Schönberg to make the call. As I had planned it, no one was home. I put on Joni Mitchell's *Blue* album and turned it up loud so Lainey could hear it over the phone. I knew she would take playing *Blue* as an offering of peace. It was a reminder of her latest betrayal. This one still hurt — she *forgot* to invite me to see Joni Mitchell in concert. She and Evan went without me. I couldn't believe it. But this new offering would be a true act of generous love. She would understand that I forgave her, and she would be grateful. She would realize the superior love I was capable of. When it came to matters of the heart, certainly, Joni cured all.

Indeed, Joni soothed us with her warmth and familiar sentimental woe — Lainey and I talked in gentle tones over Joni's songs. Lainey told me that I was important to her. She said she would always care for me so deeply. She knew we would see each other often, and that nothing could keep us apart. Soon she would be back in The States, too, and we could be with each other without all this mess surrounding us. I loved her so profoundly. Now she had finally revealed she felt the same about me. Her games with Laszlo were just a temporary distraction. We only needed a better opportunity. I had said it all along, and now she finally agreed. . . . And then there was nothing left to say. We had found our destiny together.

The title song, "Blue" played and I turned it up even louder.

"Can you hear it, Lainey?"

"Yes. Oh, yes. I can hear it" she said slowly.

And Joni's voice trembled on the last note of "Blue," and I moaned. "Ahhh." The tears rolled down my face. I quickly got up to turn the record over. We listened in complete loving silence. Joni sang:

*Oh, I could drink a case of you*
*And I would still be on my feet,*
*I would still be on my feet.*

By the time the song had ended, I knew Lainey could hear me crying. I *wanted* her to hear me cry. One more song and the last note faded into a crackle. I heard Lainey's voice again. Maybe she had been crying, too.

"Come over to my house, tomorrow. I'll have a surprise for you," she said.

At last, we were going to make love! That must be what she means.

"It will be in the bushes by the front door," she said.

Was she speaking in code? Would we do it in the bushes? Why not in the house?

"Good-bye. I love you," she said.

My body rumbled ecstatically. My ears began to thump and my skin tingled. "Tomorrow," I whispered to myself.

I didn't care if anybody came home. I got undressed and went to bed early. I made beautiful love to myself and then lay there facing the ceiling. I let the sperm dry and crack on my belly. She was wonderful, lulling me to sleep. I dreamt I was in shadowy corridors, cubicles — in love with Lainey Wintergreen and she in love with me . . . and Sam Laszlo. Dammit. She is stretched out, reclining over us, side by side on his and my lap supporting her. She takes off her clothes and lies back down. She is younger. Like when I first met her: Her hips have hardly widened and her breasts are like small tea cups. In the faint light she stretches and Laszlo and I caress her in long strokes down the length of her body. She is in ecstasy, writhing, so beautiful, undulant. The darkness between her legs is hypnotic. But soon, she says she prefers his touch over mine. I am furious. I find a cut-glass vase, and I crush her head, beating her repeatedly until she is unrecognizable.

I didn't dare reveal my dream until now. I was filled with remorse and guilt for having experienced it. Still, I went to meet Lainey as planned, but when I arrived, no one was home. I waited a little while and rang the doorbell again. I tried to remember her exact words: "I'll surprise you in the bushes?" I pushed aside a few shrubs, and there I found a package. Inside was an 8" by 10" framed photograph of her smiling in that inviting way. On the picture she had written, "I could drink a case of you. . . ." I wrapped it back up. I did not understand anything. I did not know what to do. I walked over to Laszlo's next door. I hoped she wasn't there.

"What's in the package?" he asked?

"Nothing."

"Look, there are no secrets here. Got it?"

"Come on, Laszlo, cool it," I said. "I don't feel like fucking around." And I tried to push past him into his house. But he recognized no suffering in me, or chose to ignore it.

"Lainey hasn't been here, has she?" I asked.

He ignored the question. I pushed on the door. He said, "You're not getting in until you show me what's in the package." He pushed me back and slammed the door in my face. Had Lainey told him she was going to give me something, but wouldn't say what? Was she inside there? I stared at my reflection in the glass door. I knew what to do. I hid Lainey's picture back under her bushes, and then I got the garden hose and unrolled it to Laszlo's front door. I opened the mail slot and shoved the hose right in. Laszlo must have been upstairs, because it was a long time before he came running out of the house, screaming at me to turn off the water. Once he was in the yard, I jumped from behind the bushes and ran inside his house. Victory, but over what I didn't know. Was she in there? He ran upstairs after me. Our shoes and socks were soaked. At last, we began to fight in earnest. Back and forth we exchanged punches to the face, and I was happy. He was stronger than me, and so managed to force me out of his room and throw me against the banister. I plowed back with all my head-butting force and we rolled down the stairs. I got up laughing and punched him some more.

"You are fucking nuts," he kept saying, pushing me closer to the door. We fell into the puddle and wrestled with the door handle until I relented, and he shoved me outside. I read his lips through the glass, "You are fucking nuts." And then he smiled. Was she in there? I didn't know if he had enjoyed himself as much as I had, or if he was smiling because he had triumphed again.

I crawled back under Lainey's bushes and sat there for a while. I took the picture back out of its wrapping and stared at her teeth and lips. Her teeth were big and her lips were thin. Beautiful, still. I had never thought of it when I kissed her. I wondered what she would do if she came out and found me there, my eye swollen — I could feel it throb — and my nose a little bloody, clinging to her picture with a stupid puffy smile on my face.

I wanted to go to Amsterdam one last time, but didn't know what the hell for. Just to pass the time. I was hanging out at the PX, getting up the motivation to catch the Straßenbahn down to the Hauptbahnhof access road and stick out my thumb. I was surprised to see Lainey at the PX, and she commented on my black eye. I thanked her for the gift. No more words. Stop it. No more hope.

It was going to be interesting hitching with all the roadblocks of heavily armed Polizei as they searched for the Baader/Meinhof group. A couple of them had already been caught, and it had only been a few days since the most recent bombing in Heidelberg. I got my push to go when yet another bomb scare was called in to the PX. No sense in waiting around any longer, so I said my good-byes. A few friends said they were envious that they weren't going with me. It was too weird to stay in Frankfurt. I looked at Lainey, daring her to say something, but she kept quiet.

Not much happened on the road. Instead, I missed the excitement in Frankfurt. The Polizei caught Baader and a couple of the others of the group up in a North Frankfurt cemetery. Apparently, it had been a thrill for all — there was a shoot-out with helicopters and tear gas and hundreds of Polizei and plain-clothes cops and German military and a throng of spectators. And the whole thing was broadcast live on TV. I heard they even made Baader strip naked in front of the cameras before dragging him away.

Later on, I read that the bombs used to blow up the I. G. Farben building had been gift-wrapped and topped with pretty flowers, and made in a sculpture studio very near the old fire-bombed Öpernplatz. Baader/Meinhof were probably working away at destroying historical imperialism that very night we saw the tripping fool walking the edge of the crumbled opera-house facade.

Joe and Evan came out to visit me in Schönberg territory. We wanted to smoke a bowl out in the woods and say our good-byes. The Dive-bomber caught us on the way out. He saw our improvised emergency pipe made from a toilet paper tube and aluminum foil. "Where you going with that?" he asked.

"Out in the woods," I said.

"Oh, no you don't," he said. And I was ready to tell him to fuck off; we would do what we damn-well pleased.

"If you want to smoke, you're gonna do it here," he said. "Not outside where you can get arrested."

What had come over the two of them? They were so loving to each other and tolerant of me. What about Mom's so-called discovery — the other woman conspiracy? Peace. The thorn, which was me, had been extracted.

So Mom and Vic and my friends settled on the patio to take part in our sacrament — Vic offered his meerschaum lion-head pipe. When the pipe came around, the old Dive-bomber smoked like he had been smoking hash for years. Even Mom took a couple of hits. She was so funny, puffing like the little train that could, but she said, she didn't like it much. "I don't know what all the fuss is about," she coughed. "I don't feel a thing." Yet, after twenty minutes or so, she asked, "Ya'll hungry? I just got to where I have to eat *sumpin'*."And she disappeared into the kitchen. All of us, even Vic, began to laugh.

Quite a bit later, she came back onto the patio with enough food for twenty people. She brought cheeses and crackers and fruits and canned oysters and various leftovers she had heated up, and chocolate, a couple of bottles of wine and so on and so forth. "Now if this in't enough, ya'll let me know," she said.

And we burst out with a roar of laughter.

"What's so funny," she demanded?

"Mom," I said. "You're stoned. You got the munchies something serious." And nutritional neurosis to boot.

On June 15th, the Polizei caught Ulrike Meinhof. At first, the cops weren't sure who they had, but when they searched her apartment they found an x-ray of her head. It revealed from a 1962 operation a metal clip had been placed over an engorged blood vessel. To verify it was the same woman, the cops forcibly anesthetized her and took an x-ray of her clipped head. Terrible, the indignant demand for love.

I had badly burned my face by covering it with a liquid black shoe polish. I'd been staring at myself in the mirror and I wondered how I would look as a black man. I looked ridiculous, and a few minutes later my face started burning like fuck. I washed off all the black I could, but couldn't get it off where it had burned into my flesh. And so, when it was time for me to leave Frankfurt, it appeared that I had scraped up my cheeks after falling into a coal mine. Nobody hassled me about it. They just stared.

Mom and Vic took me to the airport on June 19th, as scheduled, two days after their fifth anniversary. On the way, and once there, Mom needed to nervously chatter, but there wasn't much left to say.

When we got inside the airport, one of the few things Vic said to me was, "Here. Take this," and he handed me a carton of Winstons. "That's your brand, isn't it?" I nodded and thanked him. I didn't want to tell him I still preferred to roll my own shag with just a pinch of peppermint.

Joe and Evan and Mole showed up, waiting to send me off. I kind of angrily hoped I'd see Lainey, but figured she was *busy* with Laszlo. Bastard.

It was too painful for everybody to hang around talking about nothing, wishing we could, at last, find the perfect thing to say. Mom couldn't stop crying, so I told everyone I was going to say good-bye now and pass through customs. I got up from my seat, and Vic offered me his hand to shake. He said, "I'm sorry things didn't work out." I nodded slowly, but said nothing. Mom was crying too hard to articulate anything. She just sobbed and said the word "love" several times in incomprehensible phrases.

Then, like justice in a bad movie, I turned to see Lainey and Laszlo running toward us. They had ridden Laszlo's Honda 50 and it had taken longer than they thought it would, they explained. They were all smiles, colliding with the somber mood they had not yet witnessed. Lainey smiled large. Out of her rucksack she pulled a jar of straw-colored liquid and two wine glasses. She poured the wine into the glasses, and I feebly reached to toast.

"No" she said. "Like this." And she linked her arm with mine to drink. There we were, romantically elbow to elbow. Laszlo moved forward and gave me a big bear-harbor hug. Lainey cut in, and she hugged me the longest and tenderly. She was crying. She said, "I love you."

Slowly, I pulled away from her. "I have to go," I whispered to her softly and then repeated it to everyone else, "I have to go," and slipped through the door to customs.

In the waiting room I tore open the carton of Winstons as fast as I could. I was trembling so badly I couldn't light my cigarette. The man sitting next to me stared looking worried. He said, "Are you okay, Son?" I nodded.

He said, "Here. Let me light that for you."

*Jiggling*

# THREE

*Jiggling*

# Hell or High Water

---

Threads of clinging sleep stretch and snap into falling droplets. My cheek is cold, wet. I lift myself slightly and notice a tiny pond of drool has slowly absorbed into the sandwich-size pillow. Someone has covered me with a blanket, but it is thin. I scrunch up close to the humming wall of the plane as it tilts and balances in sudden, short jerks. Someone closed the plastic shutter next to my seat, maybe the same thoughtful person who covered me. I slide the shutter open a bit, just a peek at the day I'm stuck inside of.

I wait for the ocean to close up and the day to take hold. I search for land through the fogged double-thick plexiglass. And, at last, bright solarized peaks of icebergs come into view. They poke above a blue so very clean and delicious; their rooted wads below the surface are scoops of vanilla ice-cream dropped into Aqua Velva blue.

Gradually, the icebergs thin to a few speckles, and a green rocky coast appears far below us. Solitary roads, some deserted or guiding a single vehicle, twist over humps that appear smoothed out from above. Silent waves crash without threatening me. I dream of parachuting down there. That is where I belong. I want to hitchhike forever along the backroads of Newfoundland. Down there I ride in a fisherman's truck, or a minstrel's van, or a restless meanderer's car across a land so full of beauty and gentle promise. Some day.

But the wild freedom of Cape Breton and the Bay of Fundy, the captain named them, has maniacally exploded, then withered as hope receded. The undulant promise of the wild has become pocked with towns. Now it's too late to jump. The towns have become the cities of the seaboard — Boston and New York — approaching Philadelphia, where we land.

The tension was palpable. The anxious faces in the airport had no greeting. They were endless layers of putrid meat. I had made it back, and I wanted to tell anyone. "So what?" the faces seemed to be saying. I asked a man how to get to the bus station.

"Limo," his sneering eyes slashed across me for not knowing.

At the exit, flight crews were protested the lack of security, loudly complaining that just that morning there had been yet another bomb scare. "Don't Hijack Our Jobs," the signs declared, "No More Unnecessary Risks." I slipped past them and found the Limo.

"I just got back from Europe," I said to the driver. No response. "I've been gone for three years." He looked at me blankly. I withdrew into fear and hostility. That seemed the way to get by.

The ugly stretched station wagon, parading as a vehicle of luxury — a limo? — slopped through the rancid buttermilk streets. The passenger next to me carelessly blew cigar smoke into my face. Nothing to say. You don't like it? Get out. Right here. In the South Philly slums, the poverty spilled out and bounced upon the windshield. I caught the specter of a Black man flipping us off.

The bus would not get to Wilkes-Barre, PA until late at night, and I would have to take my chances getting to Berwick from there. No more information. "You want the ticket or not?"

"Yes, please," I mumbled.

The first friendly face I saw was worn by a hippie. "Hey dude. How's it going?" He offered his thumb for the short version of a wrap-around soul shake. "Where you truckin' off to?"

Momentarily lifted, I searched for the conversation groove. "Uh, here for a few days, and then I'm headed down to Florida, Man."

"Why Florida, Man? Florida sucks."

I wanted to ask him why he thought so, but felt I should have known better. He kept looking around while talking to me, like he was in a hurry, or he was afraid someone would see him there.

"Why don't you come out to California with us?" He smiled widely and then stared over my shoulder again.

"Wow, that would be great, Man, but I'm gonna have to postpone that one." My father was expecting me, but I hadn't told Dad I was going to stop in Berwick for a few days.

"Come on, Man. We need someone to help out with gas."

"Sorry. I really need to go to Florida. I wish I had run into you. . . ."

Before I could finish proclaiming my allegiance to the cool, he had disappeared into the crowd.

My heart drooped. I turned to find my departure gate. There I dropped down on my backpack and waited in the silent line.

The bus stretched into Wilkes-Barre shortly before midnight. The first bus to Berwick would not depart until eight the next morning. No, I could not wait in the station, I was told. The station was about to close. Damn, only 28 miles to Berwick. I couldn't afford a taxi. Thought I'd walk. Take about as long. But

I was too tired. Best to try and find a place to sleep. I couldn't afford a motel. Maybe the "Y". Too strange to sleep outside. I looked around  the fume-soaked loading dock zone for some help. The most approachable person, it seemed, was a guy about my age. Thin. Fair, short hair. Jeans and a yellow windbreaker. He was acting a little nervous, like me. I felt more cautious than I had been upon arrival — reluctant to speak. He didn't look like a traveler. I asked him anyway.

"Hey, you know where I can find the Y-M-C-A?" I stumbled over the letters. He began to give directions, but he saw I couldn't follow his quick, jabbing speech.

"What the hell. I'm not doing anything. I'll show you," he said. "My name's Billy."

A coffee and doughnut shop was still open "Special on Crullers," I read. Next to that a medical supply store, its window cluttered with walkers and shiny bedpans, and an old-style commode. "How do you attractively display products for the infirm," he asked me seriously? Every shop window was an occasion for him to pause and chat.

"Mind if I jump in here for a coffee?" he said.

I was getting impatient. "Why don't you just point the way, and I can find the Y on my own."

"No, never mind. I'll show you. You know it might be closed by now. I think they close right at midnight. It's two minutes past. But you might make it."

I was exhausted and disoriented. I picked up the pace and my guide led me to the door. But it was locked. Had Billy wanted me to get there too late, dragging along, window shopping, stopping for coffee? Don't worry about it, I told myself. No sleep. Jet lag. Move on.

We went back to the coffee shop, and I told Billy about my long trip from Frankfurt. I told him about the icebergs, and Newfoundland, and how strange it was to be back in America, and that the next bus didn't leave until eight. He paid for my coffee, and offered to pass the time together, wandering around Wilkes-Barre. Billy decided I was to be his guest.

It was going to be a long night, but he was generous and strangely interesting. It seemed like he was speaking from another world, and struggling to maintain contact. Where was I going to go, anyway? This wasn't like Europe. You couldn't throw your sleeping bag down most anywhere.

Billy didn't seem to need the coffee. He was already zipping like a speed freak. We passed in front of every pitiful window display of industrial fashion and derelict bargains in that rotting downtown. Incongruously, a green light haunted the luster of piano wood through a silent window. Steinways to stare at amidst urban decay.

"Do you play?" Billy asked.

I shook my head.

"These are shit. I play some, but I know more about the mechanics," he said, "the workings of the instrument itself. There was a man here from Steinway not too long ago. Maybe three weeks. Maybe two. I don't remember exactly. That man knew my grandmother." His voice trailed off and then he recovered. "Well, he used to know her. She's dead now. I was very close to her, you know? She was everything to me. She was my solace. What do you think about that?" he said acidly.

"I'm sorry," I said.

"It's okay," he said indignantly. "You don't need to be sorry about it. *I* am sorry, and that's enough. So. As I was saying,

Grandmother, rest her soul, invited a Steinway rep. over from Vienna, Austria to meet with me. Have you ever been there? Oh, he was quite full of himself. But I let him know what he needed to know. Don't get me wrong; I was very polite. We were talking about my future, you know? I offered him some suggestions for improving these old junk boxes. He was impressed. That's for sure."

Billy paused to check my reaction, and I smiled faintly.

"If they're smart," he continued, "they'll take my advice." Billy turned his back on the pianos, feigning disgust. "Yes, the gentleman was impressed. In fact, he invited me to Vienna to become his protégé."

"Are you going to go?" I asked. It could happen, I guessed.

"Well, Grandmother had become ill, you see, and someone had to take care of her. Her own children had neglected her shamelessly. It is truly disgusting the way she has been treated." Billy sucked in on his already sunken cheeks. "I may still go one day."

Perhaps it was just my exhaustion, but he had some tense hypnotic power about him despite his absurd vanities. Maybe he was tormented by an intuition he could not yet articulate — an understanding of himself that could free him at last — but for now, he experienced whatever was calling, as pained, vague emotions, scratching inside him. At least, with hindsight, that's the way it looked to me.

"I am very tired," I said. "Is there some place we could sit down?"

"Why don't we go to my house? It's not too far away. Yes. That would be good." He had suddenly become exuberant again.

"I could feed you. I have some fertile eggs and sprouts and whole-grain bread."

I did not understand. What was all that?

"Yes. I shall give you the proper welcome home you deserve," he said.

The colored lights of downtown faded behind us as we walked away from the river and into the residential hills. Billy was suddenly in a hurry, so we walked quickly along rows of wooden duplexes with porches. The walls in front of the houses changed in height; as we climbed the hill, it made it seem like we were walking beside a concrete escalator.

Billy resumed his performance. "My grandmother died eleven nights ago this night," Billy whimpered. "I miss her terribly. But you know, what did you say your name was, she hasn't left me altogether. She talks to me sometimes. She guides me. It is a very beautiful thing. In dreams, and sometimes, when I'm awake, too, she helps me know what I am to do. I love her very much."

He stopped under a lamp post and stared as deeply into my eyes as the streetlight would permit. "Do you believe me? Do you believe that she talks to me?"

"Yes. I believe you," I said. I had heard voices myself. Who was I to doubt him?

A cab came around the corner. Billy praised our good luck.

"I can't afford this," I said.

"Oh, for God's sake, don't worry about it. I'll pay for it," he said.

We travelled over several more identical hills, past many more identical houses until we stopped outside his. I had no idea where I was or how to get back to the station.

"Come in, but be quiet. My parents are probably asleep," he said.

"You didn't say you lived with your parents"

"Shh. Don't worry. It's okay. Come on in."

I walked ahead of Billy through the back door, through the kitchen and into the living room.

"No. Let's stay in here," he whispered from the kitchen. As I crept back toward him, he pointed at the piano. It was old, beaten, and cheap.

"Piece of shit," he whispered.

I came into the kitchen. "You sit over there," he motioned nervously. "And please, don't get up. I will make you something nice. Just mind what I say. Do you like fertile eggs?"

Billy smeared what he said was cashew butter on toasted seven-grain bread. He laid a slice in front of me with a smile. He talked non-stop, and loudly, about the food. He seemed to have forgotten about the plan to be quiet. Before long he served over-easy orange—yolked eggs topped with what looked like a pubic grass he called "sprouts." I'd never heard of such food, not even in Amsterdam. I entered this new world cautiously. The yolks were heavily mucoused ova, but the grassy pubes helped to cut the slime. I was grateful when Billy placed a glass of water in front of me. "How do you like it?" he wanted to know.

But before I could answer, a woman's voice from beyond the living room asked, "Billy? Is that you?"

Billy jumped up from his chair to greet the sleepy voice before she could enter the kitchen. "Yes, Mom," Billy spoke rapidly. "I brought a friend home. He just got in from Germany, and he didn't have a place. . . ."

"Dammit." The voice awoke into a shriek. "I told you, 'No bums in this house.' Get him out before I call the cops."

I stood up, but Billy quickly threw a sharp look at me from where he stood. He quietly told me to sit down. He explained that everything would be fine. He would take care of his mother, and then we could enjoy our meal. Back in the living room I heard him say softly, "Mom, I want you to go back upstairs and leave us alone. There's nothing here to concern you." I could hear her retreat back up the stairs.

Billy sat back down and asked me how I liked the food. Without waiting for an answer, he told me with as much zeal as he had exuded over the need to improve the Steinway, that we must not corrupt our bodies with inferior food. He said we must cultivate a righteous diet. I wanted to tell him about nutritional neurosis, about the Hare Krishna meal. Too late. Someone was coming back down the stairs.

This time a weak male voice mumbled sleepily towards the kitchen, "Damn you, punk-ass kid. Look at what you've done to your mother," he muttered automatically. "Why'd you come back at all?" Billy did not bother to get up. He let the voice fade, shook his head, and then continued talking tensely about food. But again we heard his mother, in turns snarling and growling, then sobbing and muttering. Her sounds moved closer to the kitchen.

Billy leapt up and rushed toward her, shouting, "Get up those stairs, now. I've already told you once." And his mother grumbled away.

Billy turned back to me, "Pay no attention to her," he said.

"I think I'd better go."

"Don't worry. I tell you she's harmless."

"I guess, but still. . . ."

Billy caught my eyes and pinned me to my seat — "You have your food. You said you were hungry. Now, eat."

I picked at the cold eggs and considered my options, but again the mother interrupted with a rant about bringing home scum in the middle of the night. Strange how she was one minute so docile and the next like a frothing attack dog.

Her son shouted back, "Shut up, bitch. Go back to bed."

"Get him out of here. And you get out, too, Billy," screamed the mother. "We don't want you here. You are trouble itself," she whimpered.

Billy moved toward the stairs as his mother moved across the mezzanine. "Keep your voice down, you crazy woman. Don't you dare wake my little sister."

I could hear the man's voice again. I searched for how to make my move.

Billy complained, "Christ, leave us alone. What the fuck is this?"

The man's voice pitifully ventured, "Don't you use language like that in this house."

"Fuck you. I bring a friend home who needs a place to stay and you want to throw him out. You call yourselves Christians?"

Billy sounded like he was beginning to cry. Just slip out the way you came in, I thought. Go. But I was stuck. My feet would not respond.

He regained his strength, and his voice dropped down to threaten his parents, "I think you should go back to bed now. Go now, or I swear I'll kill you." There were gasps and the sound of galloping up the stairs.

I could feel the fear ache in the soles of my feet the way they do when I'm up too high, too close to falling.

A little girl's voice faraway said, "Mom, is Billy back?"

Confused, I got up and walked the wrong way, away from my exit, and braced myself up under an archway. The little sister stood at the top of the stairs, sleepily gazing. Her hair was long and yellow-white. In the half-light it looked the color of old teeth.

"Dammit," screamed Billy. He knocked me into the piano as he ran back into the kitchen. I saw him grab a kitchen knife, a big 12 inches of glinting steel, and his nuclear family fled into their separate rooms. He retreated downstairs, then Mom and Dad and Sis snuck out of their rooms again. Damn curiosity. I stood as they sobbed and screamed by the railing of the mezzanine while the son made silly dainty jabs at the air. "I shall kill you. I'll kill you," he gibbered. Then he faked a more vicious charge all the way up the stairs, shouting and stabbing the air as the others safely fled.

Billy returned the knife back to its proper place. He was grinning. He turned to me and said, "Go outside and wait for me, please. I'll be right there. You will wait, won't you?" I nodded that I would, walked past him and out the kitchen door.

I could not pull away. This was too familiar. I sat paralyzed on the steps leading down to the sidewalk, and I waited. Did someone move behind the darkened window across the street? I bet all the neighbors were sitting up in their springy beds, listening for more as the night swung slowly toward another belated dawn. Through a window I saw the silhouette of Billy on the phone.

"Is this Angie?" he said. . . ."I want to talk to Father Barnes. . .
. Yes. I know. . . . But this is extremely important. . . . But I
would prefer to talk to him. . . . No, it can't wait till morning.
That's why I've called now. . . . If I must, I suppose I have to tell
you, don't I? This is the way it is; the way it has become, I mean.
I want my parents banned from the church. . . .Yes. Excommu-
nicated. . . . Yes, that's right. With their behavior they don't deserve to call themselves Christians. I want them excommunicat-
ed. If they cannot help a friend in need, well then. Angie, . . . I
*am* calm. . . . No. Tell Father Barnes. . . . Why don't you just let
me talk to him?. . . Yes, wake him up. . . . Well, okay. I want you
to tell him first thing. . . . Please listen to me. They have no re-
gard for anyone but themselves. Is that Christian; I ask you?. . .
Will you just tell him? . . . "

I stared at the stark, emphatic silhouette spewing a sudden
religiosity. I laughed softly to myself. Please, release me, I
prayed to no one.

I suddenly heard the door slam, and Billy blazed toward me.
"Let's get the hell out of here," he said.

We walked downhill in silence, both of us thinking too rapidly
to speak. "Down to the river," Billy mumbled. And I obeyed.

After a few blocks his thoughts finally exploded, "They make
me feel so fucking crazy," he complained. "I don't know what to
do about it anymore. They won't respond to reason. It's useless.
I'll never go back there again. This time it's forever. I'm with you
now. . . ." He wanted to say my name, but he seemed to have
forgotten it. He went on, "I can't believe the way they acted toward you. They don't even know you."

"Hey, forget about it. I don't care."

"Well, I care. They never listen. No one listens. Except you. You listen. I can talk to you. I think *you* are the only one who understands."

"You know, maybe you're right about leaving. Maybe you should get out on your own. Leave them behind," I said. "That's what I finally had to do."

"Yeah, but it's not just them. It's everybody and everything. It all turns to shit, every time I try," Billy whimpered. It was a pitiful display. I had seen it before. Thrust yourself into a pit of pained emotional turmoil for the sensation of it. It makes you feel alive.

We could see the far hills ascending in the dawn on the other side, the Berwick side of the Susquehanna. We kept walking.

"Christ, I feel like dying. I want to float away," Billy said. "I want to die, god dammit. I want to die. Tonight. Yes. This horrible night I shall join Grandmother."

I knew he wanted me to feed *him* now. He wanted comfort. He demanded comfort, and it was my turn to give it. Maybe he would jump into the fucking river, if we ever got there. At first I calmed him with miscellaneous tender words, and when he persisted, I said to him what I wished I could have said to my mother, or myself for that matter. It was a lesson from Allen Ginsberg. "Billy, listen," I began. "Kill yourself if what you think comes next will be better." And then, with just enough of a pause, "But I don't think you will."

That shocked him a little. He was entertained. But he knew he was in trouble with me. He had chosen to surrender his paternalism in exchange for garnering pity. That game, too, I knew too well, and I was sick of it. "But I hurt so bad," he said. I knew if I told him to shut up, he would fight me and pity himself all the more, trying to suck me back again with guilt.

I ignored him.

A flinty light began to focus, beginning to cause the darkness to disappear. Billy hung his head, embarrassed and pouting too long. He tried a couple of more oozing pity jabs at me, but I didn't respond. The light seeped onto the pavement, and we two stumbled on. I was so tired and now bored with his company. "Billy, how much further?"

"Not too far. I know a place where we can watch the sun rise."

"I don't know," I said. "I'm pretty tired." I repeated. It was time to escape, even if I had to run. "Which way is the bus station? I want to go back downtown."

"But it's still too early. We can take a nap together. It will be very beautiful. Please, stay with me. Don't you abandon me, too."

My chest tensed and my heart beat faster. I stared at him begging me, a stranger, to help him. I felt miserable for both of us.

"Please. I'll walk if you want to," he said. "Come on. It's this way. We can talk some more. Please, I need to talk to you. You've been so kind to me, and I really like you."

So we walked towards town for a few blocks until Billy said, "Do you think maybe. . . . Would you hold me? Just for a moment. We could go to the river. You're so nice." He paused and then blurted it out, "Make love to me. I've thought of it all night. Wouldn't it be so nice?"

I'd never thought about having sex with a man, except to disdain it. If Billy had been a woman asking for comfort, I would have said, 'Yes, please. Let's go back to the river and find a nice secluded spot. I'll love you for a little while.' More likely, if Billy had been a woman, I probably would have done the same thing he had done to me. I would have waited for an opportunity and pleaded that I needed to be held, to be suckled, to be loved. Such greed! I turned to him, afraid to touch him, though he was trembling. And though my contempt was mixed with a little em-pathy, I kept my distance. I said, pointing toward downtown, "I'm going that way. And I want you to go away." I took a few steps, and heard him whimper at my back. I hate to admit it, but right then, part of me preferred he kill himself.

The bus station was open by the time I found it. I got my pack from the locker, and sat down to wait. A few elderly women stared at me from their brightly-colored bucket seats. I guess they were concerned, maybe afraid, at the sight of me. Maybe it was just the black burnt shoe-polish that had lingered. I don't know.

The bus left on time, and I was the only passenger. The river was swollen. I asked the driver, "You ever seen the river so high?"

"Long time ago, Son. During a heavy spring run-off. This is real high for summer time, I reckon. Must be on account that hurricane by the name of Agnes."

"Hurricane?"

"Yeppert. She's a-moving this way."

When I woke up that afternoon, collapsed onto the Dive-bomber Seniors' guest coach, the Dive-bomber Grandma told me that Andie Carnelian had dropped by. Andie had left the address of where I should meet her — an apartment on Market Street across from the stone Victorian City Hall.

Andie's wide beautiful smile made a crescent that nearly connected the falls of her flaming-strawberry hair. I had forgotten how freckled she was. Her sun-red face was spotted with hundreds of pinpoint flares now darkened with emotion. She was crying. She said she was so happy to see me. She had missed me terribly. We hugged each other tight, and I felt her jolly breasts press warmly against my ribs and belly. I surely had not expected this. She stood back from me and seemed to be staring quizzically at my pocked face. I wasn't going to say anything. She indicated her friends, waiting to be introduced. They were older than her, and it was their apartment. I shook the offered hands and then hugged Annie again. "Well, someone's having a happy reunion," one of them said in a very adult, sarcastic tone. I was relieved when they retreated to the kitchen.

Andie invited me to come talk with her on the couch — a foam pad covered with a hippie batik and some pillows with little mirrors sewn into them. It was most comfortable to lie all the way back, flat with my knees bent at the edge and my feet dangling. Arching up, I could just touch the ground with the toe of my shoes. Reaching like that kind of made me feel like a little boy.

Andie was boiling with affection. Side-by-side, she stroked my arm. Her caresses felt like little flaming licks. I wondered how Sally would feel if she knew I was back, or if she even cared. Andie was eager to hear about Germany, she said, but I postponed the past Turning abruptly, I found her lips. Her mouth opened, relaxed and soft. Her lips were full and tender wet. Not at all like Oatmeal, Laszlo. She trickled little passionate sighs of relief. We paused to smile at one another, sheltered in each other's arms. Then, without warning, she rolled over on top of me and our bodies settled into the grooves and contours of our blending shapes. Her large breasts at my upper chest forced her soft little belly to press into the cradle of my ribs. Her legs fell on either side of mine, and a pulsing warmth beat against my lower belly. I began to grow towards her like a searching beanstalk.

"Mmm. That feels good. Our bodies fit perfectly," she cooed.

We kissed and kissed until our ears burned and our eyes were drunk. Then Andie paused. She sat upright and the full heat of her cleft caressed my cock as the fire between us coursed down our thighs in slow, pulsing, yearning insistence.

Her mature friends had been trying not to watch as they slowly made their way back to the living room. Suddenly aware of them, we felt embarrassed. "Let's go over to my house," said Andie. And just like old times, she added, "My mother's at work until six."

It had started to rain, but her house wasn't far. We walked without a care, kept warm with desire. I couldn't believe my good luck. I was laughing and happy with a girl, knowing we would make love. Fruition. Fulfilled in the anticipation and the certainty of what was imminent. No greater satisfaction, I still believed. Two blocks from her house the sky really dumped its barrels, and we ran down the street, up onto the porch, and into the house.

Andie got us towels, the kind that are so big you can live in them. She disappeared inside hers, and I saw her as an animal jumping and rumpling under terry cloth. I joined her inside her little cave. Her hair frizzed out into my face and I had to hunt to find her mouth. As I kissed her, she dried my head. Her ears had cooled from the rain, and I savored the fleshy drops of her dangling lobes. She squirmed and gently pushed me back. We lost the towel, and her wet sweatshirt came over her head. She was wearing a black leotard, and her shoulders radiated all the more pink against the shiny blackness. Skip and I used to tease her about how large her breasts were on her tiny frame. She had complained that it wasn't funny, since their weight hurt her so. I was afraid to touch them. Until then, the girls I had felt and fondled had small breasts like Mom's, but Andie's announced themselves loudly. She felt my caution and invited me to touch. As I pressed and poked, she began to undress me. "You'll catch cold," she said, and she helped me out of my wet shirt. I was eager to take off my pants. My dick had forced itself way up and out beyond the plastic underwear band. Andie grinned at the head peeking out to greet her. She took off her jeans and lay back. We were warm again, nestled there in pillows with a blanket draped over us. I wanted her to take off that leotard. I wanted to see her. I wanted our soon to be naked bodies to touch. I tugged at the black shiny skin. "No, like this," she said and reached her hand down between her legs. The leotard had snaps there. Three in a row, waiting.  I heard three little explosions: "Pop, pop, pop," they said. I saw her white underpants printed with little colorful flowers that danced on a softly breathing mound. And at the edges, wisps of hair, the color of a blushing pumpkin, licked her thighs.

"Let's go upstairs," she whispered. "We'll be more comfortable there." I wanted to see her ginger cat more than I wanted anything. Upstairs, downstairs, anywhere. More than my own happiness, I wanted to see it. More than my history revoked and tried again. More than fucking her, I wanted to see her pussy. I chased her upstairs. She jumped into the bed, lay back and lifted her up her hips, and she slipped down her underwear. A furry maple leaf had fallen between her legs. She reached out her arms to me. She wanted me to make love to her. She wanted me! I slipped off my Fruit of the Looms and crawled toward her. I looked down. Furry wet leaf, rippling as she writhed with anticipation. Furry wet leaf.

It was getting close to six o'clock. I must have fallen asleep. Yes, she said, I had. We gathered up our clothes.

"Tomorrow night there's gonna be a dance at the Y," Andie said. "I think it's to celebrate the first of summer. Remember that guy who used to do 'Hey Joe' with fake blood and strobe lights?"

"Oh yeah. That guy that looked like Tom Jones," I sniggered.

"Well, he's got a new band."

I ran through the cemetery to the Dive-bombers' and got soaked all over again. Dive-bomber Grandma was serving cabbage her husband had macerated, cucumber slices in vinegar, and rhubarb pie.

The next day Skip picked me up uptown — that's what they called it in Berwick — in his new car. When he gave me a welcoming "brother" hug, I saw that his pony tail snaked far down his back. Though I was enthusiastic to tell him about my bizarre first day back in the US, Skip was guarded. He had little to say, so I withdrew. We drove over to a treeless suburb where he said we could find Sally. I guess our friendship had always orbited around Sally and Andie.

We pulled up to the ugly artificial expensive house where Sally was baby-sitting. My chest constricted and my ears began to heat up. Sally Chesterfield had become a very beautiful girl. She was much taller, and her high-pronounced cheekbones reminded me of Joni Mitchell's. Sally stood defiantly at the end of the driveway, turned slightly away, ready to deflect any unwanted attention. Don't you see me? I'm back, I wanted to shout to her. Of course, I wanted to kiss like before. Maybe now we could finish what we had started in Andie's mother's bedroom that last night before I left. Wow, that would make two wonderful chicks in two days!

Sally never bothered to turn her lithe wonderful body all the way round to face me. Instead, she mirrored Skip. She seemed annoyed at the interruption. She and Skip moved further up the driveway where I could not hear them talk. A few minutes later he was ready to leave. "She looks great, doesn't she?" said Skip. "Too bad you didn't write her."

"Yes," I said, too stunned to confront him. Was that it? Was that all I could expect from her? Yes.

Skip drove around the corner to another part of the same subdivision and stopped the car. Another good-looking girl with dark features was suddenly at the window. She bubbled over, dying how happy she was to finally see me again. I looked at her closely, trying to remember. But I was thinking of Sally. "Don't you remember me?" the pretty girl beamed.

"I'm sorry," I said. "I don't"

"Oh well," and then she said something to Skip and excused herself to go back inside her house.

"Man, you can't do that to a chick," said Skip.

"I couldn't remember who she was. She looked so different. Who was that?"

"Wendy Zadren," he went on. "That's really rude."

The name was vaguely familiar. Too bad I had scared her off. She looked hot. I wondered, was Skip trying to set me up with Wendy or what?

"Didn't you learn nothing about chicks over there?" he persisted. He was beginning to remind me of Laszlo, the way he could act like a mean father, the way he kept me from what I wanted. I hated it.

We drove around a little more, and then Skip told me he had some things to do, and would see me later. I was sure he was going to turn around and go get Sally.

I walked up Front Street to stop in at Rea & Derricks drug store to have a cherry coke with a paper straw. Didn't Skip care about Andie anymore? I guess not. Maybe that's why Andie was so happy to see me. It was her vengeance. I was kind of glad we had switched partners. Still, Sally was incredibly beautiful. A goddess. My straw-house had started to collapse. Clearly, I'd never see Sally again, but did Andie really love me?

I went back to the Dive-bombers' in the rain and called Andie at work. She said we should just meet at the Y later on that evening. I told her what had happened, how Skip, and especially Sally, were so cold. Andie said they thought they were better than us, and she wouldn't give either one of them the time of day. Skip had confessed to Andie that he had wanted Sally ever since she was introduced as my new potential girlfriend three years ago. They fought about Sally all the time, she said. He had waited until I left, and then started making his moves on Sally, Andie said. But Sally hadn't given in, until now.

"They just started dating about a week ago," she said over the crackling phone. The storm was making it hard to hear. "I think it had something to do with you coming back," she said.

I stared at Zizi the poodle's rubber chew toys piled in a box in the corner of the living room. "Maybe we won't stay long at the Y," she said, "just in case they show up."

The band sucked. We only stayed for a few songs and since it had stopped raining for a while, we decided to go for a walk. Both of us were hungry to romp some more, but there was no place to go. We ducked into a few dark spots here and there to kiss, but the town was small, and getting caught, even kissing, meant grist for the rumor mill. The only place I could think of where we might get it on was the Pine Grove Cemetery.

Andie pulled back on my hand when she saw I was leading her into the graveyard. "Oh, I don't know. This is scary. This place has always creeped me out."

"Come on," I coaxed her, and I pulled her past the wrought-iron gate. After one delicious fuck with her I had decided she was mine to lead. I searched for the darkest hollow. We were going to do it again, because we had done it before. That's how it works. But when I laid her down, landing between two soggy graves, and began tugging at her jeans while kissing her neck, Andie resisted. "Slow down," she told me. But I wanted to see more of that harvest. I wanted to inspect this thing of hers that I had done so little to cultivate. I wanted to see what it looked like inside. I wished I had brought a flashlight.

"Let's just kiss a while," she said. And so, for what seemed like forever, we rolled around over someone's old bones as we negotiated the pace. When, at last, she let me unzip her jeans, she told me that it was on condition that I understood she didn't want to go all the way there on somebody's grave. Day after day she had walked by those same graves we were romping on.

Maybe she had learned to respect the spirits, to fear their ret-ribution.

"Come on, Andie, Why not do it here?" I teased her. "It could be fun."

"It's just too weird."

I sat up, acting dejected, and leaned against a tombstone and secretly tried to think about what she must be feeling. I could respect that it was too weird. I turned around to see if I could read the stone. Nothing. Too dark. We didn't even know whose bones we would be doing it on top of.

"All right, " I said. "I've got another idea."

She seemed to know what was coming next, and she helped me lower her jeans and underwear down to her ankles. She lay there cuffed like that, and asked me not to hover above her. I should hold her, or just go ahead and do it

I hesitated. Under the night sky her leaf was very dark like wine. I half-expected her to taste the same way, but instead, she tasted more like pickled sea-monkeys. I had had a small plastic aquarium of them in Key West and another one in Berwick. Someone told me they were really called "brine shrimp" and that you could eat them. I liked the taste of Andie much more. She seemed to like what I was doing down there, but after a while, she told me she preferred I just hold her. I hugged her a bit, but I wanted her to taste me, too. I scooted next to her and pulled down my pants. The ground was cold and wet on my naked butt. I could see how uncomfortable all this had been for her. Andie's mouth was warm and wet on my silly stick. I soon forgot where I was, who she was, who I was, and there was no pain. Just mois-ture, warmth, a wet gentle pressure. And all of a sudden, my body began to tremble, and then it passed. I climbed back to her and sat up.

"Thank you," I said, nearly weeping. "You are so nice to me." And for some reason, I remembered the loss of Lainey. Dammit! Why wouldn't she go away? I couldn't get her out of my head no matter what I did. I looked guiltily back at Andie. I wanted to kiss her again, but I did not know what had happened to the sperm. Better not risk it.

We pulled up our pants and she asked me to walk her to the other end of the cemetery, because she was tired and wanted to go home. At the east-end gate she made me kiss her in spite of where her mouth had been. I turned around with a clownish spin and ran back the way I had come. I passed the same graves, and then stopped at ours and smiled. "Andie's really cool," I said to myself softly.

I walked down the two blocks to the Dive-bomber house. They were still up, excited about the news. Had they seen us? "Yeppert," Dive-bomber Grandma said. "Got a hurricane by the name of Agnes a-headed our way."

It didn't feel like a hurricane. It didn't feel like Donna or Betsy or even any of the smaller ones. It was too quiet. "Are you sure?" I asked.

"Of course, I'm sure, young man," she protested. "Came right up through Florida, too. Maybe you ought to call your folks."

"Yeah, I was planning on heading out day after tomorrow."

"You call your folks, ya hear?" Mr. Dive-bomber Senior grumbled. It was the second thing after "Hello," he had said to me since I arrived.

But I waited.

I wanted to spend the day with Andie, but she said she was busy, and we couldn't see each other until later, when, as she suggested, she would take me to a guy who was selling an old violin for cheap. I had told her how much I loved music, and how Laszlo had busted my violin. She felt sorry for me, for what had happened. I didn't tell her the violin belonged to the school or that we had been tripping.

Andie borrowed her mother's car, and she took me out to the violin guy's trailer. He, opened the case which looked like a little coffin. The violin was resting inside like a corpse in an advanced state of decay.

"I know it's beat up," he said. "But I'm only asking 20 bucks for it."

"I'm sure I could get it fixed in DC. I'll be passing through there in a couple of days," I said, trying to sound adult and worldly.

I paid the man, and felt my career was just beginning again.

Andie dropped me off and only kissed me lightly. "Too many neighbors," she whispered.

I forgot about calling Dad, but figured he wouldn't mind if I showed up late. It had been six years since he and Mom had split. What difference would another day make? Besides, I wasn't ready to think about him just yet. Tomorrow, I'd call for sure.

But by morning Hurricane Agnes had curved back toward Pennsylvania, and the Susquehanna Valley was under water. All phone lines were down and the river continued to rise. I got nervous. I walked down to the bus station to ask when I could get a ride out. Better leave right away. But the station was closed.

Someone saw me looking in the window. He offered, "No buses leaving. None arriving either on account of this storm. All the roads are flooded out," he said.

I walked over to where Andie worked and told her the news.

"Wow, that's great," she said. "Looks like you might be here for a while, yet."

She took her lunch break early, but, instead of going somewhere to eat, we wanted to be with the rest of the town, down at the Nescopeck bridge where we could watch the river swirl.

"The radio said the storm's just northeast of us," Andie reported. Still, there was no howling. There were only heavy rains, mostly somewhere else, and the river was rising and rising. We seemed out of harm's way high up on the Berwick plateau. From the Nescopeck bridge we could see that the little islands forming the foundation of the old wooden bridge had been covered over completely. In fact, the Susquehanna had swollen over its banks and drowned the railroad tracks. Did the hobos still hang out down there? Were our forts okay? I hoped the hobos made it out in time.

From the bridge, we saw the flood debris come racing downstream and crash into the concrete pilings directly below us. Most of the junk was branches, and, once in a while, there was a whole tree. We even saw a refrigerator floating along like a small boat that had lost its captain. But it was too rusted up to be from someone's house. Andie said it was probably a fish smoker. Hurricane Agnes was just cleaning up the river banks of all the crap people had abandoned, we thought.

Andie had to go back to work, and she said we couldn't meet later because her mom wanted her to stay home and help take care of her little brothers. She'd heard we might have to evacuate. I figure I'd better go back and help out the Dive-bombers. I knew they would be worrying and angry.

It rained hard all night long, and it made me feel happy, I was clean and warm and relatively safe.

Andie came over to the Dive-bombers' the next morning and asked if I wanted to volunteer at the Salvation Army. I said as long as I could be with her, and she liked hearing that. It was true. She was so much fun to hang out with. We laughed and flirted, and, also, for a couple of hours the two of us loaded up trucks with donated clothes, and we felt real good together.

When we got tired of volunteering and were ready to leave, I asked someone where the stuff we loaded was going.

"Up to Wilkes-Barre. They're hurtin' pretty bad up there. Got 18 feet above flood stage," the volunteer said. I wondered about Billy: Had he got his wish? Was he able to let the waters roll over him? For one clear moment in my mind I saw him floating down the Susquehanna atop his new, improved Steinway, the ghost of his grandmother guiding him down into the muck.

Andie and I went to the bridge again. We couldn't believe how much the river had risen. Now, more than branches floated past us. The wrack of people's lives bobbed and raced away under the bridge. Slabs of painted wooden walls, toys of bright plastic sinking and then rising again in the churning brown flow, a dresser whose drawers had burst out to show daisy-patterned contact-paper floated down the river. With each marvelous passing the crowd on the high bridge "ooed" and "ahhed" at the baptizing spectacle below. The bloating death around us was still too abstract for most. Then something truly astounding floated our way — a house's roof bobbed into view, and careened toward the pilings. The roof surged higher up and revealed the face of two windows and a door. Silently, it passed beneath us. We ran to the other side of the bridge and saw it emerge down river, an entire house rocking away from us.

Andie wanted to leave immediately. We walked away from the river, and a couple of blocks away she stopped me and raised her head with tears in her eyes. I kissed her, but with all that was going on it seemed stupid to ask if she wanted to make love. Besides, there was still no place for us to go. Because of the flood, her mom was off work. I kissed her and when Andie lowered herself back down from her tiptoes, I finally understood that she was distraught.

"What's the matter, Andie?"

"I don't know. It just made me feel so sad to see that house floating away. Those poor people," she cried.

"Yes," I said, and I hugged her for a while. But in that moment, the rain began falling with a vengeance. Slowly, as we tried to ignore the onslaught, we walked back most of the way to her house.

"Better not come any further," she said.

I lowered my head.

"I'll pick you up, tomorrow," she called out after me. "You want to go help out again?"

"Sure," I said, and I turned back around and walked toward the cemetery.

The next day we heard the river at Wilkes-Barre had begun to subside, but 10 miles south, Bloomsburg was still 12 feet above flood stage. That was my direction out, whenever the gate finally opened. I was getting restless.

I went to volunteer at the Salvation army, but my heart was no longer in it. Most of the danger seemed to have passed. Andie and I kissed each other after a few hours work, and we went home separately. I spent the rest of the day napping, and I felt lonely again. I even offered Zizi my toes to lick.

Another day passed without Andie. It had been a week since I left Frankfurt. It looked like I would be able to leave for Florida the following day. I was impatient. I saw Andie, and she was friendly, but when we kissed there seemed little left for us to exchange. I guessed our desire, too, had washed away. I hated the world. And so,

I waited.


On the 27th of June, 1972, the phone line had been repaired, and I called Dad. My sister answered the phone.

"Where have you been?" she asked. "We've been worried sick about you. Dad called the Red Cross and the Pennsylvania State Patrol."

"I'm all right."

"We didn't know what had happened to you," she said.

I explained that I had been stuck, and that I was catching a Greyhound that morning and would be in Florida in a few days.

Andie cried when I kissed her for the last time there at the depot. It had to be on the cheek since the Dive-bombers were watching. I wondered what had happened between all of us. I tried, but I couldn't make any sense of it. Part of me didn't want to know. I just wanted to get on the bus and go.

"I hope you get your violin fixed," Andie said.

"Thanks," I said. And maybe because of our loss, we both whispered our love.

The first bus out originated in Wilkes-Barre. It followed the same route I had taken before on my way to Florida — along the

Susquehanna Valley to Harrisburg and then on to DC. Nobody on the bus wanted to talk. We travelled to the sound of the low-humming splash and shifting gears. The river had dropped about 20 feet in a few days. In some places we rode over mud that still covered the road. From bank to bank a brown path of ruin and grief stained what was left of the greenery. At least 50 people had died. It was said to have been the worst natural disaster in Pennsylvania's history. In my mind, I saw Andie crying again, soaking the ruined houses along the river bank with tears. I felt bad for them all. Part of me wished that somehow I could have stayed with her. But how? Those wrecked houses did not belong to me, and Berwick was not my home either.

# Orange Greenery

---

I looked up from my grubbin' hoe. I could see combed rows of orange trees, green with no fruit yet — parallel and slightly rising far off in the distance. I'd been hacking at sucker roots all day. Once I reached the crest again, I knew I would have to turn around and work back in the opposite direction. I dragged my grubbin' hoe tree to tree, handsaw hanging out my back pocket, hacking and chopping, sawing sucker roots. Sometimes the branches met the ground, forming a gumdrop, and the dark green cave bid me crawl inside. Oh, I was ready to back out in a hurry if I startled another snake or armadillo or I mistakenly found the origin of the world. Most days nothing rustled or jumped or coiled up, and the great canopies offered several brief, I mean 30 seconds, escape from the sun.

"Hoe up them weeds," they told me. "Saw off any sprouts that mightn't stunt they growth. And you damn well better keep up."

Of course, the old timers passed me on the first row up. They called themselves "old-timers," but they just looked that way. Most of them were in their 30s or 40s. Maybe. They weren't quite sure. The work had beaten them down, but bad. Nobody would have been surprised to hear one morning, "Ol' Joe Bob passed on last night. Guess he 'uz just worn out."

We'd meet at the 7-11 before dawn. A rusted red farm truck picked us up and took us out to the groves. The truck bed had a roof over it, so some workers liked to sit way back on the dark benches inside, where they could steal a half hour of bumpy sleep. I sat near the tail end, where leaky exhaust thinned in the breeze and it was a little easier to breathe.

As the sun came up, we jumped and bounced and rolled down a sandy road. I stared at the narrow slice of crab grass and sand spurs rolling away beneath us. The ground sometimes twisted, waved and turned in ways that didn't seem logical. I figured these displays of swirling insubstantial earth were either acid flashbacks, or the truth revealed to me, or both. It worried me a little to watch this show, because the ground only stopped undulating if I closed my eyes for a minute, then forced myself not to stare.

Every so often, I'd be playing this game when the truck abruptly stopped. An old-timer, that tall muscular black fellow, would jump out the passenger side of the cab and aim his shotgun at an armadillo or a 'possum crawling through the high poke salad.

"I got eight *younguns*," I heard him explain as he got back in without getting off a shot, and we quickly pulled away. "Can't feed 'em on the minimum what I makes here."

I later asked how armadillo and 'possum tasted. He told me "'Possum's real greazy. And that armadillo, hims got bouta million bones. Still, they's good eatin."

There was a white fellah about my age they called "Professah," because he was the only one of them that could tell time.

"Hey, Professah, what time's it gotten to be?" somebody would shout after we'd been in the grove a while.

"Let's see here," he'd say, letting his hoe rest against his leg. "The big hand's just past the three, and that little one there, well, he's clear 'round to the nine."

"You reckon it's time for a smoke, Professah?"

"Seem so to me." And everyone would let his hoe fall to the sand where he stood and pull out his "P. A.," that is to say, his Prince Albert loose-cut tobacco from its bright red tin.

"Ya'll better watch for that straw boss, now," the nervous, stooped one would always say. "Hain't been but a little bit since we smoked that last one."

And that would start them talking about the big blue car the "straw-boss" snooped around in.

"That ain't no Cadillac."

"The hell it ain't"

Sometimes we'd have contests to see who could roll a P. A. faster with just their hands, or with one of those little red machines that came with the tin. I tried both. I liked rolling with the magical machine, but the feel of paper and tobacco in my hands soothed the constant bug bites. Either way I rolled it, even with practice, it took me a while. I barely had time enough to smoke before the break was called too long for their comfort; and the hoes went up on the shoulders.

Dad got me the job through his work at Lykes-Pasco, the sprawling stinker orange processing plant on the north side of Dade City. All the plants in town were run by a steaming den of incestuous landlords. They and their cousins farted out so sweetly-sick the basis of the local economy. Dad wasn't related. He was in sales and computers. He was high up enough that I was protected from being fired or even reprimanded by the straw boss when it became clear I couldn't work as fast as the other grove workers. Once they found out my dad was a "big shot," the others began to resent me — they thought I might be a spy — and so kept me at a safe distance from most of their conversations.

Dad lent me enough to buy a motorcycle, a used little Kawasaki 90, and I didn't have to ride in the truck anymore. I savored zipping along in the early mornings, the fog splitting and scattering around me. And then, in the afternoons, the wind cooled as I returned home gritty and sore.

One morning I followed the 'possum truck out to an old blighted grove. We were told that the whole gray, haunting forest had to come out of there. That meant I was to walk along in back of a tractor and hack away with an ax at all the roots the plow couldn't pull up. Already the crew leaders had lit huge bonfires of piled up dead trees that blazed across the wasted field and baked the red summer morning. The cloudless sky choked with black smoke billowing toward the sun. It must have been 95 degrees with the air humidity-saturated at 7 a.m. I looked around and thought we must have landed in the hell Maw-maw had threatened would eventually consume all but the chosen few.

We weren't allowed to take breaks that day because we had to "keep up and get the job done." Before long I was getting dizzy and hallucinating again, and I could hardly swing the ax. I stumbled over the wrecked earth chopping as best I could until, blessed relief, I swung the ax into my ankle.

Now, you'd think that would have been enough excuse for me to take a break, or maybe even go to a doctor, but straw bosses were everywhere. They only conceded to let me rest by pulling snake-infested vines off the few healthy trees. I didn't like the idea of pulling a snake down on top of me, so, I just gave up. I collapsed in the sand, took my sweaty blue bandanna from my neck and bandaged my ankle. I sat there for a few more minutes with my rake in my lap. The ground eventually stopped swaying, and I hopped on my motorcycle and rode off to what I thought was forever.

By the time I reached town, I was delirious with what I thought was sweet unemployment. Then, I was riding under a tropical storm that had suddenly opened up. I drank up the in-flight bath with "whoops" and "yahoos." But I was having a hard time seeing the road, so I pulled over at the high school.

There it was for me: the institutionalized future. The ugly machinery would start up in a few weeks. I was just about to escape back into the storm when I spotted a red-headed lovely decorating for the school's opening sock hop. There was hope again, and I felt shy. I felt I had to explain myself standing before her, soaking wet, a blue bandanna sticking out of my tennis shoe. Her name was Jeanne Bendlocker.

"Let me look at that," she cooed. She found that my ax wound wasn't too serious, though no one could doubt the event must have been very dramatic, and told me I should still see a doctor in case of infection. Did I know she worked in the groves, too? She worked in the nursery. She got her job with her daddy's help, just like I had. Maybe we would see each other out there under the hot summer sun. I guessed I was going back there after all.

When our grove crew was finally put over to the nursery — our job was to stake and prune seedlings — I saw her working at the far end of the field. When we had a break, she came over to say hello. She looked wonderful — halter top and cut-offs and full of smiles. She reminded me of Andie Carnelian back in Berwick.

By the way, I got a letter from Andie warning me she was going to get married to a guy who lived in Minnesota if I didn't respond quickly and affectionately. Although I didn't realize she had loved me so much. But I never wrote back.

I decided to linger out in the nursery field by Jeanne, but the break was short, just time enough to get a drink of water; someone had spotted the blue Cadillac sedan. "Fire in the hoe," I heard one of the crew shout. "Fire in the hoe."

And I decided, that Jeanne would be my new girlfriend. But though she still seemed interested, not much came of our promising start. I don't know why. Did it have something to do with our fathers came from competing sides of the county? We did kiss, at last, several months later in her very old curvy Chevy truck. The radio still worked, and we smooched, in secret, to the music fading away again.

Each day after work, I rode into Dade City and then north again past Lykes and what was left of the company-owned migrant worker shacks. First I'd ride six miles to Trilacoochee, between Trilby and Lacoochee.

Trilacoochee was a peeling-blue bar with a stack of beer cans out back that reached the roof. A cop hiding back there stopped me one night for riding with a burnt-out headlight. Dad and I had to appear at their cinder-block court dressed and mannered as conservatively as possible. Dad portrayed me as the purest angel who had made a little mistake; I was just a hard-working young man trying to make an honest buck to pay back my dad. We got off paying just court costs.

It was four miles further to the nothing development of Ridge Manor where Dad, my step-mother and I lived in an American Timber Home. My father had contracted it, and he intended to sell it someday in order to move upwards to the top-of-the-line model — according to the brochure, "a Swiss chalet in the Florida woods."

We lived in the split-level model on a small lake. Though I'd seen an alligator swimming there, the first thing I did when I rolled in was to walk straight into the lake and collapse. The bath was better than in a tub; it canceled out the day of sweat and mosquito bites and sore muscles. The murky brown hot water kissing the shoreline of tall grasses soothed me in a way that no porcelain tub could ever do. Every now and then, I paddled a funky whitewashed raft to the middle of the lake and smoked some pot. I had purchased it in downtown Orlando on one of my visits to Sam Apricot, of Watt, White, and Apricot fame. He had moved to Sanford, 70 miles from Ridge Manor. It was fun to take my rattling miniature motorcycle over to Sam's to see his familiar face and talk the jive and joke around the way we used to. But his life, like mine, was changing. He was "going into business" of some kind or other, and the past seemed to threaten him and, especially, his new girlfriend.

On the raft, I smoked the pot alone, and wrote letters to Frankfurt friends; I read in the sun, and relaxed. Soon school would begin, and I could then quit the groves without shame or reprimand.

My father did not quite know what to do with me. He did not have a lot of experience playing at the role of father. He hadn't been a son to his father either, who he never really knew. His step-father, the Southern Baptist preacher, was prone to torment my dad with Christ. Dad left the day he graduated from high school. He checked into the Y and never looked back. When it came time for him to be the responsible papa, he was usually off selling something. And after the divorce, it was often my sister who took care of him, and not the other way around. He was clearly bewildered as a father; he covered for it by being witty and otherwise remaining aloof. Yes, I was treated politely, the way a guest would be, and I certainly preferred that to a kick in the ribs. But I wanted more. Again, I wanted affection, solace, and gentle guidance. I was back home again didn't know what the hell to do. I wished for a map, a guide to slip under my pillow when I slept. I needed a truth fairy to guide me: wisdom in exchange for my two remaining baby teeth. But my hide had thickened. I knew that. And when Dad approached me with his first efforts at discipline — curfews, restricted territory and the like — I took it as more repression and simply ignored his directives. It was too late to control me. I had struggled for liberation, and what remained was a weak child inside, and a stubborn, resilient young man on the outside, one riddled with guilt for abandoning his sobbing mother. I was insecure, constantly in search of a woman's caress and, I believed, the harbor of her vagina. I was tense and anxious, and I kept others desperately nearby, yet at a safe enough distance, with a jocularity that was both aggressive and translucently hostile, just like Dad. Given the odds of understanding me, my father no longer had a chance.

As the ugly school days quickly approached, my step-mother took me to the Dade City Army-Navy store to get me suited up. I pleaded with her to buy me an Air Force jump suit I found that was striped with zippers, and that fit me like a bag. She eventually said she would, on the condition I not wear it to school. I promised, waited a week, and then wore it to school anyway. Festooned with wires sticking out of every zipper, save the dastardly one, I wanted to make an impression. I had to establish my defiance, attract and repel.

No matter what my neurosis, I felt a continuous need to dissolve repressive civilization through wit. Two teachers, in their 40s or 50s, who had recently married each other, were threatened with the loss of their jobs for holding hands as they strolled from class to class. The administration feared their display of love and affection would set a bad example for the children. With shit like that threatening to choke us all, I was compelled to struggle for liberty and fun. Besides, the easiest way for me to jump through hoops at the high school circus was to play the clown. I did not want more biology. I did not want an incompetent music theory teacher who could not even play the piano. I did not want to be strapped into the required indoctrination for all Florida students in a course called "Americanism vs Communism." I was impotent except for my hi-jinx, and I dreamed of omnipotence.

Jump Suit Man immediately paid off. I was approached by a couple of  guys who looked like jocks; I expected some more abuse. Instead, one of them said, "We would like to invite you to a feast in the woods." I was skeptical at first. What did they want to do, marinate me in Budweiser then roast me on a spit?

"Why?" I asked.

"We need a jester. We think you're funny."

For the occasion, I dressed in a cape made from a blanket dripped with multi-colored waxes and sparkly things. I hauled out the old knee-high Gyrorab sneakers, and added a few tropical touches — palm frond appendages and plastic fruit and such. On the glorious feast night in the woods, I sang Zappa's "Willie the Pimp," hopping from live oak to live oak. I screamed for joy, running and whirling across a clearing in the groves. I honked at a tuba, hanging out the sunroof of a Volkswagen bug. The driver, who had been careless enough to step over into the jester world and thereby lost any hope his friends would ever take him seriously, drove the two of us wildly around and around until he rammed us into some swampy muck where we sank up to the axles. "So what?" he screamed. We ran back and leapt onto the feast table, high-stepping to avoid a foot in a pie or spill the oil lamps.

As for the main dish, I borrowed a twenty-gallon cast-iron pot that we suspended on a tripod over a fire, and in it I prepared Transylvanian goulash. It was delicious — boned pork in tomato sauce, lots of caraway and sauerkraut and topped with sour cream. And there were all kinds of fruit and cheeses, roasted foul, and cakes, and fresh baked breads. I imagine we looked like the cover of the Rolling Stone's Beggar's Banquet album, and if that was true, the thing to do was to toss apples into the air and catch them onto the blades of sharp knives. So we did.

We danced, too. Well, some of us did. The butcher's son who had provided the pork for the goulash slowly began to loosen up, but not his girlfriend, or her girlfriend either. Yet, a few girls were persuaded to sway and sashay and sing until, too soon, all the fun had exhausted itself, and the spell slipped away; we fell back into the dull world. Too soon we returned to being students who never spoke to each other in the halls. It was understood. That was how it should be, we guessed. We were only friends for that feast night. At school we denied each other's existence.

Nevertheless, to my surprise, a site for a second feast was selected next to the Withlacoochee River of black-vein water and gray mossy-treed banks. There was no goulash and less of a costume. In fact, I stripped bare-butt naked and danced on top of somebody's car that night. Below me, I noticed even some of the more strait-laced girls were enjoying the spectacle in a kind of understated tittering way. Although I hoped and wished for it, no one else wanted to get naked.

That night, a rosy-faced jock brought his father's sword. Maybe, it was from the Civil War, he said. He was crazily stabbing the damn thing into the ground while I danced on top of the car. At the cue of some frenetic guitar rift was jamming out on the stereo, I leapt from the hood just at the moment Johnny Rebel decided to stab the alleged phantom Yankee. And the sword went into my poor Georgian-born foot. Oh, but not to worry. The girl I wanted to kiss the most that night, nursed me with warm concern, hugs and a bandage, and a sweet peck on the cheek. I struggled to stay soft-cocked in the darkness, bleeding for her. "Take off your clothes," I whispered. And she blushed so hotly sweet.

Alas, that was the end of it. In fact, the feast folks committee decided our little parties were getting out of hand. In fact, by the next day, our night's revelry had again slipped into the folds of secret dark memory. At best, we feasters permitted ourselves only subtle grins of acknowledgment. And my beautiful nurse didn't dare kiss me again if she cared anything for her reputation.

Well. Sure. Helen Ljungbe did write me from New College in Sarasota, asking me to come visit. New College was having a Palm Court party. Maybe I should give her another try, I thought. But when I arrived, she quickly introduced me to her boyfriend, a huge Viking with a great red beard and long outrageous hair. Nice guy. He asked me a lot of flattering questions about my interests. Before the party, we went to see him perform in *The Bacchae*. He could act. He played the messenger who frantically reported the arrival of Dionysos and the horrible acts  the god's followers had committed. But what I most remember is that when he passionately delivered his speech, spit flew everywhere, and was caught magically in the stage lights, like arching diamond threads.

The Palm Court party was raucous. Someone had filled plastic garbage cans with orange juice and vodka, not my favorite drink. Of course it reminded me of runny scrambled eggs and past loves. Just dip it out; don't puke it up, I told myself. I danced with Helen, and in between songs, she talked about how she and her Viking  planned to write a sleazy best-seller romance to make some money. They were smart. I knew they could do it. Everyone around that place was smart. It intimidated the hell out of me.

I admit, I hoped for signs of trouble between Helen and her boyfriend, but I couldn't find much. We met another time in St. Pete to see a *Yes* concert and I sensed no real discontent then either. Helen swayed to the music in those ultra-tight corduroys while smiling and caressing her man. When I heard the words "Alone is no adventure," sung over and over, I wished I hadn't run away from Helen back in Frankfurt, when I had the chance to be still, to learn to love her. Man, I wish I'd written earlier, back before she met her perfect Viking.

One day at school, a guy, tall and thin like an I-beam, asked if I wanted to be in his movie. He looked straight out of the movies himself. Way up on top of him was a head of white hair, *and* he had an angular Germanic face. Would I do it? Would I play the co-pilot to his friend, Jack?

"He's the perfect ham to play an anti-hero, circa 1944," he said.

"Sure, I will," I said.

"Can you meet us tomorrow? We need to shoot some scenes out in Lacoochee."

"Yes. Yes, of course," I said.

And, all of a sudden, I had a new friend by the name of Claude Duval.

We spent several days filming in the jungle. It did not at all resemble the Rhein-Land, though we often felt we were working behind enemy lines. Claude said the film was to be called *War Hero*. He shot it in black and white to resemble an old B movie, and so he could "experiment with textures of light." I liked that idea.

When not working on a new scene for the movie, a bunch of people could be found hanging out at Claude's place. He lived in a converted garage in front of his mom's day care center. The middle of the room was dominated by an undulant water bed. It was best just to lie back and talk and listen to music. Once, Claude told me, he had a girl over, they were making out, and when they paused for a breather, fluorescent tube came crashing down on her head. It didn't hurt her, and the bed didn't pop either, but the two of them broke up, and everyone took the story as a sign that strange powers occupied that room.

I was treated to a whole stack of listening pleasures in Claude's room. Van Morrison growled like a lion and sang about TB sheets, proving that a love song can be written about anything. Dan Hicks and his very Hot Licks complained that

"Moody Richard" was just an innocent bystander, the kind of man we swore we'd never let ourselves become. And Randy Newman let us see the Cuyahoga River spontaneously combust in Cleveland, burning on through the night. Claude joked about Mick Jagger trying to imitate a southern accent, and he wondered about Stevie Wonder's imagery of colors and the beauty of things Stevie couldn't actually see. Leon Russell was up on a "Tight Rope" and sang a "Manhattan Island Serenade." I loved his *Carney* album. Leon Russell wrote "Out in the Woods," after his Zulu backup singers told him that in their language it was impossible to be *lost* in the woods. "How wonderful! I can be anywhere, go wherever I want and never be lost," I shouted. Claude told me he was the only white boy at the Ike and Tina Turner concert. When they played "Rolling on the River," he said it had to be the Withlacooche they were singing about.

Claude performed "The Entertainer" on the piano out in the daycare center. Other times, Jack, my pilot, strummed a guitar and I sang, blew the harmonica, or faked a few notes on my newly restored fiddle. One day, Kate and Julia, two beautiful girls, surprised us at Claude's, dressed in very seductive nurse uniforms, with their interpretation of "Stop in the name of Love." Then they went backstage (the laundry room) and changed into country-western garb to perform "Funny Face," scrunching up their faces at the chorus and losing control, swore they'd pee their pants, and had to start the song over several times.

Claude and I had a lot to talk about, and I immediately trusted him. When I ventured to tell him about my weird arrival in America, he not only listened, but delighted in all the details. He wanted me to tell it to him dramatically, and I did. "You should write that down," he said, and I did. I told him about Mom's performance in *Streetcar*, and he told me that Tennessee Williams was the playwright he admired the most. He said he could relate to the character Tom in *The Glass Menagerie* because Claude, too, had always escaped to the movies. And, by the way, did I know that until a few years before, they made Blacks sit up in the balcony at Dade City's only cinema? "If you sat below them, you'd get pelted with vengeful volleys of popcorn and Red Hots."

"Do you remember the bathrooms marked 'Men,' 'Women,' and 'Colored'!" I asked.

"Oh yeah," Claude sighed.

"And the cool Oasis water fountains with a sign over them saying 'White' and then a bend-down-low rusty spout attached to its side marked 'Colored'?"

Claude shook his head. I could see the sorrow in his eyes.

I went on. "You know what my mother used to say to me?" I imitated her southern accent, "Son, never make friends with a Negro, because one day they's just as nice as they can be, and come the next, they'll turn 'round and stab you in the back!"

Claude stared at me for a moment, and then he said to me, "You're very bitter, aren't you?"

Several of us went to Tampa to see *Cabaret,* the play. I told Claude I would love to play the role of the Emcee someday. I'd do it the way Joel Gray had, but a little more bizarre, more raunchy, maybe. In the meantime, we got the score and worked up "The Money Song" and a few others. Claude was fascinated with decadent Berlin in the 20s. He wished he had been there. He taught me about the *Weimar Republik* and *Bauhaus*, and I grabbed every book I could find on the subject. Eventually, I spun off with Bauhaus theater and landed back home in the lap of Dada. That was the thing, to be an iconoclast. Creative destruction. Any way to chop through the mundane and the dogmatic. Fuck heaven and hell, I wanted to go beyond myself, beyond my fears. Was that Zen? But I did not want to engender more terror and lying hope. I could see me traveling the way the Beats had done. Wandering around in the chaos, loving it all to death.

I tried to explain to Claude about Nutritional Neurosis, and again, he suggested I write it down. This is what I came up with:

A universal deprivation of brotherhood has become apparent among humans recently, thus provoking a frantic search for intimate relationships with inanimate objects. Certain persons disgusted with their counterparts have, in this search, become deeply involved with their daily nutrients to the point that some persons have deemed neurotic. They have produced wondrously intriguing devotion to their victuals and have become so extremely satisfied with these relationships that the fantasy of "Nutritional Neurosis" as a means of *comogonal* delight and harmony is rapidly becoming a reality.

"Wonderful," he said. "Now I get it. What's 'comogonal'? Is that like communal and. . . what?"

"I can't remember if I looked it up, or just made it up. But yeah, sure, it's communal and common. Maybe."

By the next day, Claude had started his own Nut Neuro series by dipping pictures, such as one of an ornate chocolate cake from *Good Housekeeping,* into acetone and rubbing them onto watercolor paper. He called it "American Gothic." It was beautiful. He made several others and gave the fainter prints to me to write scripts and stories on. And I did.

# Jiggling

We decided to make a short film called *Lunch* in between filming the more complicated *War Hero* scenes. We gave ourselves one Super 8 cartridge, just 50 feet of film that we promised not to edit, to make my horror of Dive-bomber peas flying in Key West come to life through the persistence of vision. Some of the script read like this:

*[Menu consisting of one large plate of peas with small deep red pimento complement is brought to the dinette table.]*

*[Consumer proceeds slowly, isolating each pea, then tasting, smelling, and finally devouring.]*

*[Gradual increase of dosage — double, quadruple, etc., — with attitude of consumer changing from boredom to interest to fascination and climaxing with a frenzy of rapid consumption.]*

*[Once this frenzy occurs, a violent, abrupt fascination should be displayed, and then the consumer attacks the entire plate of peas and suddenly hurls them at the camera.]*

*[Final shot of peas and glass and pimento scattered about kitchen, panning to consumer who sits at table with original glum expression.]*

For the part, I greased my hair back with vegetable oil and darkened the circles under my eyes. When we got the film back from Tampa we were very happy with the results, especially the long pan revealing the thousands of frozen peas strewn across Jack's mother's kitchen floor.

One night, Claude and I came up with another Nut Neuro scheme to be called *The Capers of Alfredo Fettuccini*. There would be twenty-four one-minute capers, each rolled on a separate spool and distributed in a case of four six-packs. I wrote out two of the capers. The first was called *José Torpedo Discovers Plumber's Island* wherein, the scenario read:

*several persons are intermingled with plastic and metal plumbing in a tropical potted-palm setting. The people are stagnant; rigor mortis has set in. The only movement is of José dressed in large garden hosés waders and a mask. He is squirting water out of hoses in frantic fashion — dousing plumbing (flesh and other) with water turning to blood.*

The second caper had Alfredo cast as *a "curious college-type youngster" who strolls a kitchen looking for excitement in dust balls. Behind the refrigerator he discovers a most rewarding collection, but, in his enthusiasm, trips the cord to the fridge. The door flies open, revealing a time-lapse of Tomato Bisque rotting — soundtrack of screams.*

Claude and I made collages from old National Geographics, creating our own worlds of juxtaposed places and dissolved time. And while we were busy shuffling around images, Claude introduced me to another kind of music — Lou Reed sang about heroin and strange chicks named Holly Woodlawn and Candy Darling. Claude explained that they weren't really chicks, but drag queens. Okay. I could see that. I listened to *T. Rex* and *Mott the Hoople*, but some of the best rocking sounds were from David Bowie. Claude had me listen to a strange song about Andy Warhol, and showed me pictures of the soup cans, Marilyn Monroe and Andy Warhol, himself. He said Andy Warhol was his favorite artist and that he wanted to emulate him.

I liked everything Claude introduced me to, but something about David Bowie made me uncomfortable. On the cover of Bowie's *Hunky Dory* there was a picture of a good-looking woman, — I was really attracted to her — but then I realized it was probably a man.

"Yes, I'm sure that's Bowie," said Claude.

"But why'd he do that?" Claude wouldn't answer. He showed me another picture of Bowie on an album called *Ziggy Stardust and the Spiders from Mars*. I had to admit, he looked really cool. And the music, the music knocked me out. On the back of the cover it said, "TO BE PLAYED AT MAXIMUM VOLUME," and so we did. Mick Ronson's screaming guitar solo at the end of "Moonage Daydream" launched me every time. And I could never sit still listening to "Star" or "Suffragette City." I got into Bowie's fantasy of blasting out beyond forever. I could derive a little bit of hope, in spite of myself, from the idea of being watched over by extraterrestrials, but a lot of the lyrics confused me. Part of the time he was singing about making it with women and sometimes with guys. How could it be both ways? Who or what was "she" to Bowie, anyway? I was afraid to ask.

So much wasn't clear, and, on the spur of the moment, we decided to show off a part of that ambiguity of appearances in the last scene of *War Hero*. As Claude slowly revealed the plot I understood that Jack's character and mine had been shot down behind enemy lines. Jack and I were wounded and Jack's character left me for dead. A lovely German maiden, played by Kate, nursed Jack's character  back to health in more ways than one, and then returned to the allies to find his company. Meanwhile, the same gorgeous maiden, we called her Helga, discovered me still alive and took me back to her cabin *in der Wald*, which looked a lot like Jack's mom's shotgun house. And that was cut with exteriors featuring the jungles of the Withlacoochee. Anyway, Jack's character decides to desert and to return to love, so he heads back to his Helga. By this time, the viewer discovers that I am not dead, but in fact, am getting it on with the same Fraülein Helga.

Oh, I loved filming that scene. No sooner had gorgeous Kate and I jumped into bed than we started making out very passionately in front of everybody. Claude never had to say, "action," and we ignored his command to "cut." I could not believe how hot Kate/Helga was in the scene.

So, back to the plot; I was under the covers with Helga when we hear something outside. I grab my gun, thinking it's the enemy. The door bursts open, and I shoot and kill "Jack," the War Hero. The camera lingers over the horrifying scene for a while, but then Kate and I jump out of bed to reveal that we were fully clothed. It just *seemed* like we were naked: implied nudity. Jack stands up from death and shakes my hand. Claude pans around to show Jack's little brother holding the ciné light, and we all smile at the camera.

And where was Julia — Kate's best friend, the other nurse? Why wasn't that wonderful girl in the movie? Well, she came from a strict Catholic background, and declined to be in the film out of fear she would be caught and tortured. I wished I could have made out with her, too.

Kissinger announced, "Peace is at hand," and Nixon was re-elected in a landslide. Yet, within six weeks, Nixon conducted massive B-52 attacks on Hanoi and Haiphong, hitting many populated civilian areas and destroying a major hospital in the bargain. Kissinger explained that these bombings were a necessary brutal ending to assure South Vietnamese President Thieu's acquiescence to the peace agreement. Meanwhile, my friend Claude and I sat upstream from a gutter and wrote poems, in the rain, as fast as we could before the rain drops melted the ink away. Hitting the last period, we floated our protests down the stream and watched them disappear through the iron gate and sucked down the drain.

On the home front, things weren't too bad, but I felt increasingly uncomfortable and restless. Dad incessantly groaned at the length of my hair, and constantly preached about responsibility and career plans. And as if to show me what success meant, he and Step-mom were ready, at long last, to move up to the bigger, better American Timber Home. We would have to vacate Ridge Manor by New Year's and move into a trailer on the new property, while the Swiss chalet was being built.

It seemed like the perfect time to escape. I felt like an intruder, and I didn't think I should stick around to live in a small trailer. I would have just taken off, but thanks to my failing US History class in Frankfurt — I had refused to write 500 times, "I will refrain from using profanity in Mr. McCoy's class," I was one-half credit short of being allowed to graduate early. I don't know why I cared. I suppose my teachers had succeeded over the years in making me feel afraid of what would happen if I dropped out. A high school diploma would somehow protect me, they insisted. So I had to find a place to spin around a little longer before they released me.

Did I pursue Vermont? All I know is that Paul Underhill, my long-time traveling nemesis was up there and invited me to come stay with him and his older brother at his mom's house. His folks had just divorced, and Mrs. Underhill — she didn't want to change her name — suggested to my dad that it would be good for us boys to lend each other some moral support. Dad said he'd help me get the cheaper night-flight to Boston at Christmas.

Claude came out to the house at Ridge Manor a couple of times before I left. Once he was there when my sister was home on break from the University of South Florida. She was ironing and watching soap operas the way Mom used to do. The sight disturbed me. Our lives had decidedly drifted apart since the divorce five-and-a-half years ago. She had done well in high school as captain of her tennis club, and I think she was even a homecoming queen. Claude and I were hanging out in the kitchen above and behind her, while she ironed in the sunken living room. Sis was annoyed because we were talking too loudly.

Claude was upset that I was leaving so soon. "What about *War Hero*?" he asked.

"What about it?" I recoiled. I was sensitive to anything that sounded like criticism. "We're done shooting, aren't we?"

"Yeah, but it's not finished. We still have to work on the soundtrack and the editing."

"But you should do that, don't you think?" I said too loudly; my sister huffed over to turn up the TV. I rolled my eyes at Claude. "Look. I'll be back. It's not like I'm going to Vermont forever."

"You have to be back for the World Premiere Extravaganza," he said.

"Wouldn't miss it for the world," I said. And he and I began to make plans for what the extravaganza should include. While we planned, I got some cheese, baloney and mustard out of the refrigerator. I found some bread and made us some sandwiches. "We need a cake," I said. "A big one that a beautiful woman can jump out of."

"And music," Claude added. "Kate and Julia can work up with some numbers. And you gotta show *Lunch*, too."

"You think we should? This is about *War Hero*."

"It'll be the short."

I still had the mustard bottle in my hand, I looked at the fridge and felt inspired. I carefully cut out a half slice of baloney and a corner triangle from a cheese slice. I pasted them on the fridge with mustard, just so, and then gave it a good final squirt. Claude laughed at my very own DuchampPollockTzara. My sister turned around abruptly.

"You wouldn't do that if you had to clean it up," she said.

"You wouldn't say that if you had Nutritional Neurosis," I countered, and Claude and I laughed.

She looked at me as if I were out of my mind, shook her head and sighed.

I hadn't been too successful with the girls in Florida. Somehow, I kept sending away those who were interested in me; while pursuing those who refused me. Of course, I still yearned for Lainey. So. Besides my kissing romp with Kate in *War Hero*, there hadn't been much action other than kissing Jeanne, the straw boss' daughter, and the nurse at the feast by the river, and there was that cutie who kept inviting me out to her house called Taliesin, Florida. Oh, and there was another girl I liked a little, but I wasn't quite sure about. To test her, I gave her a lamp on her birthday I had made out of a butternut squash. The lamp-shade was assembled from an old pale blue shirt and a coat hanger. On the shade, I wrote her a love and death poem called, "A Butternut Squash Will." She didn't get it. We tried to kiss, anyway, but there was nothing much to kiss about.

In a few more weeks, all the boxes had been packed. And my step-mom bought me what winter clothes she could find at the Army-Navy. It was a cool evening. The house was all but empty. I was alone, and stood downstairs playing *Hot Rats* on my ridiculously tiny stereo. I got out my violin and jammed to fill the loneliness. As best I could, I tried to imitate Sugar Cane Harris. For dramatic effect, I slid down the high e string almost to the bridge, playing frantically. Then I shot the bow out of my hand and let it fly up into the air. As it came rushing back to earth, I caught it, just in time, and I acknowledged my imaginary audience.

When "The Gumbo Variations" finished, I went into what had been my room. I sat down on the wall-to-wall carpeting and leaned against the tongue-in-groove. Out on the lake, lightning flashed, and soon, the wind whipped the shadowy moss like horse tails swishing in the live oaks. The longer tails beat against the window of my room with soft, but insistent blows. From the farthest high corner of my dead empty room, white doves began to fly in two arcs toward the door, and then flew back to the center of the room. At first, they disappeared there as they reached the center with all the doves following exactly the same path. I squinted and realized they were headless. Where they were dissolving, a great shimmering tubular prismatic light began to form. As it took shape, I saw a double helix twisting in the center of my room. It extended to the ceiling while turning ever upwards. As soon as the helices were complete, the doves began to fly out a little further down on the other side of the turning light. But as they emerged, they became two-dimensional doves, sort of like paper airplane doves. They flew out the window, and were swallowed by the mossy twilight. There were so many birds — countless abstracting doves flying before me and away into the coming night. I decided to go into the next room. Were there more in there? No. I went back to see if they had left my bedroom. At first, my room only had a few laggards; yet, the double helix grew again, and the doves began to reappear in the upper corner from where they had originated.

I smiled to myself. I wasn't afraid.

# Lainey Love

---

Paul Underhill from Frankfurt picked me up late Christmas night at the airport. What a hellacious blizzard! I'd never seen so much snow. It lit up Boston's stacked brick darkness with covers of white. The dance outside dazzled me with its textures of light and shadow, alive and tactile.

"Come on. How about doing something?"

"What do you want me to do?" I said sleepily. I peered out the fogged window. There was no one in sight.

"I don't know," he said, turning the wrong way down a one-way street. "Jesus," he shouted. "Just help get us out of here. These fucking streets are insane."

We found ourselves in a ruptured neighborhood with few lights. The snow fell like broken shadows. Paul suddenly stopped the car. "God, I give up. Ask in there," he said.

"In where?"

"In the cop station."

I started to roll down the window. "Where?"

"Don't roll down the window. Just get out and ask."

So, I got out. When I looked up, I saw the snow-capped white light ball marked with snow-eroded black letters: Police. The falling snowflakes crashed and singed silently on my face. I lowered my head. The bricks seemed vaguely reddish. I let my fingers trail along them as I climbed the steps.

After a few minutes, I came out and got back into the car.

"So, where to," asked Paul.

"I have no idea."

"What?"

"I couldn't understand a word they said."

Paul angrily jumped out of the car. He opened the door to the station, and in a flash of office light that momentarily doused him, I was relieved to see him shake his head and laugh.

Through the night we traveled off to somewhere. I did not know how to drive, so I couldn't help there either. And the blowing snow, and the flight, and the hour, and the death doves had made me sleepy. I was drifting off, but Paul wanted me to stay awake to help keep him on the slick road.

"The plan," he said, "is to stop off at my place in Dorset, pick up some things, and maybe get a few hours' sleep, and then we'll head north to Averill. Everyone's waiting for us up there."

"Who? Where?"

"My relatives," Paul said impatiently. "They wanted me to come north earlier, but I had to pick you up."

"Yeah."

"It's up near Norton. Almost in Canada."

"Still in Vermont?" I said sleepily.

"Yeah."

The next thing I recall, it was morning and we were in a large, wood-heated old cabin filled with Paul's friendly relatives of few words. When they spoke it sounded so strange to me. Mostly, they talked about how good it was to see each other again and the next warm beverage we were about to enjoy.

"By the Jesus," an older man said to, I think, me, "that cider's good with a piece of cheese."

No sooner was the cider in my belly than I was told it was time for us young fellows to go cross-country skiing out on what they called a pond. It was way too big for a pond. A pond is a little thing with ducks and lilies; this was a good-sized lake. "How could is it out there?" I wondered, getting a restrained chuckle out of them. Then they told me the bad news.

"'bout 20 below, I guess."

"I'll just hang out inside," I said. But Paul quickly let me know that was not a possibility. The older folks wanted some time to themselves, he explained. Well, off we went, me in every layer of clothing I could possibly button or zip or tie around me.

While the others skied ahead, I clomped after them for about a mile to the center of the so-called frozen pond. I was sure I was going to die. I felt my bones become brittle and splinter inside. I heard them cracking. No longer did I have any flesh. I was only a skeleton wrapped in a porous shroud. Gratefully, they showed me how to get my blood circulating again by taking off the skis and doing jumping jacks.

"Won't we fall through?" They thought that was hilarious. Poor pathetic Florida boy. The jumping did little good. Our dove heads were sinking down inside our bodies. We were dying. Who was the fool? Not me. Not today.

"Let's go back, please. I can't stand this."

After some manly posturing delays, we started back. By the time we arrived at the cabin, my feet were frozen stumps, and my fingers, my nose, my eyelids had left me. I drank some hot chocolate, and my body passed through several stages of pleasure and pain before arriving at stasis. Is this why people live in this, I wondered, to feel this extreme and silently avoid anything temperate, save their social demeanor?

A few days later, we were back in Dorset. "Pronounced 'Dahsit'". Dorset only had a few hundred people; they lived, mostly, on one beautiful street lined with very old white wooden houses. On the corner, down from a cannon, was a fancy inn that used to be some revolutionary war hero's place. Across from the inn was a little general store run by an old man who, I was told, knew everything about the history of the town and the people who lived there. But I was too young, and much too foreign to listen when the village stories began, or when some casual gossip slipped. I only saw the cautious neighbors whispering across the counter to the kind shopkeeper who they depended on to guide and counsel them. I envied my neighbors' measured familiarity with one another. The notion of staying in one place for so long amazed me. What a wonderful, alien idea!

Paul showed me how to build a fire that winter, and every morning we took turns scrambling to get the fire roaring and re-heat the old house. Paul's older brother always got up very early to go jogging. It didn't matter to him how cold it was, every morning he jogged. I went with him, twice. The second time the temperature dropped to way far below zero. I could imagine a pale blue fluid filling my lungs, with each frigid breath, freezing and cracking me apart.

At school, the principal called me "Mephisto" on account of my little white goatee and my "demeanor," he said. One guy called me "Billy Goat." He didn't like a single thing about me. He must have been a redneck. "Up here we call them "'woodchucks'," Paul explained. I dutifully performed my half-credit pre-release penance, taking a creative writing class and a speech class. Speech consisted of fetching donuts for the teacher and us students, and sometimes, teaching the class for half an hour while the teacher got the donuts himself. I caused quite a stir one day when I read from Ferlinghetti's *Improvisations* about the origin of the word "jazz" — jasm, jism.

As for the creative writing teacher, I didn't get along with her so much. Once, she wrote on my paper, "It seems your writing could be ventilated with some 'straight' thoughts!" What could she have possibly meant? I had written,

> *rrrrRadiographs of ink*
> *pass through my hand,*
> *thinking of you. Of mellower*
> *Mommmm.*
> *Extractions, expectations of life —*
> *A bottle cap inside a bottle, or*
> *An excuse on the floor.*
> *And dreams again, my*
> *security in sleep.*

That said, my father expected me to work while in Vermont.

His attitude about work was compulsory, habit forming. We must work because work is good, even if there is no real aim to the work. Working was better than not working at all. Besides, he said, when I turned 18, he would no longer be obligated to provide child support, which was arriving in the form of rent for Mrs. Underhill.

So I worked at the mill. I was a bander, sealer, sorter. I coated the ends of bundles of wood with a pitch sealant that made my trousers stand up by themselves. I wrapped big bundles of wood in metal bands to prepare them for shipping. I sorted pieces of wood according to size and shape as they came off a conveyor belt. I didn't like my father's idea of work too much if it meant nothing but mindless tedium. I didn't like the goal of winning power over others through money, or the idea that nothing exists unless it has utility. It seemed to me that the culture of work was an anti-erotic culture of guilt and bankrupt human beings.

By the end of January 1973, the Paris Peace Accords had been signed, and the troops were further withdrawn. The draft expired at about the same time. The news affected me the way a whimpering dog finally shuts up and wanders off to another part of the room. I felt we were still involved somehow. It wasn't clear to me just how, but I didn't care. I had tired of hearing about the whole lying mess.

At about the same time, Lainey called and told me she was back in the US. In fact, she was close by in New Hampshire. Yes. She was just across the river from Brattleboro, about 50 miles away from me. Could I come visit? She said there was still something we needed to do.

"Okay," I said. "Tell me the day, and I'll come over as quickly as possible."

The day arrived. I quit my job and stuck out my thumb. Hitching was exasperatingly slow. By the time I got to the top of the very white Green Mountains, I found myself stuck in yet another snowstorm. I helped some people get their car out of a snowbank, hoping they would give me a ride, but no way. They barely even said thanks. I was freezing. My feet were numb. I was wearing tennis shoes that had gotten wet in the slush. I made it to Brattleboro, and I immediately went into an Army-Navy, picked out some toasty Sorrels. Then I called Lainey.

"What's taking so long?" She was annoyed. I tried to explain, but she cut me off.

"Just get over here as fast as you can, or my folks will be back and we won't be able to do anything." I didn't like her tone at all. She must have sensed that, because she softened it up on the good-bye, and I rushed over the bridge into New Hampshire.

I huffed and puffed up the hill to her grandparents' house. Lainey opened the door before I had a chance to knock; right away she led me into the bedroom and took off her pants. All antagonism dissolved. I got undressed and stood naked before her. She was happy to see I was ridiculously ready. I savored the act of her reclining on the bed, lifting her hips to slip off her underwear. Oh, Lainey, thank you, thank you, my heart wept. Her sweet fur transfixed me. All I could say was, "I love you, I love you," over and again.

She said in a most gentle voice, "Do you mind if I keep my socks on?" I adored her for her simple request. "My feet are a little cold."

"Oh, I don't mind."

Her socks were red. Between those socks and her waist, her legs were so white and smooth.

"Come here," she said. Little white hairs were standing up and breathing, her flesh become bumpy. Lainey was so slender and delicately curved. Ah, Lainey.

I couldn't move; I was paralyzed before her, before my dream sprawled out before me.

"Come here," she insisted. "I'm cold."

I fell to the bed. I embraced her with all of my endlessly burning heart, opening to her. She could never again mistake the certainty of my love for her. After this act together, she and I would belong to one another, as we always had. We were just waiting for the right circumstances. Her big basset-hound jumped up

260

onto the bed. I tried to push him away, but Sam, or whatever his name was, was insistent. Lainey suggested we let him stay. Lainey giggled, and I caressed and kissed her.

"We don't have a lot of time," she reminded me. "I'm afraid they'll come home." And I saw her legs begin to spread apart, ever so slightly. Contrary to her warning, I tried to make it last as long as I could. Perfect love, I told myself, even if only for a few moments — her warmth and liquidity seeped into me, twirling down my legs, up into my chest and throat, and I relaxed into all the time I had been craving her. I never wanted to stop kissing her. I lifted myself up a bit to see that damn relentless searcher for a moment, and disappear inside her. I looked up and saw her beautiful loving ecstatic face. The sight of her becoming overwhelmed caused me to tremble, and then, at last, after two years of screaming yearning, I roared up inside her. I heard her sigh, and I fell to her side. The droopy basset sat up and stared at us. "I love you," I whispered again, and Lainey told me she loved me, too, and that we had better get dressed.

We sat on the couch with a view of the Connecticut River Valley, quietly, nervously waiting for her family to return. I tried to cuddle with Lainey with every bit of love I knew and understood, but maybe that wasn't much or enough for her somehow, because she was a little stiff. Still I luxuriated in my belief of mutual belonging and completion. I was convinced. Never had I felt so certain about my place in the world, my arms around Lainey felt deliciously calm, the river valley bathed in gorgeous perfection.

Lainey was getting antsy just sitting on the couch. Too damn cozy for safety. I knew I'd have to leave her as she so often had left me.

A few minutes more and we heard the car pull up in the driveway. When her mother entered, she could sense the sex in the air. To everyone's relief, I quickly left.

For my next job, I worked as a dishwasher at the Track Fore Lodge in Manchester near Dorset. About that I have nothing much to say. I liked staring at the sparkling clean variety of glassware I was responsible for stacking at the waitress' station. Nothing else to report. I was working. That's all. It gave me some money.

I took violin lessons from a friend of Mrs. Underhill. But the teacher said my fingers were rather fat and more suited to playing the viola. Furthermore, she insisted, I really must practice if I ever hoped to make any progress. Then I started missing several classes, and my teacher said if I missed another, she would drop me. The night before my last chance with her, Paul and I took some nostalgic acid, and I hadn't quite come down by the time of my lesson. I felt I had to go, so as not to embarrass Paul's mother. I hoped I'd be coherent enough to play, but the lesson was a disaster. I couldn't keep the violin from drooping like taffy. I wasn't stupid enough to confess that I'd been tripping. Certainly, she would not have appreciated any reverie from me about altered states, how I wanted to capture, somehow, the sounds of *The Dark Side of the Moon*.

Right outside Dorset was an artists' studio where Mrs. Underhill encouraged me to take life-drawing classes. She was making a big effort to help me along with a little high culture. I sheepishly appreciated the human form in that strange room of brightly lit smocked-artists considering the object before us. But my charcoal strokes were too 'heavy-handed,' It was said, and I gave it up.

Next on the cultural survey was a round of Film Classics every Tuesday night. I watched such films as *Gaslight* and *Philadelphia Story*. I was good at watching. I could have watched for much longer, but the lights always came up, and it was time to go.

I thought about Claude, and wondered how the editing of *War Hero* was going. There seemed to be no opportunity to make even a short film in Vermont. No camera. Besides, I felt I needed Claude's help to pull it off.

The next best thing was the stage. My speech teacher, who was also the drama teacher, cast me in a play. He decided to produce and direct e.e. cummings' *Him*. He asked if I wanted to play the lead, but I said I was too busy. He could sense the truth. I was terrified to play the lead. So he cast me as one of the drunks, instead.

When I saw who he had cast for the female lead, "Me" the her that "Him" corresponds to, I deeply regretted my fear. Again, another more than beautiful girl threatened to knock some sense into my misdirected longings. She was perfect for me, I decided. She challenged me when we spoke, she insisted on intelligence, and had no taste for crude seduction. She was interested in my affection, but I could find no way to comfortably allow her the possibility of risking more than a backstage kiss. When I saw the guy who got the lead trying to be loving on stage, I was disgusted. He was pitiful. When the director told Him to affectionately rub Me's shoulders, he used his fists. And when it came time for them to kiss, it was the worst insult to kissing anybody had ever seen. She hated that guy, and I did, too. It was an insult to her and to Me to be treated so indifferently, so clumsily. If only I had had the chance to act out my affections for her on stage, we could have made the transition from stage to life-long play. But it didn't happen, and she became increasingly bitchy as I approached her with more need than affection.

I talked Paul into going over to Brattleboro so I could meet up with Lainey. The moment I jumped out of the car we began to kiss. And when we got back in, she sat on my lap. Though there was nowhere else for her to sit in the junk-filled car, I took her sitting on my lap as permission to do what I wanted with her. I rammed my hand down into her pants. Paul just drove around and tried not to get in a wreck while Lainey struggled. After a while, I gave it up. I wondered why she seemed so hostile when it was time to drop her off.

Nevertheless, we planned for her to come visit Dorset in early spring. But that visit didn't go much better. She arrived a couple of days late because she had met a "really cool dude" in the Berkshires who took her back to his farm. She couldn't stay long with me, she announced. She might want to stop in and see that dude again on the way back. And as an 'Oh, by the way,' she impaled me with the comment that it had been great to go skinny-dipping with him in his indoor pool.

I didn't hear from her for a while except for a very brief note requesting either Paul or I to immediately send her a wrap-around skirt. She had refused to remove it for me, yet left it behind in the guest bedroom.

Oh yes, at the Track Fore they served quahogs. You know, those huge clams. I loved the name and decided to use one of the thick grey shells in my sculpture dedicated to Lainey. I had been inspired by Duchamp's *The Large Glass,* for which he pressed objects between sheets of glass in a ritualistic process. Sculpture did not have to be something carved out of stone, I realized. I took the cue to express my frustration with Lainey and women in general. I took out her framed picture she had given me in Frankfurt, the one with "I could drink a case of you," and so forth, written on the back, and I smashed its glass. Paul was in the room and he protested, "You're going to clean that up, you know."

I nodded but otherwise ignored him. I took the shards and pressed between them paint and bow hairs, and paper with bits of charcoal drawings on them, and a scrap labeled "Meat Ticket" from a butcher's shop. I made kind of a mobile out of them and suspended it from the underside of a chair. Below the mobile I placed the quahog stuffed with a wadded-up violin string, and I glued pieces of glass extending out of the open shell. On the tip of the longest shard, I glued what looked like a gem stone, but was just painted glass.

"What the fuck is it?" Paul wanted to know. We weren't getting along very well. We were acting the way we had on the boat over to Denmark — a creeping betrayal, he wanted Lainey, too, I guess. There was a gradual understanding of our dissimilarity. I wondered if he was jealous of his mother's attention on me. Or had he decided I was a neurotic ass he was embarrassed to be around? Probably both.

Anyway, I tried to explain my desire to liberate Lainey from the confining frame I had placed her in, and transform myself into a sharp reminder of what I must do if I ever expected to secure her permanent love.

Paul made a noise as if he were gagging, and wouldn't let me continue talking.

It wasn't long before I received a letter from Lainey saying she and her parents would be moving to Texas in a few weeks, and asking me to come see her there. No time remained for another visit to New Hampshire, she wrote. My hopes and dreams had been restored. No matter what other obscure objects my longing had lit upon, Lainey was still the one meant for me.

I got busy preparing for the trip to Texas. I ordered a sleeping bag kit and a backpack kit from Frostline, and sewed them together myself. My last day of class was to be in mid-semester on April 6th, 1973. I decided I'd graduate with style, and then get the hell out of there.

Yet, Paul and I agreed to trip together one more time. At least we still had that in common. But the acid was marginal. Tripping was no longer a usually pleasant experience. More often than not, it was a ten to twelve-hour bout with whatever poison the bastards were selling that week. One more time, we thought. Paul and I did enjoy playing with orange juggling balls on the snow-covered golf course.

Early in the morning, as I was coming down, I tried to do some writing. I made myself a diploma and wrote a speech to give on my last day of high school.

When the time to go to school arrived, I was still swimming a bit, but I was coherent, and the world the same, more or less. At school, I put on a Ph.D. gown an acquaintance had either borrowed or snitched from his father. I burst into my creative writing class, late as usual, and went straight to the front of the room to read my graduation speech. I said:

# Jiggling

*Publicly Speaking: Yes Yes Yes Yes Yes Yes Yes Yes*
*Yes, the word to combat suicide. Yes,*
*I'd like satisfaction of my soul which*
*I don't believe exists, although it's true.*
*Then maybe, yes maybe when tonight I*
*open that refrigerator door, and as*
*I peer and they peer back, maybe*
*I'll find something worth eating.*

*I'm tired of hamburger, of*
*cottage cheese, of turkey from that*
*dinner I missed because of*
*forest fatigue. And I'm tired of burnt*
*and saddening events in the pantry:*
*the granola gone stale, the tomato*
*soup with tuna too big to eat.*

*"Well, well, have an aluminum*
*chip," I've thought. "Accept what*
*industry is doing to you. Take the*
*evolutionary train and stay on it.*
*Find a nice little compartment with*
*cheese for light posts. Take along a*
*female, show her your refrigerator,*
*hope she'll understand the blood*
*stains on the lower shelf.*
*And then, when you and her*
*settle down for an evening*
*of delight, make it last*

267

*'till you derail."*

*Goodnight.*
*Yes Yes Yes*
*Yes Yes Yes*

No one said a word.

I then presented myself with the diploma I'd made. I had bound it with an ugly paisley tie. I slipped out the diploma, and set it on fire above the science sink. At that point, the teacher tried to stop the ceremony, but the diploma had quickly disappeared. I bowed, and then flew out of the room.

I chuckled to myself. I was so happy to walk out the door down that long flight of steps leading away from the school. I no more than made it to the first landing when I saw that damn woodchuck, the guy who on the very first day of school decided he hated me.

"What the hell you think you're doing, Billy Goat?" he called me, eyeing my robes up and down.

"I'm grad-ye-ate-in," I said and smiled.

"Oh, yeah?" he said. And then he punched me in the stomach as hard as he could.

For a moment, we just stared at each other silently, and then he began to hurry away. Then, I laughed so hard I thought I'd go rolling down the steps like in a happy cartoon. What a perfect conclusion to my formal education!

The mud season had arrived, and Vermont was ugly. I was ready to go. I had an address book full of friends from Frankfurt.

I had finished both backpack and sleeping bag, and the road was calling. Paul had agreed to give me a ride over the mountain to Brattleboro where I could get a straight shot down the Seaboard.

"Oh, I've got to get a picture of this before you go," insisted Mrs. Underhill. She later sent it to me at my dad's place in Florida. My pack was enormous and awkward. I had tied a big red water bottle to the frame and a cup and other unnecessary crap that dangled like a junkman's chorus line. At my side, I held the little coffin-case containing my violin. My hair had grown past my shoulders and I wore a little tweed cap. I had also taken to wearing disintegrating cowboy shirts, and my jeans needed a patch or two, as well. I had gotten a fresh pair of red tennis shoes and discarded my Sorrels. It wouldn't be cold soon, especially in Texas.

When Claude later saw the photograph, he immediately came up with the perfect caption.

"Look at that," he said. "Bum on a Beat Trip."

# Bum on a Beat Trip

---

I-91 south through Massachusetts toward Hartford. Please, shoot me forever past that hitchhiker's hell of the interchange with I-84. No decent on-ramps. Nowhere to stand in Hartford, except on the freeway. NO HITCHHIKING signs everywhere. Cops everywhere.

"Quick. Get in."

Jumped over to the Garden State Parkway. Gave New York City a wide berth. Too frightened to enter Manhattan. Saw it towering to the East, tempting and sullen in the afternoon haze. Not yet. The first visit there would be the coming summer with Claude. We would land in a midnight *Pink Flamingos* nest, then wander around Spanish Harlem, lost. Forced to sleep on benches outside Madison Square Garden; Horn & Hardart's at dawn.

But then, dropped off in the Jersey suburbs. Waited just briefly for a slingshot away. Swift freedom all day, southward past the Philadelphia story, strange Wilmington, and a loop around Baltimore — seen from the freeway, its snaking row houses. A few more hopping rides and I was at the door of Sharon Worley, Lainey's best friend, and occasionally, mine. She was happy to see me, and she wanted to get it on.

Sharon and I, forever with the thrill of being caught, rolled around on her parent's floor, not really caring if they'd gone to sleep or not. Her hips were wider than Lainey's. A neat, soft slope from hip bone to bone reminded me of a cradle. But our bones clanked together. Our bodies did not fit together very

270

well. I took it as a bad sign. I was careful not to tell her I loved her. Instead, I told her she was beautiful and thanked her for a pleasant time. Wasn't it great to have friends you could make love to? She agreed that it was.

Off again. Around the beltway, then west to the Blue Ridge spine and into the Shenandoah Valley. Brief stop in Harrison-burg where I met the lovely Starlight Sunshine, who gave Jimmy Delighter, that expert guitarist from Frankfurt, paper cups filled with survival spaghetti. Otherwise, it was so easy to slip through this world barely noticed. I slept somewhere outside of Knoxville. Nobody bothered me. I felt entitled to protection in Tennessee. After all, my people hailed from there. That's what I had been told, anyway. Hard to remember much about my peo-ple. I didn't dare call on those lost to me. They had settled onto the bricks of my distant memory, like the condensed steam of stranger Grandpa's industrial laundry.

Stretch. Heat up a can of something. Look at the map. Peace-ful; leaning against a pine. I was on my way to certain sex with Lainey. She had to. What excuse could she possibly have not to? No more bullshit. She was mine or else.

Interstate 40 rolled across the Cumberland Plateau — some of the most beautiful country I had ever seen. I should have asked my ride to stop the car. Let me out. I want to stroll about these hillbilly hills, touch the rusted tin roofs and the weathered wood. I saw a man and his dog, and old tractors — slipping by too fast. Yet, if the car were to stop, then what? The slippery sluice, a new pretty face, an occasional phrase to savor.

The construction workers in Nashville hooted at me. "Hippie scum." Doubtful I could ever live in Tennessee. I guess I would always be an Enemy of the People.

My ride zipped over the bone-fertilized Natchez grass on to Memphis. I should get out and walk across the bridge. It would be my first Mississippi crossing. Hire a boat and sail me across the Mississippi, maybe build a raft with some neighbor boys. But not a word out of me. The car just slid through Memphis and then crawled up onto the big metal bridge. The sun set into a slot between the trusses that announced the West.

The town of West Memphis, Arkansas; somewhere out there I sank into a blank mud flat. "This is far as I'm going." No more sunlight, just a motel and a gas station, glowing in the distance. Walking in that nothing, I sprained my ankle. I hobbled toward the bland hollow light and, with some resistance from the clerk, checked into the motel.

Next morning, a pick-up truck honked for me to hurry up and jump in. I stumbled down the gray road as fast as I could. Oh, my ankle. Damn pack was too heavy — the junkman's chorus, mocking me. A young man extended his hand to help me and the pack to the truck bed. No one spoke. I'd catch someone staring at me, and I'd have to lower my glance when they saw me staring all the same. Not one word.

About half way to Little Rock the driver pulled off the interstate, and I thought he would let me out, but he pulled away fast. What the hell! Try not to be afraid away from the freeway. The truck stopped at several dusty farming communities — silent places like Cotton Plant, Des Arc, Hickory Plains, Cabot. At each town a few workers got off, but then more got on, so by the time we had circled back to Little Rock the pick-up was crammed full. Arriving downtown, everybody knew to get out except me. The driver came back to tell me in a friendly voice that that was as far as he was going. I smiled and reluctantly dismounted. I decided I needed more safely disorienting rides.

From Little Rock hitching was slow. It took all day to get another 100 and some miles to the painfully named town of Hope. Mine had run out for the day, and I began to scope out a place to crash. I wished someone would at least get me out of Arkansas. Only another 30 miles to Texarkana. The name rang out. Sleep on a soft bed of cotton? Lovely Lainey soon. But the light was fading fast, and I knew it was hard to see me. Then the hitcher's dream car, a Volkswagen Bug — they almost always stopped for you — came rushing down the highway and coasted to a stop a long way off. He swerved and corrected backwards, his white reverse light, one burnt out, bearing down on me. I was hurried inside. Maybe he'd drive all night, he said. Okay with me?

The small talk didn't go too far. He evaded giving me details about anything, not where we were going, where he was from, and especially not his name. Still, I trusted him. You gotta read people fast when you're hitching. I told him I was headed to San Antonio. He said I could be sure that we would head in that general direction.

He took the weirdest route — not straight over to Dallas and then directly south to San Antonio. He said he wanted to avoid the interstates. Mt. Pleasant to Tyler through Palestine and Crockett. As the night wore on, he began to trust me enough to tell me, bit by bit, what was up with him. He needed to confess. I found out he had been driving non-stop from New England or upstate New York, he wouldn't say specifically.

"Well, damn. I've been hitching since Vermont," I said. His face soured. Maybe that was his secret place. Something had happened, and he had to leave in the middle of the night. "Tell me about it," I tried to coax him.

"You know how to drive a stick?"

"No, not really."

"You got a license, though."

"No."

"Man, how can you live in this country and not have a license?" he said. "Well, I need you to drive."

"Okay," I said doubtfully. "But you'll have to tell me what to do."

I didn't know how a car was supposed to feel, but it seemed his hardly had any brakes. "Just pump em," he said. "When you get out on the open road, you won't have to worry about it."

Bryan. Old Dime Box. Giddings. I was driving, all right for my first time, but besides the sloppy brakes, I couldn't quite get the hang of when to downshift. I felt a terrible chug-chugging like the engine was going to fall out into the road.

Finally, he told me he had been involved in robbing a bar of some stereo equipment. A couple of the guys were caught and some asshole snitched on him. A call from a friend came late at night. The heat was on. He had to leave. It was hard not saying good-bye to his girlfriend. It was too risky. He was determined not to go to jail. The cops had already been on his case for some other shit. They were out to nail him, he said. Maybe he'd call his girlfriend come morning.

La Grange. Yoakum. Cuero. I asked him what he was going to do.

"Just keep driving," he said.

"I am."

"No, I mean, I guess I'll just keep driving. I've got a couple of sheets of blotter acid I could sell. You want any?"

I declined. Seemed to me he was headed for the border. I was curious how he was going to get across, but I didn't think I should ask. When I started to doze, he told me to pull over and we'd switch. He told me he didn't want to get too close to big cities — too many cops. But he assured me he would drop me off not too far from San Antonio. He'd get as close as he dared. We would cruise into the 'burbs as long as the sun wasn't up, and he'd let me off where it would be easy to get to my girl-friend. It felt good to hear him say it: "Girlfriend."

I found a pleasant stand of trees by the road. The sun had just come up, and I could smell the sap rising. I let my pack collapse to the ground, and I fell on top of it. I slept like a fugitive, that is to say, with one eye open. After about an hour I gave it up — too much light and increasing traffic. I  then collected myself, and was shot over the last bit of road to Lainey Love.

She was so happy to see me, she said once again. Did I thrive on happy reunions? Was it better that the visits were always brief? I wanted to tell her about my adventures. Let me brag a little about what I had gone through to see her again, but the words came out scrambled, not cool. She said I should rest, and she made a place for me to sleep. To calm me, she pulled up my shirt and began to rub my sour belly — so kind and loving — but her mother walked in and embarrassed all three of us.

The mom quickly exited and Lainey cooed, "Get some rest, Sweet Pea. We can talk later." She bent down and kissed my forehead, my belly, too.

The door closed and my mind raced. My dick swelled. The feeling was somehow disconnected from the rest of me. Need to sleep. The room began to fall away, and I closed my eyes.

It was dark when I woke up, and Lainey suggested we go for a walk. She lived in an ugly suburban neighborhood and there was nothing much to see. But it didn't matter. It was very clear what both of us wanted.

"Over here," she said, and she pulled me down behind a scraggly hedge. Our pants and underwear were off lickety-split. The ground was hard and spiny. So I curved my hands under Lainey's warm butt, so as to avoid any blemish. That precious butt. The briars and stones beneath us cut into my hands. I pounded at her furiously, wanting this one to pass quickly: my hands were starting to bleed. Lainey squirmed and responded to my insistence by pushing up against me as I pulled hard into her as deeply as I could. I would like to have screamed. I think if I had, she would have, too. But the neighbors.

We picked ourselves up out of the bushes and quickly got our jeans snapped. I wanted to linger, maybe saunter, hug and kiss. But Lainey was in a hurry to get home. It would be impossible to spend the night together in her bed. The best I could do was arrange to make love to her again in the morning.

"My mother has to pick up my Dad at the airport tomorrow morning."

"Perfect. Wear a dress and nothing underneath. Will you?"

The next morning she did as I requested: she wore a long country-girl dress. So succulent. She was acting shy, I thought. That was unusual for her, but I liked it. It made me feel strong; perhaps she liked the low commanding tone of my desire. I was ready to possess her. To stake my claim. I led her back to her bedroom and began to kiss her sweetly, but her kisses were shallow and soulless.

"What's wrong?" I asked.

"Nothing. Let's do it," she said.

I asked her to lift the calico dress up above her waist. I kissed her belly and she let the dress fall over my head; I was forever lost in that diaphanous cave. — Wasn't it like Mommie's dress at the department store? Waiting for the purchase to become final? — She let out a quick rumbling laugh; I could never understand the tone of it. I mean Lainey's laugh. I'm writing about Lainey here. Was her love sincere? Generous? Kind? She pulled my head tightly against her and we stumbled backwards. Down onto her bed, I nuzzled my face, and my tongue explored her every tasty petal. On my knees, I worshipped and gave thanks to it. I grabbed her butt and pleaded for redemption. Better yet, a cessation of Guilt. But her desire had already trickled away. Was I doing something wrong? I looked up from my work. I saw her motionless. I felt her cool to the touch. Maybe she preferred just to fuck. I guided my dick inside her. We moved arrhythmically and she moaned a bit, but when I hesitantly opened my eyes, I saw she was staring up at the ceiling. I felt angry and afraid, yet I kept on fucking her. Perhaps, if we did it hard and fast as we had the night before, she would respond. I began to knock hard into her.

"You're hurting me."

I stopped, and I tried another angle. I began to fuck her like a trip hammer — shattering glass. I could feel I was about to come.

"Stop," she said.

277

"Wait," I panted. I had my little orgasm, but it felt like nothing. A little cut, bandaged.

"You were hurting me."

I felt awful lying next to her. Nothing made sense. She had been mine last night, but this morning my affections seemed grotesque to her. I wanted her love so badly, but I wasn't going to put up with this. I had traveled, what, two thousand miles for a bit of her love, and now she was so cold to me again. I didn't understand her.

"Lainey, why the hell won't you let me love you?"

"Not right now,"

"That's not what I meant."

"No. I mean. . . ." Her voice trailed off.

I didn't want any more pain. No more refusals. Dammit, if she wanted me, she had better let me know.

"I think you should leave today," she said. And she quickly got out of bed. "I have a lot I need to do."

"I was planning on it," I lied.

"Don't be mad. Last night was wonderful. I'm just worried my father will come home."

"No, you're not. You know they won't be back for hours." Then Lainey moved closer and rubbed up against me.

"Don't be mad."

"Do you want to try it again? I could do it twice."

"No. I said, No."

"All right. You don't have to yell at me, Lainey," I said, and suddenly I began to cry. I couldn't help it. The tears just began flowing. I sobbed uncontrollably. She took me in her arms and quickly soothed me back into devotion. That's what I really wanted, some post-coital coddling. I promised somewhere deep and dark within myself that I should always seek her out. I shall pursue her over every last road, I whimpered. As long as it takes, just as long as she, for a few moments, like this little moment now, would hold me and protect me and let me believe we were together. I said it to myself — forever united against the on-slaught.

At last, I settled into her arms and we talked about where I would go next. I hadn't really thought about it. "Maybe I'll go to 'Cal-i-for-nia,'" I said , singing the word just like in Joni Mitchell's song.

Lainey thought that was a wonderful idea. California. She told me she wished she could go, too. Did she mean together?

I asked myself that question over and over. While waiting for my next ride, the memory of the brief visited coursed through me. I was alone again, but felt relieved. Scared and relieved.

I got a few short rides west on I-10.

The warmth of Lainey's sweet ass still burned in my hands. Yet the movement away from her made me want to forget her. Just let me walk out on her, onto the highway, stick out my thumb, and go away. Yes. Maybe I should just forget her. The thought ripped at me. Strangely, I could feel my prick begin to swell, as it would over and over for her, for many years. What would it take to break away from her little pats on my obedient head?

About a hundred miles out of San Antonio, a guy stopped on the interstate and asked where I was going.

"West," I said.

"Get in."

My ride explained he wasn't going much further on I-10. He was headed up to Big Spring at I-20. I could eventually get back to 10 about a couple of hundred miles east of El Paso. I looked at the map. It was a crazy way around for me, but he was good company. "Sure," I said. I decided I wanted to get as far away from Lainey in any direction that I could.

We stopped in San Angelo at one of his favorite barbecue pits. It wasn't much to look at, just another cinder-block white building with a couple of split-drum grills out front. But, boy, did it smell good. A woman came out and opened up a cooker. Inside were the biggest hunks of meat I'd ever seen. No single steak was less than three pounds.

"Go ahead, pick one," my ride said.

"Oh, I don't know."

"Don't worry about it. This is on me."

"Wow, thanks," I said and, I took too long trying to find the smallest piece.

"Give him that one," he said, and the woman hauled out a nice smoking brontosaurus steak and flopped it onto a platter.

"We're gonna split this, aren't we?"

"No sir. That one's yours."

We went inside the building, which had a few picnic tables, and I looked to see what else they sold. Not that I needed more, but did you just eat the meat and nothing else? The answer was, yes. Sure, you could get a soda and some white bread if you bought the whole loaf. But this was strictly a meat fest, a carneval. Juicy, delicious meat as big around as my torso. I ate what I could and packed away the rest for the road.

My ride happily finished all of his. He explained he had felt like doing something good for someone to extend his own good luck. "Good deeds bring good luck," he explained.

He waited until we were almost to Big Spring before he told me what had happened to him and the reason for celebration. "I won the toss in Nuevo Laredo," he said. "My buddy lost and had to take the bus."

"I don't get it, why couldn't you both go in the car?"

"The police check the cars at the border. They usually don't bother you on the bus." He made an expression that was meant to say, "You get it?" But I didn't.

"For what?"

"Pot, man. He had two suitcases full of weed."

"What a trip!"

"Mother of God," he crossed himself. "I hope he made it all right." He sighed, "When I see him again, we're going out for the biggest steak dinner ever. That one back there was puny," he bragged.

"It was great. Thank you"

"It'll do for now."

At Big Spring I looked for a place to park my lard and sleep. I found a ditch outside of town, and crawled into my mummy bag. I was afraid I might get hassled because of the looks some grease monkeys had given me. I had asked if they had any ideas where I could crash. But there was no trouble, though I woke up that night in a start; I felt someone was watching me, but saw no one. Just me in my green bag that had turned a frosty white.

It took a couple of days to get across the desert. The drivers blended together in the heat; they searched for gas money from a hitcher, they longed for company, they were desperate against the solitary nights. They needed to preach to me about "my savior." Listen. Hear the rumbling rear wheel? Outside of Gila Bend, it fell off when they hoisted her up on the rack. And remember the Mojave sex slave murderer? I'm sure it was him. He picked me up at a rest stop; he was just waiting for someone ripe like me. Did I want to come back to his place and fuck his wife, while he watched, he asked?

No.

Took I-8 to El Cajon; skirted San Diego and headed for Tijuana. Caught a ride with a construction worker who had neglected to tie down the several boards atop his truck. Of course, when he had to suddenly stop, the boards shot off the truck and went through the rear window of the car in front of us.

"Man, you better get out of here quick," he said. "I'm not allowed to take passengers."

So I jumped out into the stalled traffic, and went the only way I could go: up the embankment, treading over ice plants. I took it as a sign, and didn't make it to Mexico.

Or later, that fat pig of a man who managed to get me out to his trailer, "for just a moment" Once there, I went for a piss. He told me to bring back the suck butt-fuck books he had laying around. I declined. He told me he liked to go down on bended knees and suck marines from 29 Palms as they cleaned garbage bags full of pot. Here was another one who told me he needed me so badly. So many discontents. I finally convinced him we should get back into his car. He suggested I jerk him off in payment for the ride. He was getting more and more agitated. I refused. He was desperate. As he drove, the news came on the radio of that poor woman who was raped by an *it* —subhuman— who cut her arms off when she resisted; then tossed her out of his van to the side of the road. All night, the radio said, she screamed for help, struggling through the dark ice plants. I was terrified. I played the game of gently convincing him to take me back to the interstate. I reminded him that he had promised he would. That seemed to make a difference! I knew that if I panicked and treated the situation as abnormal, or if I tried to flee, he would rape and then kill me.

Further up the coast, an older hippie chick who lived by the ocean in a little jungle complete with exotic birds and a brightly painted peace fence. I really wanted to go inside, meet her friends, wash the slime off my mind, but she made me wait in the van. Secret worlds, I thought.

Then I beat it along the Pacific on US-1 to Topanga and got a ride up the canyon for a rest. My ride told me I could get washed up at his place. Could I use his stove, too? "I have some great barbecued meat I got in Texas that I'd better eat before it goes bad."

"Sure," he grimaced, but didn't care for any himself, thank you.

He asked me if I had ever heard of Charles Manson, but I hadn't. My ride said, "Right up the canyon is where he murdered Sharon Tate. Brutal." He described the scene; the way he talked, I thought it had just happened.

At his sprawling bungalow, I watched for signs to make certain I was safe. I was comforted when he moved on and asked me, "You know who Cher is, don't you?"

"Sure. Sonny and Cher. 'The Beat Goes On.'"

"Sometimes, she comes into the bar where I work, down on the beach. She is so beautiful."

"I'd like to see her," I said hopefully.

Without bothering to look at me, he said, "I don't think they'd let you in."

It was getting dark. After I finished eating, and he was ready for work, he took me back down to Highway 1. The restaurant where he worked was in Malibu on the beach. He let me off and suggested I sleep among the pilings there below.

"It's a wonderful view," he said as he rolled his eyes toward the ocean.

All night I slept with one eye open as beach rat people poked around under the restaurant. Flashlights darted about the barnacled posts and shone into my open eye. All night I heard them mutter incomprehensibly.

The next day in Santa Barbara, I talked to some old drunks hanging out on a park bench. "Hobos," I said to myself excitedly.

"Whatcha got in the box?" one said as the other handed me a paper-sacked bottle.

"Thanks," I said, and I took a swig of the foul syrupy burning goop. "Oh, that." I hadn't taken the violin out of the case the whole trip. "It's a violin." I opened the case and showed them.

"Play us a tune."

I resisted.

"Come on."

I really couldn't play for shit, but they insisted. So, I attempted the bit from Rod Stewart's "Tomorrow is Such a Long Time" that I hadn't played since Watt, White and Apricot. They weren't impressed, and neither was I. So I put the violin back into its case.

One man wrinkled up his face and said, "You're not sleeping on the beach are ya? Don't do it."

"No, no, don't do that," the other chimed in.

"Some bastard chopped up a couple kids," he moaned. "Right there in their sleeping bag." The saliva dripped off his lips. "Two of them in one bag together."

"Yeah. Sonem bitch. Still out there," slurred the other. "No. Can't go out on the beach at night no more."

I thanked them for the warning and the drink, and hurried away.

Nothing to do except continue up the coast. Another bastard near Big Sur: the psycho insisted it was my job, as the passenger, to entertain him with amusing stories, provocative questions, and gracious conversation? Remember when I failed him over and over as sleep pulled me down, and he woke me up repeatedly? In the end, he threatened to kill me if I didn't participate. I had to jump out with my pack as he slowed on a curve. Off Highway 1, I ran into the woods. He drove slowly back and forth, shining a flashlight after me while I lay shivering behind a redwood.

What kind of endless nightmare was this?

Got a ride into San Francisco with a loan collection officer. He had to make several stops at Hunter's Point. Each time he got out of the car he hesitated, choosing whether the client merited taking his silver gun. I hid in the interior shadows of the car. No way was I getting out until he could take me to where there was light.

Somehow, I made it over to Berkeley that night and slept in the youth hostel. In the morning, I went back to San Francisco, because I had to see Haight/Ashbury. Haight was clogged with junkies, drunks, and thieves. Every few feet some jerk tried to hustle me. Many buildings were boarded up, and the street stank of garbage. The love had certainly festered and popped.

1973. What the world needs now is power. I wanted to get out of California as fast as possible. I did not want to stay in that world of death-sucking alienation. Yet, one more hope remained. Maybe the Beats still swarmed in North Beach. I did not yet know that both "Hippies" and "Beats" were a media invention made mostly at the expense of those of us who strained to belong to something, somewhere.

I found the Café Trieste and The Bohemian Cigar Store. I drank too much coffee at each and witnessed the espresso addicts feverishly taking notes for their tormenting books, waiting to be written. I grooved at City Lights and tipped my cap to Mr. Ferlinghetti for letting me roam and read for hours without having to pay. If ever I opened a shop, it would be just like his.

In a City Light's publication of favorite Japanese and Chinese recipes, I discovered — great, good fortune — the name of a Chinatown restaurant where I could dig the "Zen lunatic" waiters that Kerouac had raved about. At Sam Wo's you had to walk through the kitchen — Chinese women formed won-ton by the hundreds with a few deft twists of a chopsticks; I was greeted by great clouds of steam and flaming aromatic wok explosions. I passed through the kitchen and up the stairs leading to the dining room.

One step in, and the instructions began to fly at me: "Check it out. Sit there. What you want? This is a test." The waiter threw down the menu. "Check it out. You tell me."

"I'll have the Lo Mein," I said.

"Write it down," he said.

I copied it down and how much it cost. He turned quickly from his hand-operated dumb waiter, snatched the menu and the order, and demanded to know why I had left out the tax.

"Here chart. Be precise on every little thing. This is a test."

So I wrote down the tax. But he grabbed the little slip of paper from my hand and shouted, "You write, I rewrite." And so he scribbled down the whole thing again in Chinese, put the ticket on the dumb waiter, rang the buzzer, and made it rumble away.

I could see in my waiter's eyes that he was actually the gentlest of men. So that's it, this Zen business: Expectations disarmed in daily events. A fun little game, much of the time, yet painful, nevertheless. I began to understand that I was entangled in the fear of loss and greed for comfort. I'd read about the *Ten Bulls* of loss and liberation and it began to sink in. A few years later, sitting at the San Francisco Zen Center, facing the wall, I could hear the whack, whack of the *keisaku*, the "encouragement stick." The sound and possibility of a spanking flared in my mind as that of a red-welted sinking, a descending terror of the Mommie Switch. Well, I asked for it. Whack on one shoulder, whack on the other. How wonderful it felt! A blast of volcanic release shot out the top of me. I had been released for a moment, a speck of Satori. But it was nothing, not like some kind of special discipline from One on high.

And, so. I-80 to Sacramento. Over Cannibal Pass to Reno. Screech to a halt. Dumped off in Sparks. What to next?

Sarah Christensen, my kissing friend from Frankfurt days now lived south of Salt Lake City. Now that we were back in The States and a little older, maybe Sarah would want me, too. Maybe she missed me. Maybe she thought we should take it further, after all. Oh, that would be nice. And as I was dreaming of her love, something to erase the most recent smudge of Lainey, the car that stopped for me honked to wake me from my reverie.

He was going eastward across Nevada and Utah and further still. He, too, wanted to drive all night.

The land had turned brown since California. The trees thinned to scrubs and low pastel tufts growing in the rocks and in the sand. No water. No sound of water's presence. No humid death, no saturated pores floating in the wind, no fecund stream or drenched light. The driver turned off the static radio, and I heard the artificial wind pushing past us blending with the automobile hum. Out there was an austere, dry silence. Once again, but not since Tennessee, I wanted to wander off into it. But the momentum of 70 miles per hour and the sexual urge, again, carried me ever forward. Yet, wouldn't it be better to linger in this place of open minimalism and listen to the solitude? Once there, I could hear my hopes and desires calmed for a moment. Out there in the desert, I could listen to the exquisite silence of daily dying — continuous and free.

We stopped for gas in Winnemucca. I got out of the car and the heat instantly baked me to a crust. I ducked inside the cool station and played a couple of quarters at the slots. We got a burger in town, and I called Sarah to warn her I was coming.

Eastward through Elko and Wells. I loved these little towns. I imagined I could live in any one of them. Maybe, I could settle down into a drug store romance. I'd be the short-order cook. She, the waitress. On our days off, we'd drive up and down the lonesome roads protected by our eternal love.

I saw the Great Salt Lake appear at morning. The driver was enthusiastic that we had already crossed into Utah. We had gone 500 miles. I was almost tempted to keep on eastward with him. I liked his zeal, but he said he wanted to take in Salt Lake. Besides, I had already made my decision to go visit Sarah. She was expecting me.

Was it just habit at that point? I hitched the remaining 150 miles south to Salina through Nephi and down into Sarah's britches. I was getting pretty damn fast at unsnapping and un-zipping the obstacles to ram my insistent hand down into the aromatic fuzz. In her family's living room our kisses had started off kindly enough. It took but a moment to rekindle our affec-tions. But I wanted more.

"What are you doing?" she wanted to know, surprised and a little angry. She pulled back and grabbed my wrist. We struggled a bit, and I relented. She zipped herself back up, and bravely made a try a kissing me again. I held her close and pulled her in tight with my hand on her ass. What was I doing? I was rotting our kisses, spoiling the affection of our ecstasy that blissful day long ago in the Frankfurt library. The thought made me angry. I was disgusted with myself.

"Stop," Sarah said. "Get your hand off my rear end, If my brother catches us, he'll hurt you." This was not erotic play. She was serious. I stopped, and she explained to me that she was a Mormon and, she did not do those things before marriage.

Her brother did come home, and he sensed the threat to his sister's virtue. Sarah and I made an excuse to leave. She took me downtown to get a bite to eat. The place was called Mom's, an old soda fountain fancied up with cheap paneling and fixtures to suggest something of the sophisticated-rustic. Mostly, it was hollow and oppressive. I couldn't postpone it any longer; it was time I left. Sarah told me she'd give me a ride to the road leading out of town.

And so she stopped at the secondary road on the way to I-70 east. I apologized for my aggression, and she kissed me again, long and slow. I could not help it; I still wanted her. Why not? We were alone; I searched for a place that we could slip off to. But I could see in her eyes that it was not what she wanted from me. She wanted to be held and to sigh in my arms. I needed to hold her, too, to staunch the flow somehow. Years later, another attempt, and I never saw her again.

Next? A visit to Chris Marascino. Who was she? The girl who hugged me in the school halls, for which I was suspended. I barely knew her. She was in Colorado Springs. She had written once. It might be fruitful, I thought. Even though I hadn't known her very well in Frankfurt, that wouldn't stop me from insisting we have sex. I was at her doorstep the following afternoon.

She didn't mind a rudimentary kiss, but became quite angry at my presumptuous hands. She didn't want to be mean, she said, but she made it clear that I should leave immediately.

I felt empty, the way someone who has stuffed himself feels hungry. There was nothing erotic about self-disgust. What was I trying to do with all these women? Did I want them to submit, so I might garner up a little power, shore up a store of flimsy meaning because they had spread their legs for me? And then I'd hate them for consenting too easily. Or I'd hate them if they didn't consent. I'd arrogantly place her, my object, on a pedestal and worship her, but never really learn to respect her. And though I'd found myself alone, given several chances not to be so, I had never really tried to learn who these women were.

I scoffed at the name of a town called Loveland on my way to Fort Collins. I was running out of money, so I called Dad to ask if he'd send me some dough for my 18th birthday. Was I coming home, yet, he wanted to know?

"Not yet, Dad. I'm going to see another friend; then I'll be back."

"Why don't I send you a bus ticket home?"

"I want to hitch."

He told me again that once I turned 18, that was it. No more money. There was a long silence. He then asked where to send the dough. I gave him Evan's new address in Minnesota.

"That's the wrong direction if you're planning on coming home."

"It's just a little further . . . north," I said, savoring the word as it slipped out.

"Whatever."

"So will you send it?"

"I guess."

"Thank you. Bye."

"By-e," he said with a sour twist of the word at the end.

The next day meant the plains of Colorado and Nebraska. I followed the Platte, the Oregon Trail in reverse, and soon enough I made it to Omaha. I wanted to get off on a back road for a while. I was tired of the monotony of the interstates. Besides, it was my birthday. I owed myself something pleasant to look upon. At my request, the ride dropped me by the freeway interchange with a road leading me to the scenic route.

"You sure you want to get off here?" the driver asked. "Storm's coming up fast."

I turned around and saw the dark forbidding wall behind us.

"Yes, this'll be fine."

I didn't quite make it to the underpass before the clouds caught up to me, drenching me and my pack. I worried that the violin case would leak. Don't know why I cared — ridiculous prop. Even below the underpass I had trouble staying out of the blowing rain. The only dry place was where the slanted concrete wall met the bridge overhead. There wasn't much space up there. I couldn't even sit up straight. I pulled out my mummy bag and tried to get warm. While resting on my elbow, I wrote in my notebook. I noted how fitting it was that this place was the site of my so-called gateway into manhood. "Happy birthday to me," I sang. I laughed derisively at myself, at my situation, at the rain. I wished I was already at Evan's. He'd promised to treat me to Flatt and Scruggs in Fargo — "Foggy Mountain Breakdown" in a big gymnasium.

I'd laugh with Evan for a few days, and then he'd go off searching for his Ojibwa roots within the White Earth.

And I'd be surprised at the windy terrain around Barnesville, Minnesota — how it took the greatest effort to put one foot in front of the other. The few trees had grown bent over facing in the same direction, and how the rolling land was dotted with so many tiny lakes and ponds. And I would be horrified at what those ponds could breed. Evan's poor little dog, fighting for his balance against the wind would be covered with hundreds, maybe thousands of beige-colored ticks, some swollen up huge. I half expected them to explode and gush blood and pus all over the driveway. I would want to pet the poor thing, reassure the creature, but I wouldn't dare touch it. Poor miserable pup longing for a caress.

"Can't you get those off him?" I'd say.

"No, I don't think so." Evan, clearly, would not want to talk about it.

"Isn't there anything you can do?" I would plead.

I would not be able to pull myself away from that thing. The beast would look at me with the helplessness of a creature invaded. If there was ever a being that needed to be killed out of compassion, it was this grotesque tick-sucked victim.

"Why doesn't someone shoot him, Evan?" I'd say, nearly crying.

"Do you want to?" he'd ask me.

Maybe I would.

But for now, I was huddled, shivering in the cleft of an underpass in Nebraska on my 18th birthday. Then the rain in Omaha subsided, and a pleasant, peaceful silence filled the cleansed air. Shortly, someone took me to where my scenic route began. Then, there wasn't much traffic, but I didn't really care. I got a couple of very short rides and found myself between the towns of Fort Calhoun and De Soto. I was pretty hungry, but I would have to wait until the following day to eat a decent meal — my belated birthday meal purchased by yet another nearly anonymous donor.

Yes, that day after my birthday, the stranger and I stopped at a diner somewhere south of Sioux Falls, South Dakota. I kind of let him know I was celebrating my 18th. "Order anything you want," he said. He fed me well — roast beef and mashed potatoes with gravy, corn and a roll — and told me the news that some of Nixon's staff just resigned. People in the diner were talking about it agreed it looked like Nixon would be the next to go. Someone said, "You remember when he said the average

American was like 'a child in the family?' I sure don't want to be in that SOB's family."

My ride placed an order of strawberry shortcake in front of me. "Happy Birthday," he said.

But that was the day after the day I'm trying to remember. That 'pleasant peaceful silence' I followed outside of Omaha; I'd almost made it on foot to De Soto when I came across an old two-story school house. It was a pleasant brick building; I wondered if it was still in use. As I walked past, I felt a presence. I looked up and down, but no one was on the road. I looked back at the school and nearly every window was filled with faces. I saw children and their teachers standing still, watching as the longhair passed by. I waved, and a few kids waved back. I saw their teacher slap down the hands of the few brave hearts.

Maybe they were phantom children and teachers that had appeared so suddenly. The hungry ghosts, if that was what they were, stared at me in the silence. They were so horribly still. I became afraid. Would they attack me? I could not abide. I fumbled through my hippie medicine bag, an army surplus satchel I'd bought in Amsterdam. I took out my harmonica, my final defense and protection, and improvised a silly little blues shuffle. I played with the silence as best I could, for me and the kids, and for the teachers, too. In fact, I played for everyone I wished would love me.

I played as I walked. I did not dare stop. Not there.

Made in the USA
Lexington, KY
17 October 2019